MOST ELIGIBLE BILLIONAIRE
BILLIONAIRES OF MANHATTAN

ANNIKA MARTIN

CHAPTER 1

VICKY

I'M SMUGGLING a tiny white dog named Smuckers into a Manhattan hospital to see his owner, Bernadette Locke. Thanks to a standing appointment at a chandelier-draped dog salon on Fifth Avenue run by a woman who ostensibly loves dogs but might secretly hate them, Smuckers's facial fur is blow-dried into such an intense puff of white that his eager black eyes and wee raisin of a nose seem to float in a cloud.

There are three things to know about Bernadette: She's the meanest woman I ever met. She believes I'm some kind of dog whisperer who can read Smuckers's mind. (I can't.) And she's dying. Alone.

The people in her condo building will probably be glad to hear of her passing. I don't know what she did to earn their hatred. That's probably for the best.

Bernadette has a son out there somewhere, but even he seems to have washed his hands of her. There is a photo of the son on Bernadette's cracked fireplace mantel, a toddler with a scowly little dent between fierce blue eyes. Surrounded by people, the little boy manages somehow to look utterly alone.

Back when Bernadette got her terminal diagnosis, I asked her if she'd told her son and whether he might finally come to visit. She brushed off the question with a contemptuous wave of her hand—Bernadette's favorite way of responding to pretty much anything you say is a contemptuous wave of the hand. *He won't be coming, I assure you.*

I can't believe he wouldn't visit her, even now. It's the ultimate dick move. Your mother is dying alone, jackass!

Anyway, put all of that in a pot and stir it and you have the strange soup of me clicking past a guard, smiling brightly—and hopefully dazzlingly—enough that he doesn't notice the squirmy bulge in my oversized purse.

Smuckers is a Maltese, which is a toy dog that's outrageously cute. And Smuckers is the cutest of the cute.

Smuckers and Bernadette Locke made a notorious pair out on the sidewalk in the Upper West Side neighborhood where my little sister and I have our very sweet apartment-sitting gig.

I remember them well. Smuckers would attract people with his insane fluff-ball cuteness, but as the hapless victim drew near Bernadette would say something insulting. Kind of like the human equivalent of a Venus flytrap, where the fly is attracted to the beauty of the flower only to be mercilessly crushed.

Locals learned to stay away from the two of them. I tried—I really did.

Yet here I am, slipping down another chillingly bright hospital hallway, smuggling the little dog in for the third time in two weeks. It's not on my top ten list of things I want to do with my day. Not even on my top hundred, but Smuckers is Bernadette's only true friend. And I know what it's like to be hated and alone.

I know that when you're hated, you sometimes act like you don't care as a survival method.

2

And that makes people hate you more, because they feel like you should look at least a little beaten down.

Bernadette's hatred was real-life neighborhood hatred; mine was real life plus a fun national online component, but it works the same way, and heaven forbid you should have a cute dog. Or that a picture of you smiling should ever appear on Facebook or Huffpo or People.com.

I know, too, how being hated can build on itself, how sometimes you do things to make people hate you more because it's better in a certain perverse way. I think only people who have been hated in their life can truly understand that.

I push into the room. "We're here," I say brightly, relieved no medical personnel are around. While Smuckers enjoys being in a purse, he prefers to ride with his head out, like the fierce captain of a pleather airship. Needless to say, he's achieved maximum squirminess. I take him out. "Look, Smuckers—your mom!"

Bernadette is half propped up on pillows. Her skin is sallow and her hair sparse, but what hair she has is energetically white. Her eyes flutter open. "Finally."

She has a tube in her arm, but that's all. They've taken Bernadette off everything except morphine. They've given up on her.

"Smuckers is so excited to see you." I go over to her bed and set Smuckers next to her. Smuckers licks Bernadette's fingers, and the love that comes over Bernadette's face makes her look soft for a moment. Like a nice woman.

"Smuckers," she whispers. She moves her lips, talking to him. I can't hear, but I know from past conversations that she's saying she loves him. Sometimes she confesses she doesn't want to leave him, doesn't want to be alone. She's frightened about being alone.

Feebly she scratches Smuckers's fur, but she's focusing hard on me, whispering something fervently. I draw near. *Eggplant*, she seems to be saying.

"Are you hungry?"

"*Eggplant...*" she says, voice weak.

"Yes, Bernadette?"

"Eggplant makes your complexion..." she winces hard, "...*wormlike.*" She manages to infuse the word *wormlike* with incredulous contempt, as though I've performed such a feat of fashion monstrosity that she needs to muster all her strength to let me know.

"Damn. I was going for slug-like," I joke as I adjust Smuckers so that he's not on her tube.

She sniffs and turns back to Smuckers.

Over the three years I've known her, Bernadette has always been judgmental about my fashion choices. *Did you get that out of a 1969 catalog for librarians, Vicky? Did JCPenney have a sale on drab pencil skirts?* At times I literally seem to hurt her eyes, what with my uninspired ponytails and glasses and whatnot.

I have this suspicion that Bernadette came from money but that her fortune dwindled over the years. Clue one: her apartment is in an expensive neighborhood, but it's really shabby inside, like it was once grand and went to ruin. Also, her clothes are worn versions of what was expensive maybe fifteen years back. Really, she seems to spend nothing on herself. But Smuckers? Nothing is too good for Smuckers. No expense spared.

I take her hand and put it where Smuckers most likes it so Smuckers will settle down.

"Smuckers," she breathes.

I have this impulse to set a comforting hand on her arm, but human contact is not something Bernadette would ever want from me.

I'm really only around as an extension of Smuckers, a conduit for Smuckers's important communications. Other than that, I'm chopped liver. If Bernadette could somehow automate me or keep me in a sardine tin with just the corner rolled up so my voice can escape, she would.

She looks up at me expectantly. I know what she wants. What does Smuckers have to say?

I'm at a loss for what to say, or rather, what Smuckers might say. I never signed up for this fake pet whisperer gig with her, and what with her being on her deathbed, it seems especially wrong.

But she's waiting. Glaring. She wants a communication from Smuckers. She won't rest until she gets one.

I suck in a breath and put on my whisperer expression, which I would describe as a curious listening face. "Smuckers says that you shouldn't be afraid to die," I say.

She waits. She wants more.

"He wants you to know it's going to be okay, even though it might not feel like that right now."

She nods, mumbles to Smuckers.

In terms of subject matter, this is getting into new territory. Smuckers has typically confined himself to lifestyle commentary —requests for certain styles of neck scritching or flavors of Fancy Whiskas dog treats.

Now and then he'll speculate on the antics of pigeons outside the window. He has certainly never exhibited any divine wisdom about death or special understanding of esoteric secrets of the cosmos.

But I can tell from Bernadette's face that she likes hearing that Smuckers supposedly said that.

"Vicky," she says to Smuckers. "Vicky will care for you."

"You know I will, Bernadette," I say. "I'll care for Smuckers as if he were my own flesh and blood."

Though not literally. I don't plan on racing around Central Park eating goose poop with him.

"He'll live like a little king," I amend.

Bernadette mumbles something and I settle into the surprisingly luxurious, leather-upholstered chair in the roomy private room they've given her. This is the hospice wing of one of the larger Manhattan hospitals where the news often talks about overcrowded conditions.

How did she get this fancy room? Maybe she has good insurance or something.

Bernadette scritches Smuckers's neck. "Love you, Pokey," she whispers.

I quietly scroll through Instagram, one ear attuned to the door, but all I hear is the sound of footsteps and muted conversations going up and down the hall, along with the occasional intercom announcement. I want to make this visit last as long as possible.

Smuckers will live like a little king, but maybe not a king of a wealthy country. More like a king of an impoverished nation, but one that loves their king. That's the best I can do for him.

I took Smuckers home two weeks ago, the day before Bernadette went into the hospital. It wasn't long before I discovered that the raw frozen food he gets is more expensive than spun gold, and I can only imagine what it costs to re-up his puffball hairstyle at his monthly standing appointment at the aforementioned dog salon, which has an original Warhol painting of a poodle in the waiting area.

I'll just let you do the math on that one.

So, no, I don't envision keeping Smuckers in the exact lifestyle he's accustomed to. I've supported my little sister, Carly, ever since she was nine years old and I want her to have everything I never did. I want her to feel safe and dream big.

And if there's some left over for a fabulous blowout, it'll be her in that chair and they won't have to tie her up to do it like poor Smuckers.

She's sixteen now. It's hard to raise a teen in Manhattan, but somehow we make it, thanks to my Etsy store of funky dog accessories. Someday I'll break into women's jewelry, but for now, it's all sequined bow tie dog collars all the time.

Bernadette's lips move. Nothing comes out except the word *alone—I don't want to be alone.*

I feel a pang in my heart.

It's strange how a long life can be reduced to a darkened hospice room, a stranger scrolling Instagram, and a little white dog.

Though I suppose it's no more strange than my playing the part of a pet whisperer, which I never in my life wanted to do, and which I a hundred percent blame my friend Kimmy for.

Kimmy is the one who put on a festival to raise money for her animal shelter, the one who looked at me so beseechingly, holding a colorful scarf and hoop earrings, when the real pet whisperer didn't show up for the pet whisperer booth.

Just make shit up, she said. *It'll be fun,* she said.

So I left Carly to handle the booth selling my dog accessories and I put on the scarf.

I'd said whatever came into my head that day. A lot of pets had complaints about their food. Most wanted the owners to play with them more. Sometimes, if the companion person seemed sad, the pet would express intense empathy and love. I think, no matter who you are, your pet cares about you.

Sometimes I'd say how much the pet enjoys it when they talk to them or when they sing to them, because doesn't everyone talk and sing to their pets?

Then Bernadette came by, steely and outraged, smashing the pavement with her cane alongside a tiny, energetic toy dog.

She threw down two five-dollar bills and demanded to know what Smuckers wanted to tell her. I honestly couldn't tell whether she wanted to debunk me or if she really wanted to know.

So I took the little dog in my lap and rubbed his fuzzy little ears and started talking. I'd found, over the course of my afternoon as a pet whisperer, that the more flattering you are, the more the people buy it.

Smuckers loves you so much, I'd told her. *He knows you think you're too slow for him, but he doesn't care. He loves you. And he mostly loves to hear you sing. Maybe you can't run around with him, but he wants you to know that your singing is amazing to him. He thinks you're beautiful when you sing.*

When I looked up, her eyes were shining. She really believed me. I hadn't felt like a scammer until then. She asked for my card, but I told her it was just for fun.

She didn't believe I didn't have a card. Like I was evilly keeping my card from her.

I told her that if she just watched Smuckers closely enough, she could do it, too.

She bit back something about *not all of us being pet whisperers* and then proceeded to try and get my contact information from other people there, who refused to give it, and who she then insulted.

She finally left, and I thought I was home free, but New York has a way of pulling random people into each other's lives. And you can be sure that the exact person you don't want to run into in the city of millions will show up as a regular where you work or shop, or in Bernadette's case, as a frequent sitter on the bench Carly and I had to pass on the way to her school.

I look up from Instagram to see Smuckers at the edge of the bed, like he wants to jump down. I go over and give him a vigorous ear rub and he circles and settles.

The last time I was here visiting, a priest came in, offering to say a few words, and Bernadette called him a sewer rat in the process of banishing him from the room. *Sewer rat* is one of her favorite insults for neighbors, mail carriers, clerks, and the revolving roster of maids she has in.

But never for Smuckers. I stay at the bedside, feeling so bad for her.

"Smuckers wants you not to be scared," I say. "Smuckers says you're not alone, and you won't be."

Her dry lips move. If I could give her anything it would be some way for her not to be scared, but it's pretty unavoidable in her situation. I don't care what religion you are, the unknown is always scary, and death is the ultimate unknown quantity.

A nurse comes in just then, entering stealthily. She spots Smuckers before I can flick the sheet over him like I usually manage to do. "You can't have a dog in here!"

I shamble on a surprised face. "The other nurses didn't say anything about the dog..." Since they didn't *see* the dog.

"You need to remove the animal."

"Get out," Bernadette says hoarsely.

"I'm sorry," the nurse says. "Animals not allowed."

I go over. "Please," I say under my breath. "The dog's all she has. You need to give her a break."

"Hospital regulations."

I look back over at Bernadette, who is doing a nervous clutching thing on Smuckers's fur, something Smuckers won't tolerate too long. I go back over and put a protective hand on Bernadette's to get her to stop it.

"A few more minutes," I say. "If he was a service animal you'd let him in here. Can't you just pretend he's a service animal? I mean, he pretty much is one."

"You'll have to remove the animal."

"A few more minutes," I say.

"I'm getting security." She spins and leaves. Security.

I turn to Bernadette. "The *animal*," I say. "Please."

She's only paying attention to Smuckers, though. Her breathing is erratic. She's upset.

Security will throw us out, and I probably won't get Smuckers in here again. Which means this is the last time Bernadette sees Smuckers, and maybe she knows it.

I feel sad and helpless, but also like everything is important now. Like I have an important job to do as fake pet whisperer.

That's when I make up the story.

"Smuckers has something to tell you, Bernadette," I say. "He has something to say that he never told you before, and he needs to say it."

She moves her lips. Nothing comes out, but I know what it is. *Tell me.*

That's what she always says when I announce that Smuckers has something important to communicate.

Whenever I channel Smuckers's thoughts, I use the curious listening face and also change my voice just a tiny bit. *I hate it when my water bowl is dry, Bernadette. Sometimes I get so very thirsty!* Or, *You shouldn't let that sketchy building handyman in anymore, Bernadette, unless somebody you trust is with you. I don't like him very much. The food in the refrigerator smells very yucky. Maybe it's old.*

Smuckers uses the word *very* a lot.

In addition to household matters, Smuckers is a good one for morale and encouragement. *Your flowered shirts are very pretty. Please open the curtains, Bernadette, I love watching the birds. I feel very happy when you sing.*

The sound of Bernadette's singing was a major passion of Smuckers's, according to me. And Bernadette is actually kind of a good singer, as it turned out, from the bits I heard over the three years I've been at it.

"This is very important. Are you listening? Smuckers wants you to know that he has a brother. A twin."

Bernadette seems to still. She's listening.

"It's painful for Smuckers to remember. Smuckers's twin brother died as a puppy. His name is Licky Lickardo."

Bernadette's lips quirk.

Does she like that name? She was a huge *I Love Lucy* fan in her day.

"What dimwit named him that?" she croaks.

Oh.

"Umm...that's not important. Licky Lickardo lives on the other side. He looks just like Smuckers. Smuckers has told Licky all about you. Licky needs a friend so badly, and he's waiting for you on the other side. Just beyond the light. And he's just like Smuckers. You'll totally think it's Smuckers. And you'll know his thoughts. You won't need me."

I once read about this ancient island tribe once where if a king died, he'd have his queen and servants and pets killed and buried with him, believing that they would then accompany him to the afterlife.

This Licky Lickardo thing kind of delivers on that, but in a less psycho way—she's getting the pet and the special whisperer services in the afterlife or whatever she believes in, but the whisperer and pet get to stay in Manhattan.

In fact, Bernadette's breathing seems to calm.

"So here's the deal. I'll take care of Smuckers, like I promised, but Smuckers needs a promise from you. Are you listening?"

She moves her lips. *Tell me.*

"Smuckers very much needs to know if you'll take care of his brother. Licky is just like Smuckers, Bernadette. Smuckers can't wait for you to meet him."

The way her hand changes, grasping Smuckers's neck, I think she likes it.

I keep on.

"Smuckers says you're going to love Licky so much. Oh, wow! Smuckers says that Licky is wagging his tail right now—he totally can't wait. He's wagging up a storm, just like Smuckers does when he sees you coming."

Bernadette's face is definitely softening. Is this wrong? I don't know. But then again, I've gone a long way down the road of wrong already with this thing.

"Smuckers has something else important to tell you. Instructions! He says you should sing *Somewhere Over the Rainbow* the minute you get to the other side. Smuckers says to follow the light and you'll see Licky Lickardo wagging his tail. And you're to immediately sing *Somewhere Over the Rainbow*."

Right then, a voice booms, "What the hell is going on here?"

I sit up, a rabbit in the headlights—or more like a virgin sacrifice, pinned by the furious gaze of a man in a perfectly tailored suit, a prince of a power broker currently standing in the doorway, though the word *standing* doesn't quite cover it. He's owning it. Dominating it. Lording over all the world from it like an entitled god.

His brown hair is impossibly lustrous, touched with gold where the light hits. There's something charmed about him, but more like wickedly charmed. His eyes are cobalt blue. Icy daggers, aimed to kill.

To kill *me*.

How long has he been standing there?

Bernadette begins again to clutch at Smuckers.

"Shhh," I whisper, putting a finger to my lips.

He straightens, as though *shhh* is a strange command to his ears, and I suppose it probably is. This is not the kind of guy you say *shhh* to.

"What are you filling my mother's head with?"

Mother? This straightens me right up. This is *the son?*

"Well…" I cross my arms. "About time you visited."

He scowls and strides commandingly across the room.

He reminds me of a vengeful god in one of those ancient paintings that hang in the Met. Current mood: destroy the earth. But this god wears a suit instead of flowing robes. Vengeful god 2.0: the hot-but-scary Wall Street edition—hard, deadly, and dressed to kill it in the boardroom.

It seems impossible that this man was ever that lost little boy in the photo on Bernadette's mantel.

He sets a disposable cup on a table next to a small stack of empty cups over in the corner. It's here that I notice there are several iThings there next to a man's cashmere coat slung over the arm.

So he's been here. For a while.

He turns back to me. "Smuckers says to follow the light? He says to sing *Over the Rainbow*? A brother named Licky Lickardo on the other side? Care to explain any of that?"

Definitely not, I think.

I turn to Bernadette, like maybe she might care to explain for me, but her eyes are closed. Is she faking sleeping? That would be so Bernadette. "Bernadette," I say. "Hey, tell your son—"

My words die as he nears, looming over her on the other side of her bed. He gazes down at her with an expression I can't read.

I wait, cowering in my sensible pumps.

"Was she...*awake?*"

"Well, yeah," I whisper.

"You're sure?"

"Yeah."

He's silent for a long time, still with that unreadable expression, but a small dent forms between his brows, like he's working something out in his mind—something troubling or distressing. It's here I see a flash of that boy in the photo.

"She wanted to see Smuckers," I explain. "I was just...trying to help."

When he looks up at me a second later, the boy is gone. Maybe the whole thing was an illusion. "*Help* is an odd term for trying to convince a dying woman you're communicating with her dog," he bites out. "Giving her bizarre messages from her dog." He pulls out his phone. "Maybe you can explain your *help* to the police."

My heart pounds. Communicating with her dog, bizarre messages from her dog—that *is* what I was doing!

"She just wanted to see Smuckers," I protest.

He gives me a disgusted look. "And you're happy to accommodate. If there's something in it for you."

I raise myself up straight as possible because I wasn't doing anything wrong.

I wasn't doing anything wrong.

"She likes to interact with Smuckers." I swallow. "She doesn't want to be alone."

"Harry," he says, strolling out into the hall and speaking in soft tones. Is Harry the police?

"Bernadette." I touch her hand. "I have to go, Bernadette."

She stirs. Did she even hear?

The son returns a moment later. "They're coming." His steely glare twists through my belly like a corkscrew.

I won't let him cow me. Years ago I swore I'd never let a rich asshole scare me or bully me ever again—not ever again.

So I glare right back.

It comes to me at this point that there's something oddly familiar about him. He's got that classic Hollywood-leading-man look—at least, if your Hollywood movie was about a darkly mesmerizing titan of industry. If your movie was about a friendly cowpoke this guy probably wouldn't work out, unless you wanted him to turn dangerous at the end and take over the whole town.

"Good," I say. "Let them come." I don't mean it. The last thing I need is the cops.

He scowls. "Mom," he says, looking down at her.

There's this awkward silence where she doesn't reply, and I think I should go, but I don't want to rip Smuckers away.

"You're telling me she seemed…conscious before?" He asks it remotely and without looking up.

"She was talking," I say. "Petting Smuckers."

The expression on his face is unreadable.

Just then, a beefy bald-headed guy in a security uniform comes in, followed by two nurses. "You're going to have to take the animal out—now," the security guard growls.

Bernadette's hand is over Smuckers's fuzzy little back.

"Leave him," I plead. "She'll be so upset."

Nobody's listening to me; their attention riveted on the son who has chosen this moment to turn the harsh light of his wrath onto the guard and the nurses.

I take a deep breath. I feel like I haven't breathed since he entered the room.

Calmly, the son cocks his head. He and the security guard are about the same size—the security guard might even be a bit beefier, but if it came to a fight, my money would be on the son. He has an aura of power and confidence. He crackles with it.

The security guard is no wimp, though. He stares right back, all testosterone. It's like watching *Animal Kingdom*, Midtown Manhattan Edition.

"If my mother wants the dog by her side," he says calmly, "my mother gets the dog by her side."

"Rule's a rule," the security guy growls. "You'll remove the animal or I'll remove it and hand it over to animal control."

Animal control? It?

The son's blue eyes sparkle with humor, as if the security guard's threats are mere clownish whispers in a world constructed for him and him alone.

He addresses the assembled staff as a group. "Do you all understand who this is?"

It's Smuckers, biotches! I think.

The complaining nurse folds her arms. "I don't care. This is a pet-free facility."

I rivet my attention to the son. I didn't like him when he was turning his hard-ass Blue Magnum gaze on me, but now his asshole power is on my side, or at least Smuckers's side.

"This is Bernadette Locke, head of the Locke Foundation, the entity that funded this wing, the medical teaching and research facility on the other side of that skyway, and probably your paychecks."

I straighten. *What?*

More people come into the room, among them, a woman who seems to be some kind of administrator. "Henry Locke," she says, grasping his hand. She apologizes for the mix-up, uttering words of empathy, admiration, gratitude. If he had a ring, she'd kiss it. She'd make out with it.

"...and of *course* Mrs. Locke can have her dog stay with her as long as she pleases," she continues. "With our sincerest apologies —we had no idea that the swing shift was not informed..." She mumbles on, all excuses.

"Thanks," I say. "It means a lot."

They all look at me, like *you're* still here?

The son points at me. "You. Out."

"Wait. I promised Bernadette—I promised her I'd care for Smuckers. She asked me specifically to care for him, you know, when..."

He huffs out an exasperated breath and holds out his hand. "Card."

I grab my wallet, and hand over my Etsy business card, quickly drawing away from the brush of his hand, the sizzle of his orbit.

The card has a photo of a tough-looking German shepherd wearing a pink-sequined bow tie.

He scowls down at it for a long time. Really scowls.

I'm imagining that he's thinking of all the things he'd do if somebody tried to put a bow tie dog collar on him. And I'm guessing none of his scenarios end with the bow tie dog collar being in any way recognizable as a bow tie dog collar.

"She wants to know Smuckers has a home and—"

"I comprehend the meaning of *care for Smuckers*," he says. "We'll send Smuckers in a car."

A car. That's how Mrs. Locke would always say it. Send a car. I thought she meant an Uber or a cab all this time.

But it comes to me, standing there, that Bernadette Locke belongs in an entirely different world than I belong to, and that in her world a *car* is probably a *limo*.

CHAPTER 2

TWO WEEKS LATER

Vicky

I ALMOST DON'T ANSWER the buzzer. I'm not expecting anyone. And who just shows up and buzzes? A drunk or a freak, that's who.

My sister, Carly, is busy fulfilling her duty as a sixteen-year-old girl to make us late due to hair styling operations that are more complex than a Space-X mission.

The buzzer sounds again and again. Smuckers barks.

I pick him up. "Shhh!" We're not technically supposed to have dogs in the building.

Carly answers it. "For you," she says.

I go and push the intercom button. "This is Vicky."

"Certified letter for Smuckers care of Vicky Nelson."

"A letter for *Smuckers*?"

"Yes. Care of Vicky Nelson."

A Venn diagram forms in my mind.

The circle that contains people I know who would think of

such a moronic joke does not touch the circle that contains friends who would be up this early. "No, thanks," I say.

Buzzzzz.

"Reading the envelope," comes the voice. "Smuckers care of Vicky Nelson. From the law offices of Malcomb, Malcomb, and Miller."

It occurs to me then that maybe Bernadette remembered her promise to help pay for Smuckers's upkeep, after all.

She'd mentioned it when she was asking me to care for him, once the diagnosis was in. *Take care of my baby. I'll see you're compensated,* she'd said.

I never thought she'd actually follow through. Bernadette made a lot of promises and vows in her life. She liked making promises way more than following through on them.

To be clear, I didn't offer to care for Smuckers to earn any kind of allowance—I would happily do it for free. The little dog had grown on Carly and me over the years and no way would I let him go to a home that wouldn't love his fuzzy little face as much as we did.

But what if? What if she'd made arrangements to defray his food and vet costs? It would be a godsend!

"Coming down," I say.

I spin and eye Carly. She's not ready yet. "I'll take Smuckers down and we'll handle this and wait. Five minutes." I look over at the corner where Buddy the parrot eyes me. "And feed Buddy!"

I carry Smuckers down all six flights. Smuckers is for shit on stairs.

I never saw Bernadette after that day in the hospital with Henry Locke. She died soon after and Henry's assistant called me with an alert that Smuckers was being sent over, and it was indeed in a limo. Carly and I just laughed, seeing his furry little snout in the backseat window of the sleek, black, mad-money ride.

Instagram time!

I didn't go to Bernadette's funeral. Nobody invited me—not that I expected it after meeting jerky hard-ass Henry Locke. Smuckers and I said goodbye to her in our own way, sitting on their favorite bench together. Dog treats were involved.

Carly's been telling me all along to track down Henry and make him follow through on Bernadette's promise to defray Smuckers's upkeep. I told Carly I'd take a job as a gloryhole attendant at the Glory Daze massage parlor before I'd approach Henry for money. The Glory Daze is an actual place in the shitty Bronx neighborhood where we used to live before we got our very sweet long-term apartment-and-parrot sitting gig. And it's what you think.

I will never ask Henry for anything.

Henry is exactly the kind of rich, entitled asshole I've constructed my life around avoiding.

I find a courier waiting outside the doorway. He hands over a large envelope and gets my signature.

I thank him and put Smuckers on the green leash that goes with today's green bow tie.

I open the envelope while he poops next to his favorite light pole with its graffiti-covered base. My heart sinks when I see there are only some letters inside.

No check.

Oh well. I walk Smuckers up to the block to throw the poop bag in the trash. He smells the small fence around the scrubby little tree, investigates a sticky dark puddle with yellow bits in it that I'm hoping is a smashed ice cream cone.

I pull him back to the stoop and we sit, just outside of the stream of people rushing back and forth. I pull out the papers and get to reading.

It takes a good minute for me to get that it's not just any letter; it's a summons to a reading of the last will and testament of Bernadette Locke.

"Because that would've been too easy," I say to Smuckers, who is straining in the direction the suspicious possible ice cream cone.

A young woman with wild magenta hair that has a streak of yellow down one side comes by, and Smuckers forgets about his quest for food in favor of stranger petting, which he gets.

Carly arrives and smiles at the woman. "I love your hair! I want your hair." The woman smiles and walks off, and Carly discreetly snaps a photo. "Did you see that?" Carly says. "That's the exact hair I want."

"Mmm-hmm," I say.

"There's this cute place on Eighty-fourth that does it. Bess is doing purple there this weekend, and I'm thinking about maybe a change." She twirls a red curl. "Of the purple and yellow kind..."

"You know the rule," I say.

"But I want to go with Bess. She's not going to want to delay."

I raise my eyebrows. "Twenty-one-day cooling-off period. All major financial and appearance decisions."

"Colorful hair is not really major."

"That's what you're going with? Hair in two different Skittles colors is not major?"

She pouts.

I grab her backpack. "Come on. That's our pact."

"It's not fair. You never make money or appearance decisions. You have everything the same all the time."

"It's our pact. End of story."

We head down the crowded sidewalk, expertly sidestepping people on their phones and navigating around wandering tourists with the precision of fighter jets in formation.

"I'm going to tell Bess to delay twenty-one days and then I'll do it with her," she says when we come back together.

I give her a look.

"What?"

"That's a commitment. When you're good for your word, like we are, committing is the same as doing. Telling Bess to delay because you'll do it with her?" We've been over this before. "We keep our word, us two."

She snorts and huffs. But it's our thing, and she knows it.

We two sisters keep our word. It's a thing.

Also, our pact has kept her from quite a few misguided tattoos.

"What was the courier? Was it the Smuckers allowance?"

"Who knows?" I say. "Maybe she put the dog food allowance in her will. I have to take an afternoon off work and trek halfway across town to find out. Rich people have no concept of life."

Carly zeroes in on another fashionable woman with wild-colored hair and then gives me the side-eye.

"Bird," I say, which is our sisters version of *fuck you*, from flipping the finger, the bird.

But really, that's what I want for her—to only have to worry about things like hair and pop music and TikTok lighting techniques. I'll fight to see she gets that. She's decided to be an actress but she has to wait until she's a senior in high school before she can be in nonschool productions.

I know I keep her too close. She doesn't get to kick around town at night like other girls her age. The helicopter sister. But better that than our shipwrecked mom back home in Deerville.

"Tell you what," I say. "If I get Saks, we'll go get ourselves two-hundred-dollar blowouts."

"Hold you to it."

The preliminary buyers liked my collection of jewelry for humans. Sedate elegance, they called it, which is about right. It's not the big, wild, exuberantly colorful stuff that I used to be attracted to, but I'm good with that. My life these days is geared for staying under the radar. Coloring inside the lines.

I'd do anything to distance myself from when I was Vonda O'Neil, the most hated teen in America for one very long summer some seven years ago. The girl who cried wolf. Except there really *was* a wolf.

Nobody believed me.

Carly hates the clothes I wear even more than Bernadette ever did. *You're not on trial anymore*, she always says. *You can stop living like a monk now. You don't have to wear those boring-ass outfits.*

But the pencil skirts and dark sweater sets my lawyer recommended grew on me. For the record, they're not boring-ass. They project an image of trustworthiness, and that's important to me.

Anyway, there's just one more hurdle for my jewelry line—the VP of merchandising. A huge order from Saks would make such a difference. Carly doesn't know how hand-to-mouth we actually live; we're still in the hole from two years of braces, but I'll never let her know. I don't just want to protect her from Mom; I want to protect her from everything.

"Can a person even do that? Leave an allowance to a dog in a will?"

"Rich people can do anything they want to," I say, and then I swallow my bitterness, because Carly doesn't need it. She doesn't need to hate rich, entitled people, and specifically rich, entitled men, the way I do.

It still shocks me that Bernadette was fabulously wealthy. She was pretty successful in hiding it; she seemed post-rich, if anything. I sometimes wonder if she concealed it because she picked up my disdain for the wealthy.

After the shelter fundraiser fair, Bernadette suddenly started showing up on this bench that Carly and I couldn't avoid passing in getting to Carly's school, and she'd call us over and ask for a reading—*just a few impressions*, she'd sometimes say. And I'd politely decline.

Carly thought she was stalking us, because she kept on showing up. I don't know about that, but she definitely got madder and madder that I wouldn't read Smuckers for her. She clearly thought it was a personal thing I had against her. The woman had a paranoid and highly suspicious nature.

Then there was the day she was in distress, out in the heat. We were on the way to school, as usual, and she was half slumped on that bench, so pale and frail, with Smuckers panting at the end of his leash. We stopped to make sure she was okay. She told us she felt faint; she asked us to help her home.

Her home turned out to be a gorgeous prewar building several blocks down. We got her up and settled in and hydrated. As soon as she bounced back to her regular self, she offered me money for a special Smuckers reading from the whisperer.

It was then I saw Smuckers's bone-dry water bowl.

"Okay, one quick free read," I said.

Carly widened her eyes as I unhooked Smuckers's leash and picked him up. I put my hand on his head, kind of a Vulcan mind-meld thing, and closed my eyes. *So thirsty. I need a lot of water. So very thirsty, Bernadette.*

Bernadette seemed pretty upset when she looked down at Smuckers's water bowl. I made Carly fill it and we got out of there as quickly as possible after that.

That was the first step down the slippery slope of being a pet whisperer.

Bernadette's next move was a masterful one. From a different bench, she spotted Carly playing Frisbee in the park with some girlfriends. She asked her if she'd walk Smuckers for thirty bucks —just around the park.

Carly jumped at it and treated her friends to frozen yogurt afterward. Days later came the big ask—Bernadette wanted Carly to be her permanent dog walker, once a day, an easy thirty bucks. No doubt she suspected how badly Carly would want it, and probably figured I wasn't going to let Carly walk the streets of Manhattan alone with that dog.

I said no to Carly at first, but eventually I relented, after making Carly agree that twenty-five out of every thirty bucks would go to a college fund. And, really, dog walking is a legit service, unlike pet whisperer. Especially for Bernadette.

From then on, we'd stop off at Bernadette's apartment on the way home from Carly's school. We'd grab Smuckers and do an errand or two. Sometimes we'd take him to watch the neighborhood mimes. We feel sorry for them, because they are really not at all talented, but they always brighten up in a gleeful mime way when Smuckers comes around.

Little by little, Smuckers began delivering safety-conscious or morale-boosting messages to Bernadette. She was so alone, and Smuckers was the only one she seemed inclined to listen to. It felt like a public service.

Sometimes I'd wonder if Bernadette sensed our kinship—my summer as a universally hated media sensation and her present as a despised neighborhood fixture.

Either way, that money was a kindness to Carly and to me. Another reason I didn't feel inclined to press for more for Smuckers's upkeep.

True, I'd switched over his food from frozen raw rabbit meat to a sad dime-store brand, and the closest Smuckers has had to a blowout at a dog salon with original Warhol art is a brightly colored dog brush dragged through her fur, but Smuckers has a great life with lots of fawning attention from teenaged girls.

I decide I'll go to the reading anyway, though, because if Bernadette left money for Smuckers to go to his special groomer and vet and all that, well, that was the bargain I'd made.

Luckily, the reading is during school hours the following week. It takes place on the Upper East Side and the letter specifically requests Smuckers's presence.

I brush him extra well, put a dapper black-sequined bow tie on him, bundle him into his flowered carrying case, and set off. I throw a buck into the mimes' hat set on the way to the subway station. I transfer at 59th and Lex and then walk a few blocks. I budgeted extra time so I wouldn't have to splurge on a cab.

It's cool for early September—autumn is definitely in the air. My iPhone map function guides me deeper and deeper into a neighborhood where I've never been, though I'm more inclined to call it an enchanted glen; the trees are huge and healthy, the streets are clean, and the buildings have a fairy-tale sheen to them. Will a unicorn soon bound out from the foliage?

I arrive at the address on the letter, which turns out to be an impossibly vertical mansion made from white marble, of all things. I go up the walk, ascend the strangely spotless stairway, and push through beveled-glass doors.

The inside is all lush carpet and ornate woodwork, even on the ceiling. I take Smuckers out of his case and carry him in my arms as I go in search of room eleven. I'm glad I have the letter with me, because I'm thinking they might not let me in, even though I'm wearing an ultra-trustworthy outfit with a delicate obsidian necklace of my own design.

Room eleven turns out to be full of illustrious-looking people standing around talking against a backdrop of chandeliers and dark carved wood. It's like I stumbled into a photo shoot for Dior.

I spot Henry right away. He's not technically in the middle of the room, but he's definitely the center of gravity, forcing everyone to orbit around him with his asshole sheen of power.

Most of the people here have the blue eyes and gold-burnished dark hair of Henry, as well as the imperious stature, though nobody wears it quite like him. It reminds me of the way a high school girl gets into a certain style and all her friends follow her, but nobody quite pulls it off like she does.

Henry spots me immediately, or more accurately, glowers at me immediately, a disturbance in the field of poshness, and then they all turn to glower at me, as if on the silent and kingly command of Henry. And they all have this look like they *can't even!*

Henry is the one to address me. "What are *you* doing here?"

My belly squeezes. My throat feels thick. Standing there, squirming under the power of Henry's glower, I'm suddenly sick,

sick, sick of myself. How did I get back here, cowering before the overwhelming force of wealth and power?

I'm suddenly grateful for Smuckers in my arms, a canine shield of cuteness. I squeeze him tight. "I was called. Or... Smuckers was. This letter came to Smuckers care of me. A summons, I suppose is the word. I don't know. It seemed official..."

Stop over explaining, I tell myself. *You've done nothing wrong. He can't hurt you. Hold your head high.*

"In other words, you think you got your payday, after all," Henry says.

I straighten my backbone. "Sorry, Richie McRichface, we were summoned, just like the rest of you probably were."

A hush comes over the room. I look around.

"What? Did somebody murder the butler with a golden candlestick?"

Henry's eyes glitter. He's every inch the lion at the gates of the palace, the epitome of the kind of person I vowed never to be pushed around by or terrorized by ever again.

I hold out the letter, heart pounding, a mouse in Henry's mighty jaws, dangling by my tail. No way will I let him know it.

He stops in front of me and takes the letter.

"Who is this?" another guy asks. Another one of the relatives. Younger than Henry, from the looks of it—maybe twenty-seven, whereas Henry is around thirty.

Henry doesn't answer; he's performing an intensive examination of the letter.

"It's real," I say.

He turns it over. Holds it up to the light. And suddenly I'm back there, sixteen years old, everyone acting like I'm the liar, trying to intimidate me. Challenging me on things no regular person would be challenged on.

"Oh, please," I grab it from his hand. "You know it's real, so don't bother."

"You know her, Henry?" the younger relative asks again.

"She was in Mom's hospital room." Henry eyes me. "Pretending to read the dog's mind."

Umm...what to say to that. It is definitely what I was doing. I shift Smuckers to the other arm. "The *dog* has a name," I say. "It's *Smuckers*."

Henry gazes down at me imperiously. "And now she's hoping for a payday. So, how long did you have your hooks into my mother?"

Sometimes a question is a question. Other times, a question is a finger, aggressively poking your chest.

That's what this question is, a bullying finger jab. "I didn't fool her or have hooks into her," I explain. "I never expected anything from her. I took Smuckers out of kindness."

The younger relative snorts, like I'm being ridiculous, but I keep on.

"Did she think I'm a dog whisperer? Yeah, even though I told her repeatedly I wasn't. Excuse me if I tried to use it to help her now and then."

"You mean help yourself," says Henry's younger but equally burnished relative. "If there are signs you manipulated her with your shady dog psychic act..." The relative frowns, like the implications are too troubling to name.

"What?" I say, heart racing madly. I don't really want to know, but I learned with bullies that you have to pin them down. You can't just be scared. "Or what?"

The Henry clone raises his brows, like, *you'll see.*

I snort. "I thought so."

Everybody's looking at me, but it's Henry's gaze I feel, like a silken ribbon on my skin. I don't dare look at him. He's a raging inferno of assholishness and powersuitedness with a dash of hotness that makes him...uh.

I spot a tray of champagne flutes. I walk over and take a glass, just to do something.

Also, alcohol.

I concentrate on the holding of Smuckers and the sipping of champagne while I wait for whatever is supposed to happen to start happening.

Henry and his clan are all on the other side of the room, quietly affronted and maybe they really *are* eyeing the candlesticks. There are several large candlesticks, all of them good and hefty.

I was surprised Bernadette funded so much of the hospital, with her apartment being so shabby and all, surprised that she was a somebody from a long line of somebodies, the kind that show up on the society websites. I was actually surprised there were society websites at all, but maybe that's not a shock since I'm allergic to rich personages of every stripe.

Carly was actually the one who ushered me into the world of society websites and Henry Locke soon after I came home from the hospice and uttered his name.

"Wait—*the* Henry Locke?" she said.

"There's a *the* Henry Locke?"

"Uh!" Carly has about fifty varieties of *Uh!* This one I recognized as her *can-you-be-more-clueless?-Obviously-NOT!* variety of *Uh.* She fired up her phone and promptly handed it over, and I found myself staring at a smiling tuxedo-clad Henry with a beautiful, dark-haired woman on his arm, dressed in Givenchy.

"So, he's supposed to be somebody?"

She fixed her most incredulous gaze on me. "Henry Locke? Playboy starchitect? Cock Worldwide?"

"Wait, what?" Cock Worldwide is our joke whenever we pass one of the gigantic Locke Worldwide cranes that dominate the construction site of every giant project. I assure you, we're not the only ones who make the joke, not the only ones who look at the logo of circles in the shape of a building and see quite a different image, not the only ones who think it's funny to combine the sighting of a Cock Worldwide crane with erection commentary. "He and Bernadette are *that* Locke?"

"How many Lockes do you think fund New York hospitals?"

I narrowed my eyes. "Umm…"

She snorted, disgusted with my ignorance of New York's leading luminaries. Billionaire Henry Locke is one of New York's top ten most eligible bachelors, according to another image she showed me, this one from *This Week NY*.

Judging from the scowl he wears in the photo, Henry wasn't any happier about being named one of New York's leading bachelors than he was finding a fake dog whisperer in his mother's hospital room.

"Most eligible bachelor if you're a masochist," I said, handing the phone back to her. "Did you call him starchitect?"

"It means star architect," she'd informed me.

All in all, my little sister was far more enthused about the personage of Henry Locke than I was.

I'm draining the last of my champagne when the team of lawyers enters the room. They don't say they're lawyers, but I know lawyers when I see them. They take a table set up near the fireplace.

Members of the Locke clan take the front chairs that face the lawyers' table. I take the back, the disreputable kid with her fluffy sidekick.

Members of the Locke clan wear nice outfits and they're impossibly beautiful. The women all have amazing blowouts, though it's possible they just have good hair genes. People with good hair genes tend to marry other people with good hair genes, and through the generations end up having kids with even better hair, and those kids find each other.

Like Pekinese noses, but far more desirable.

So that's the theory I'm spinning as the reading of the will begins with a distribution of money from various overseas bank accounts.

Every time I think the bank accounts portion of the will reading is over, there are more overseas bank accounts for the lawyer to list off. It's like a clown car of overseas bank accounts.

I really am pleasantly surprised Bernadette thought of Smuckers. It would be good if I could take him to the Park Avenue vet who has known him since puppyhood, and if there's money for his fancy food, I'm all there. I'm guessing there will be some bill submittal process, which is fine with me as long as I don't have to interact with these Locke heirs.

The lawyer has moved on to real estate parcels. I pull out my phone and check Twitter.

That takes forever, of course, and then we move onto the *listing of unoriginal corporate names* portion of the reading. It seems the Locke empire stretches far beyond Locke Worldwide. There is Locke Companies, Inc., Locke Holdings, Locke Capital Group, Locke Asset Management, Locke Architectural Services, and more.

I'm in the middle of an important operation that involves me retweeting a meme of a raccoon in a ballerina skirt when the listing of unoriginal names concludes with, "To Smuckers, whose intentions and decisions in all matters will be interpreted by Victoria Nelson."

I look up to find a dozen threatening glares. Except Henry. A man like Henry doesn't need to expend energy on things like a threatening glare. He just flicks his fingers and you're destroyed.

The lawyer is continuing. Something about a term of Smuckers's natural life or ten years, whichever comes first, and then something something something stipulate something.

"Um, could you repeat the whole Smuckers part?" I ask.

"This is ridiculous." Henry stands. "I contest this. All of it."

The lawyer holds up his hand. "Henry." He says it in a calming tone, a warning tone. "Please recall that any challenge to the will nullifies the real estate and holdings provisions. Upon any legal challenge..."

"She can't do this," a woman says.

I stand. "Please, can somebody explain..."

"Come off it," an older man says. "You know exactly what happened."

After my dad died, one of Mom's less scummy boyfriends took us to Cocoa Beach one spring, and at night we'd shine lights into holes in the sand and little crabs would pop out and scurry away. I feel the way those crabs must have felt, suffering the glares on every inch of my skin, wanting to scurry away.

But I know not to obey that instinct. It just makes things worse. You have to stand up for yourself, or at least try.

"Can I just get that last part repeated? Whatever came before the *To Smuckers*?"

"You don't know?" Henry asks, all steely calm. "Are you sure you didn't help Bernadette write the will herself?"

I'm getting a queasy sense of déjà vu. "I would never. I didn't even know she was, you know..." I gesture at the chandelier. My protest is met with stares of derision.

The younger, less hot Henry gets in on the action. "Maybe Smuckers helped write it. Did Smuckers dictate the will?" He gives *dictate* air quotes.

Sweat trickles down my back. "Look, when she asked me to care for Smuckers, she told me she'd defray the costs of his special salon and vet. So if she left something for that..."

Henry's eyes twinkle coolly. "I'd imagine control of a multibillion-dollar conglomerate would defray a few costs."

I frown, unsure if this is a joke or what.

"People go to jail for this kind of thing," Henry's young relative says.

"Let's dial it back, Brett," the lawyer says.

"Why should I dial it back?" Brett barks. "I'm not dialing back shit!" Brett wants to dial it up. Brett will be dialing it up to eleven, thank you very much.

"This was...supposed to be about vet bills and things," I say.

And ultrapuff blowouts at the Sassy Snout salon and Baby Poochems Perfect Pawz free-range rabbit meat for dogs.

But I don't see those specific details improving anybody's mood at this point.

Henry watches my eyes. "You're trying to steal the company my grandfather founded. How about not insulting our intelligence on top of that?"

One of the Locke women grabs the lawyer's arm. "A dog can't control fifty-one percent of an international conglomerate, can he?"

Fifty-one percent? A chill goes over me as the reality of what's happening sinks in. Bernadette left a lot more than vet and dog food money.

"With Ms. Nelson acting as regent?" the lawyer says. "Yes, then it's no different than awarding control to an infant with a guardian acting in that infant's best interests."

Control of a corporation?

Brett gets in the lawyer's face about his incompetence and disloyalty to the family, handing the company to a grifter.

Brett has unlocked full-blast freak-out mode—so much so that Henry has to pull Brett back and physically restrain him until he calms down. Another lawyer, the estate attorney, takes questions, too. They're arguing about some point of Locke Worldwide bylaws. Everybody has the bylaws up on their phones.

I smooth my dress, the simple, demure dress designed to say *I'm innocent, I'm not the bad person you say I am. I really didn't lie! Please believe me. Somebody. Anybody.*

Needless to say, it's not having the desired effect.

Carly is forever on a quest to get me to buy something colorful—pastels, jewel tones. Anything not gray or black or brown. I say I don't want to, but the truth is, I can't.

My court clothes from when I was sixteen are like the ridges of the Grand Canyon, violent gashes etched by infinite splashes of hatred and derision. It's seven years later and the onslaught is long gone, but the clothes stay.

A room of angry people. How am I in this position again?

Henry has that dangerous sparkle again. "Explains why you wanted custody of the dog so badly."

"I wanted custody because I gave my word to Bernadette, and Smuckers needed a nice home," I say. "I really just expected money for fancy food and vet bills."

Henry pulls out his phone. "I'm calling the police."

"What? What did I do?"

"You defrauded a vulnerable individual," he says. "You pretended you could read the dog's thoughts." He turns his attention back to the phone. "Harry Van Horn, please." That last he says into the phone. Because men like this have friends in the police department.

Just like Denny Woodruff and his family upstate in Deerville. The Lockes might even know the Woodruffs, or travel in the same circles at least.

Frantically I review the reading in my mind. The endless list of companies. Fifty-one percent. Which suggests Smuckers either owns or controls all of them. Or both.

And I control Smuckers.

Henry pockets his phone.

I take a centering breath. "Look, you guys. I'm not here to take anybody to the cleaners. Honestly? I came here because it was Bernadette's deepest wish that Smuckers maintain his same life-style after her death..."

"And that's all you want? And you're willing to sign a piece of paper to that effect?" Brett barks.

"Only Smuckers can designate a new heir," the lawyer says.

"The police are on their way," Henry says.

The police. Smuckers starts fussing in my arms. I loosen up on the death grip of distress.

"How about you have Smuckers designate a new heir, then?"

Brett rakes his eyes up and down me. "Then again, you'd look okay in orange. Malcomb, what does the will say about Smuckers's regent reading his mind from a jail cell?"

Everybody's talking at me or about me. "Make her sign something...affidavit...criminal background check..." Only Henry is silent, apart from the crowd, just like in that toddler picture, but his glittering gaze speaks volumes.

I cling to Smuckers, feeling like it's us against the world. Even Smuckers is upset, though I suspect that's more about being surrounded by strangers who are clearly aware of him yet who mysteriously have all failed to rush over to pet him.

"Let's all take a breath." The main lawyer, Mr. Malcomb, is next to me now. "This is all getting a little close to duress for my comfort. A contract created under duress isn't valid."

Everyone looks at Henry.

"I *am* an officer of the court, Henry," Malcomb adds.

"Yeah, you're an officer of the court who stood by while Mom was getting soaked by a scam artist," Henry says. "That's the problem I'm having here, Malcomb."

"She was of sound mind, Henry," Malcomb retorts. "It's what she wanted."

Malcomb and Henry go on to debate the concept of sound mind.

I have to admit that Henry has a point. A toy dog whose head fur is frequently groomed to resemble a large marshmallow seems a very poor choice to run an international corporation.

Lawyer Malcomb turns to me. "In the decade prior to her death Bernadette assigned a longtime officer of the company, Kaleb Rowland, to cast the vote of her late husband's fifty-one percent along with his own twenty percent, with her son Henry acting as CEO. Kaleb and Henry have been excellent stewards of Locke Worldwide. Under their guidance, the firm has expanded enormously and created a massive amount of wealth. While we're working all of this out, I'm going to suggest that Smuckers might see his way clear to allow Kaleb to retain his proxy while Henry continues on as operational CEO. You'll stay on, Kaleb?"

Everyone looks at an older man with a thick pelt of shiny gray hair. Kaleb, I'm guessing. He crosses his arms and grunts.

I scratch Smuckers's neck, trying to think when he last peed. *Breathe. Think.*

Another thing I learned while a pariah is to understand things fully before making big decisions, because one of the ways people push you around is to make you think you don't have time.

"Can you please explain the terms in a way I'll understand?" I say to Malcomb.

"Oh, for fuck's sake," Henry sighs. "Do we have to go through this charade?"

I turn to him. "Okay, I'm getting a little tired of your attitude." I pull Smuckers's little face closer to mine. It comforts Smuckers, but I kind of think it makes me harder to yell at. "Here's the situation—an old woman who felt *utterly alone* in life left things in her will to her dog. You want somebody to feel angry at? Go look in a mirror."

The room seems to still. Henry regards me coolly, like he's totally in control, but a vein in his neck has become more defined, like a violin string tightened beyond factory specs. "You don't know anything about this family," he finally says.

"I know you're all...a bit unpleasant." Even Bernadette was unpleasant, but I don't say that.

Henry undoes his one suit-jacket button, wristwatch glinting in the dazzle of the chandelier. And then it's gone, back under his perfect sleeve. He says nothing, just undoes the button. I don't know, maybe it's the wealthy man's version of rolling up his sleeves. He then turns and huddles up with Brett and Kaleb. Talking about me, of course.

Talking about charging me with a crime. Maybe paying me off. That's how rich guys control poor women. Young women. Me.

Been there. Done that. Vowed never to do it again.

Back in Deerville, Denny Woodruff's family went with paying me off—half a million dollars for my silence about what Denny did. My life would have been half a million percent better if I'd taken that money, but I was sixteen and idealistic. I wanted to make sure other women would steer clear of Denny.

I sometimes miss that brave, strong girl who wanted justice. That girl who believed if she stood up for herself and told the truth, nothing could hurt her.

We'll bury you, Mr. Woodruff said when I refused to take the money.

We'll bury you.

And they did it.

Or, at least, they buried brave, carefree, teenaged me. The brave girl named Vonda who wore bright, pretty things and wouldn't back down from a fight. The one who didn't have to fake a backbone.

They made me regret not taking the money. They made me regret standing up. The regret's almost worse than having been dragged through the mud of real life and social media hatred.

Regret for doing the right thing is a kind of poison in your veins.

And standing there in the middle of that lavish room of Lockes, I want to rage at the world.

CHAPTER 3

HENRY

PERFECT. Just perfect.

Every part of her is perfect. The whole sexy librarian look she has going, all big brown eyes behind smart-girl glasses. Glossy hair caught up in a pretty ponytail. Determined frown, clutching the dog in her arms, angry about Mom being alone.

Hollywood's top casting professionals couldn't have done better if they tried. So innocent and lovely, with a fun dash of wit.

The clever candlestick comment?

Slow clap.

And she's right about one thing—it's Mom I should be angry at.

I close my eyes, trying to shake the image of her, frail in that hospital bed, so diminished from the woman I knew. Managing to depart this earth without uttering a word to me. Her last words were to a scam artist. And a dog.

When I open my eyes, my cousin Brett is looking at me,

waiting to see what I say. Everyone is always waiting to see what I say.

"Grifter," Brett says when I don't speak.

I gaze over his shoulder at her with all of her innocent allure. "We got this," I say.

He wants me to say more. He's waiting. He knows I'll do anything to protect this company, to protect the people whose livelihoods depend on us. He's nervous.

I give him my smile. I really turn it on for him. "Don't worry. She'll be crawling on her knees before this is over. Gratefully," I add.

Kaleb comes up, balancing on his cane. He, too, wants to see what I'll do. He's seventy. He gets that this isn't his fight. "Girl could do a lot of damage," he warns. "Especially if she has people."

"We got this," I say again. "The little scammer has no idea what she's stepped into."

"You can't contest the will," he points out unhelpfully.

"Doesn't matter." So like Bernadette to put a self-destruct provision into her will. Preventing challenge of any kind. It's how she was in life. If you argued with her, even about something as objective as the air temperature, she'd shut down the whole discussion. *That's enough, Henry!*

Until she finally ghosted on me and the rest of the clan nearly ten years ago. Over a missed dinner, as it happened. A calendar screw-up. On *her* part.

With a simple command I can cause skyscrapers to rise up from brownfield lots or send buildings crashing to the ground, but I couldn't get a frail old woman to answer the phone. Or the door. Go out to brunch at the Gramercy.

I'm done thinking about her, though. She doesn't matter anymore.

I turn to the window and try to collect my thoughts. My next moves will have lasting implications for the people in this room as well as the legions of employees and vendors of Locke World-wide who trust me. They need me strong and smart.

Early on, Brett and I bribed a doorman to let us in to see Bernadette—she preferred the name Bernadette over Mom. We even engaged a therapist to help us bring her back into the family fold. No go.

From our descriptions, the therapist speculated that she might have mild dementia, possibly paranoia; he couldn't say for sure, and you can't force somebody to accept help or be treated.

One of the little known facts about extreme wealth is how stunningly long you can go with untreated mental illness if that's what you want.

You can believe in bizarre things and rave and go out to restaurants and order foods not on the menu, and they'll call you eccentric and smile and thank you for the huge tips.

And obsequious lawyers on your payroll won't push back when you decide to leave everything to your dog, in care of a woman who claims to sense that dog's thoughts or whatever it is, because the checks you write are good.

The checks you write are so very good.

We had no clue she was dying, of course.

I shove my hands in my pockets.

I glare over at Malcomb, sitting there with his colleagues, hiding behind confidentiality. I get it about the confidentiality. Still. He could've found a way to alert me.

Years ago, back when Dad died, Bernadette assigned Dad's share of the voting rights to Kaleb, Dad's second-in-command. It made sense at the time—I was in high school, too young to run things.

But then I graduated with my architectural degree and took over as CEO. I started to build and acquire other companies, turbocharging our growth.

Still my mother kept Kaleb holding ultimate veto power. She and I would argue about it, back when she was still talking to me.

Kaleb didn't use his veto power a lot. He was happy to let me make Locke into the powerhouse it is, happy for my excellent ideas, but he'd veto the shit out of the things I cared most about.

I was CEO, but Kaleb was a roadblock to the real change I wanted to see.

Kaleb's a decent guy, but he's stuck in the legacy way of building. Cost per square foot.

It was bad enough having my hands tied by Kaleb, unable to fully run the company as I wanted. And now?

Now it's controlled by a dog and a scammer.

Brett's talking about Malcomb. "...probably an extensive competency determination he and his estate people put Bernadette through before allowing this...enough not to get disbarred."

I nod. Malcomb's good. He would've ensured she was of sound mind—sound enough, anyway, for the will to hold up in a court of law.

"So. Not the straight line to control I envisioned." I say it lightly, like it doesn't matter. Good old Bernadette, lashing out at me one last time for making her life miserable. My rap sheet for that stretches clear back to infancy.

Again the crafty little scammer asks what things mean. What exactly Mom stipulated. She's a good actress, I'll give her that. With her glasses and glossy ponytail and demure dress. A simple string of dark beads.

This is the woman my mother favored over her own son?

"I've prepared extracts," Malcolmb says, leading her to the table. I follow along.

Malcomb hands her a stapled sheet. "Bernadette divided her assets three ways. Henry and Brett have inherited a number of properties and a share of liquid assets save what she distributed to the five second cousins. Smuckers's inheritance is listed here. He's in control of the family business, Ms. Nelson."

She looks at the sheet, stunned. "So all the cranes and..."

All the cranes. I catch Brett's eye. The cranes? Like she thinks we run a crane company?

"She left Smuckers fifty-one percent of Lockeland Worldwide, Ms. Nelson," Malcomb says. "It's a global corporation that includes a dozen distinct entities."

"What does it *mean* though?" she asks.

Malcomb shoots me a nervous glance. Yeah, he should be nervous. He'll never work for this family again, and nobody I know, if I can help it, though he may have a future in drawing up wills for people who want to torment their kids.

He points to the sheet. "These are the companies under Smuckers's control." My stomach turns as she reads silently. I know the list by heart. It's arranged in chronological order. Locke Worldwide Construction comes first—that's the company my grandfather founded to build homes out on Long Island. The development company comes next, when my father joined in and they started building grocery stores and shopping malls. As soon as I came on as CEO, we exploded the firm out into high-rises, massive public projects, lending, even asset management, because giant buildings are investment vehicles, just like stocks, and so that's the financial portion.

It was my vision a decade ago to spread over an entire web of related sectors, and we did it. We killed it.

He talks to the grifter like she's an idiot.

Clearly she's anything but.

"It means, if Smuckers wants to, he would take his place on the board with your assistance. He would attend meetings and vote on things, and his vote would decide issues, mostly around the overall direction of the company. As CEO, Henry runs the day-to-day stuff. But as a board member and owner, Smuckers would provide the vision and direction, while drawing a monthly stipend." Malcomb points to her handout.

Brett touches my arm. "If the dog dies under suspicious

circumstances, the shares go to the Humane Society. Natural life for that dog is ten more years."

"What?" I say. "You were thinking about killing the dog?"

"Dude," he says. "Gotta explore our options here."

"We're not killing the *dog*."

He puts up his hands like I'm attacking him. "It won't help anyway," he says. "We have to pay her off. How much? What do you think? *Smuckers* can choose to hand over those shares." Brett makes quote fingers for Smuckers. Brett is a quote fingers abuser.

Kaleb wanders over. He wants to hear what I think.

I fold my arms. "This is just a business problem with a business solution. We've had disasters before, right?" Just this year we had to tear down a partially built distribution center because a subcontractor screwed up the rebar. That was a twenty-million-dollar mistake that wasn't on us to fix, but we fixed it. People need to know that Locke does the right thing.

"Don't start too low," Kaleb says.

It galls me to give her anything. "Three million cash," I say.

Brett winces. It's not the amount. We won't even notice three million. He thinks it's too low, that's the problem. She really is holding all the cards.

"Three million, and we don't press charges," I say. "If she did any kind of research, she'd know—you know."

She'd know about the deep friendships we have throughout the city. We don't own judges and cops like a crime family does; we have something more powerful—friendship in high places. Friends in high places tend to see things your way.

"At least offer four point five," Brett says. "It feels like five. She'll go to ten, then, and we meet at seven."

"It's a good payday for her," Kaleb says. "Assuming she's not part of an organized team."

"I don't think she is," I say.

"How do you know?" Kaleb says.

Because there's an echo of loneliness to her. I hear it in her bravado. I see it in the way she straightens her spine. The cold steel you grow in your spine when nobody else is pulling for you.

I don't say that, though.

"Because she'd use them to squeeze us. She'd come in like a tiger with some boiler-room financial guy or a shady lawyer. Not like…" I gesture at her. "Please."

"Right," Kaleb agrees.

The room has emptied. Some of our cousins still linger in the hall. Some of the younger ones probably nabbed a bottle of booze and went to the second-floor balcony to smoke.

Malcomb's explaining things to the scammer and the rest of the guys are doing phone things.

She looks up as if she feels my attention. *Yeah, you've got my attention,* I think. I stroll her way. I cross my arms. "Let's talk."

She furrows her brows. "Okay."

"We've called the police. They don't have enough to make anything stick—yet—but they'll have questions."

She straightens. "But I didn't do anything!"

Did she even hear the *yet*? The yet was the most important part of my sentence. It was the opening of our negotiation. "We'll let them decide that. I don't imagine they have enough to make anything stick—*yet*."

Meaning once we dig into her background, we'll find what we need. If she's a scammer, there's something.

She looks worried. "I have to pick up my sister."

I frown. "Maybe you should've thought of that before you decided to defraud a vulnerable old woman."

"I didn't defraud—"

"It's just us here, jelly bean, so you can stop with the pretense." She starts to protest but I roll right over her. "The good news is that I'm prepared to hand over a cashier's check this afternoon to get clear of all this. Malcolmb and his team will draw up papers and you'll sign over the ownership. You can probably get more cash out eventually, yeah, but it would take years, and I think we both know the risks."

She's peering at me uncertainly.

I grab a pencil off the table and flip over a sheet of paper. You always write the big numbers for people to see. You always add the decimal point and the extra zeroes, too. The zeros have power. I write it out: $4,500,000.00.

She stares at the number, as though stunned. It's a lowball, yes.

Brett drifts over. "It's a good deal, and we walk away," he says. Like he's offering a helpful reminder. "This is a good deal. Let's resolve it now."

She turns to me, clutching my mother's stupid dog. "Four point five *million?*" she says incredulously.

The dog licks her chin.

I wait. Where is the counteroffer?

Where?

I tighten my jaw. Is it so low to her she's not even bothering? Was she thinking in terms of billions? Is this an organized thing after all? Is there a team behind her?

Brett's gotta be thinking it, too. I don't look at him. How'd I peg her so wrong?

There might be a team behind her, but she's alone now.

I step up the pressure. "Here's the thing, Ms. Nelson," I say. "It's the four point five million, *plus* we don't use the very considerable resources we have to destroy your life and quite possibly ensure that you end up rotting in a prison cell."

Her eyes shine. They're the warm brown of a beer bottle, fringed with dark lashes. I wish I could read her thoughts, her emotions—I can see she's having them. I tend to be good at reading women.

Why can't I read her?

"I don't know if you're working with people, but if you are, they can't protect you. And they won't go down for this. You know who goes down for this? You. You go down, and you go down very hard. Very publicly. Very painfully." I lean in. "And you will stay down."

She watches me with growing disbelief. The wronged and totally innocent woman, shocked at this entire thing.

I smile. "What, did they get you from central casting? Don't bother staying in character on my account."

The dewy skin on her throat goes pink as she straightens her spine. "I'm *not* acting." It's a good delivery. Vulnerable and fierce at the same time. Raw, even.

"Of course you're not. My advice is you take the money I'm offering in the next ten minutes. Because ten minutes is about how long you have, given rush hour traffic for our good friends on the police force to get here."

She frowns back down at the number but she doesn't come back with another. Why not?

I watch her, curious. Her neck pinkens more, as if heat and emotion roil right below the surface.

I don't need her to make sense; I need her away from the company I love. The company I'd sell my soul to protect.

"Everyone has a price," I say. "Especially you."

Her face flares full red—her tell for high emotions, I'm thinking. "I told you I'm not a scammer."

I step in closer, full-on intimidation mode. My skin tightens with the nearness of her. "Take the money," I growl, "or I will fucking *bury you*."

Something new comes over her face. It's as if a switch flipped deep in her soul. She glows with energy. No—it's more than that —it's pure, white-hot loathing. She's incandescent.

And so alive.

The sense of her prickles over my skin.

"That a no?" Brett growls, bringing me back to myself.

"The offer goes poof in two minutes," I say. "Now or never."

Brett shoots me a glance. He doesn't like the idea of an ultimatum, and usually I don't, either, but I have this sudden perverse need to push her.

"You don't want to feel our power turned against you."

She swallows. "Well here's the thing, Henry Locke." Her voice shakes, but she holds her ground, stands right up to me. "It's not up to me."

My blood goes cold. So she's working with a team, after all.

I try not to react, but this is very, very bad. A good team could hack apart the company and extract billions in the process. I'm suddenly imagining a man in the wings, running her, directing her. Maybe even a boyfriend or husband. I bristle at the thought.

I exchange glances with Brett. He furrows his brow just slightly. Desperation. Why not bring them in? Unless they have a long game. Dismantle the firm. Sell off the pieces before we can stop them.

I swallow.

I turn back to her. "Who's it up to, then?" I ask, cringing inwardly. For the first time I'm thinking about the mob.

"Who do you think?" She glows at me again, bright with loathing.

I brace myself for the bad news.

She smiles, widening her eyes. "It's up to Smuckers, of course! Have you not been paying *attention?*"

I watch incredulously as she repositions the dog in her arms so that he faces us, eyes and nose like three raisins in a white cotton-candy cloud.

"What do you prefer, Smuckers? Would you like Henry Locke to write us a check for four point five million dollars? Or would you prefer to take your place alongside him as a visionary member and major shareholder on the board of Locke Worldwide?"

I swallow, mystified. Is she messing with us?

"Smuckers, concentrate," she says, with a sly glimpse my way.

"Do you want some money now? Or to vote on pressing issues while drawing a monthly stipend of seventy-five thousand?"

My blood races. I don't know what to think—not about any of it. All I know is that she's on fire. Fierce as an electrical storm, dark clouds flashing bright.

"You have to decide, you just have to. Do it for Jelly Bean," she adds with a glance at me.

Smuckers wags his little poof of a tail.

"That's right, boy! That's right! You decide!"

"Oh, come off it," I say.

Her lip quivers. Is she scared? Or enjoying this way too much? She turns to me. "You mind?" She turns back to Smuckers. "What do you think, Smuckers? Think hard, because they won't offer again. It's an ultimatum. Do you know what that is?"

I fold my arms.

She tilts her head, as if she's listening with intense curiosity to a communication from Smuckers that she's not altogether sure about. "Really? That's your answer? Are you sure? I know, he's a bit of a bastard."

She turns to us.

"Smuckers has decided he would prefer to take his seat on the board. As a voting shareholder, with me as his assistant, to interpret his wishes regarding Locke Worldwide."

CHAPTER 4

VICKY

THE INSIDE of the police station is an old friend I never wanted to see again. The shiny institutional surfaces, the hard seats, the sounds of police radios up and down the halls, the emotional distance that the cops and other staffers maintain, everything strangely plain and professional even as you're scared out of your mind.

And, of course, the little room they make you wait in.

I tell myself it's different this time, but it doesn't feel different.

At least I have Smuckers with me. He took a pee on the way here, but he didn't poop. I've got the poop card to play.

I wasn't on the criminal end during the incident with Denny Woodruff—I was the one who made the accusations and Denny was the one who had to sweat it out in the little room. But after my story was made to look faked, I became the criminal. The false accuser. The one in the little room.

I sat in there alone, thinking I'd be sent to a juvenile facility. Considering home life at the time, it would have been an

48

improvement, except for having to leave Carly unprotected with a mom who'd betray her own daughter for the right price.

Mom wasn't always that way. There was a sunny "before" picture of us in a tiny but bright little home at the end of a long driveway. I would ride my shiny bike up and down it while Mom and Dad hung out with Carly, a pudgy two-year-old with fat cheeks and a huge smile.

Then Dad died.

The "after" picture was a chaos of lost jobs and increasingly shabby apartments, and us two sisters eating cereal dinners alone in smelly, dirty kitchens. And Mom was either a ball of scary energy or else had the shakes and the weeps and the two-day sleeps. And the kind of boyfriends who were overly friendly to little girls when she wasn't looking.

The Woodruffs "generously" decided not to press charges; they saw to it that I didn't get into trouble for supposedly lying to the police, falsifying evidence, and selfishly causing a three-day manhunt. "You owe them a debt of gratitude," a stern police-woman named Sara told me as she led me out.

I said nothing. I had protested my innocence enough by then to know it was a waste of breath.

I followed Sara out, hungry and tired and beaten down because I'd told the truth and the whole world had turned against me, and I still didn't understand how those tests came out the way they did, or how Denny's lies became truth and how my truth became lies. And I didn't know how I'd get home or if there would be food, or if Carly was okay. She was eight that summer, and Mom would leave her alone to "do errands."

Sara held open the door for me and I stepped out into the sunshine only to come face-to-face with a crowd of reporters, yelling questions, taking pictures.

Do you have an apology for Denny Woodruff and his family? Do you feel like you deserved to be released? Do you have a message? Do you have a statement? How does it feel to be forgiven?

I didn't have much left in me by then. Just two words for the crowd: *Never again.* I just looked into the nearest camera and vowed it. *Never again.*

People wanted clarification. Did I mean I'd never lie again?

I headed off onto the sidewalk. A few of the reporters tagged along with me, trying to get me into conversation. I would say nothing more. Eventually Sara the policewoman took pity on me and drove me home.

My release and my definitely-not-grateful-enough comment made the local and national news. It was your classic study in "do and don't"—the Woodruffs outside their beautiful home with their forgiveness, hoping I could get help. They were the DO. And then there was me with my tear-stained cheeks and swollen eyes croaking *Never again* into the camera. I was the DON'T. Put a red circle around my face with a line through it.

I got asked about my terse statement a lot after that. People want contrition from a villain. They need you to feel pain for the wrong of your ways. *Never again* just doesn't do it.

But it did it for me.

Never again was my vow to the world, to myself. *Never again* would I be bullied by people like the Woodruffs. *Never again* would I allow a rich asshole to make me feel small and scared.

Never again.

Looking back, the exercise of hauling me down to the station was simple intimidation. It was the Woodruffs flexing their muscles. *This is what happens when you oppose us.*

I tell myself that's all this is with the Locke clan. I'm being detained, not arrested.

I think again of Henry, standing there all smug. *We will bury you.* Suddenly he was Denny Woodruff. And all I could think was *Never again, motherfucker.*

Never again.

The price of taking that money was way too high, because it

would be like admitting I'm a scam artist or a liar or guilty of something.

The price of taking that money would be losing myself.

When Henry's cop friend showed up wanting to "Clear up the matter down at the station," I went. They didn't fingerprint me, though I was alarmed when they ran my ID. It seemed to hold up. It always does. The person who supplied our wildly expensive new identities seven years ago said they'd be foolproof, but it's not like you can test drive that sort of thing.

I wait to see what the police will do, worrying mostly about Carly. I don't want Mom knowing where to find us and taking Carly back. She never filed a missing persons report on us, but she's a drug addict who's proved she's willing to put her habit above her girls. I'm not taking chances.

I called Carly on the way down to the station. She was just leaving rehearsal with her friend, Bess. I talked to Bess's mom and made arrangements for Carly to stay there until I could deal with my "unexpected personal emergency." I'm sure that left a great impression.

My phone is running out of juice, and frankly, so am I.

Finally the door opens, and there's Henry, still in his fabulous suit.

His smile is pure arrogance, his attitude breezy. He sets a white bakery bag on the table—a bag that's full of freshly baked chocolate chip cookies, if the smell is any indication.

I'll admit, the smell of the cookies is exciting me a lot, but mostly it's Henry. It's as if his presence is lending me new energy.

Like he's the lion who has finally appeared to my David.

Or maybe he's the flame who has appeared to my moth, but let's just go with lion.

"The playboy smirkitect has arrived," I say simply. "How lucky for me."

His blue eyes twinkle. He tilts his head. "Hello, jelly bean."

I ignore the sizzle of his gaze on my skin. "Not my name."

He puts down a leather folder and settles into a chair opposite me. I'm struck by how muscular and golden his hands are, with just the perfect amount of roughness to them.

That wristwatch still peeks out from under his jacket sleeves and white shirt cuffs, all hot heft and dials.

Like what a race car driver would wear. Henry probably owns race cars. He probably drives them in places like the Alps or Monaco.

I tear my gaze from his hands and back to his eyes, ignoring the warmth spreading up my spine.

People have reactions to each other, just like chemicals do. Some blend. Some layer. But some transform each other—they fizz and bubble right out of their containers.

That's Henry and me—something about him gets me reacting —pulse too fast, skin too tight. Wanting to spar. Something. Anything.

It's hate, I tell myself.

I hate the hotness of his hands and the wrong heat of us in this room.

"Let's end this charade," he says.

Something dark arrows through me.

Charade. To most, the word conjures up a marginally fun game where you wish there was more wine.

Not to me. It's one of the words they hammered me with. Selfish charade. Disgusting charade.

"I have the papers for you to sign right here. And a check." He slides it across the table. The implication is clear—if I sign, I'll be released.

I look up at him.

"You don't win this," he says softly. "You don't win against me."

My blood races through my veins.

Never again. Never again. I vowed it, didn't I? Never again to be pushed around by somebody like this.

I watch myself stand. I watch myself pull Smuckers into my arms. "Keep your cookies," I say. "And keep your money, too. Smuckers and I are not for sale."

Speaking those words, I feel this rush of energy, like I'm sticking up for that girl I left in the dust of Deerville. I'm sticking up for Vonda O'Neil.

It feels amazing.

I turn. I walk. My knees are shaking like Jell-O, but I walk. With every step, I feel stronger. Expanding beyond my container. Bubbling over, wild and free.

I can't believe they're letting me leave, but they are. I get out of the police station with nobody stopping me. So they never intended to arrest me after all.

I walk down the sidewalk feeling strangely new.

Never again.

CHAPTER 5

Vicky

THE FIRST BOARD meeting takes place on a Wednesday at Locke
Companies headquarters. I enter the address from the sheet the
lawyer gave me into my phone. It's an easy subway ride.

The headquarters turns out to be one of those grand Financial
District buildings, gleaming white stone and glass shooting high
up into the sky.

The doorway is actually a bank of doorways that seems
designed to illustrate the concept of redundancy. There's a
revolving door, an automatic single door, a single door for people
with handicaps, a double door for people with handicaps, an
automatic double door, a nonautomatic single door, and one last
door, added, perhaps, as an insult to the undecided, next to which
a uniformed attendant stands.

Above is a row of blue flags, flapping in the wind. Specifically
they are *Royal Blue 1*—that's the Locke Worldwide corporate
color. This is something I learned from the packet the lawyer put
together for me. The flags are emblazoned with the Locke logo,

interlocking circles in the shape of a building, or a penis, if you will.

I take a deep breath and walk under the blue awning and enter a five-story-tall lobby with a giant triangular rock five stories high with water cascading down its sides into a Royal Blue 1 fountain.

One of the men behind the security desk rises. He suspects I don't belong.

I can't blame him. I'm wearing a black sweater with dusky pearls, a gray skirt, and kitten heels. When I put it on this morning, I felt like it embodied the timeless glamour of black, but now that I'm surrounded by women in chic brights and wow-factor shoes and men in head-to-toe GQ, it seems to embody *I'm a sad panda.*

Smuckers doesn't care; he's riding in his favorite purse today, gray pleather with a comfortable place for him to stick out his head. I can feel him wagging his tail in there, sensing petting opportunities.

"Service animals only," the guard says.

I tell him that the dog belongs to the Locke family, that he's expected. He frowns for a second, waiting for me to retract my story, maybe, then makes a call. Moments later, he waves me to the crystal elevator bank.

I ride up to the fifty-fifth floor and get out.

Into another world.

Manhattan at street level can be gloomy, especially around the Financial District with all the tall buildings.

But this place is spacious and dazzlingly sunny, with floor-to-ceiling windows that have a view of the river. But what's most remarkable is the blue, blue sky, impossibly, soaringly blue with white puffs of clouds.

The floors are an expanse of sparkling white tile sweeping out to a balcony edged with grass and furniture more appropriate to a chic lounge bar. The walls are composed of giant sparkling blue tile with a glow that comes from cracks between the tiles. Yes, that's the way the place is lit—a glow between tiles!

The flora scheme is tropical, with potted palms and Royal Blue 1 calla lilies as large as dinner plates.

It's designed to impress, but really it just intimidates the shit out of me.

At the far side of the expanse of loveliness is a glass-enclosed meeting room, a fishbowl for the fancy. Six men and one woman sit around a table in there. I spot Henry at the head of the table.

Did they already start? I pull out my phone. I'm five minutes early.

"Can I help you?"

I turn, startled, not having noticed the two women corralled inside a large circular desk tucked discreetly to the side—so as not to spoil the impact of the room, I suppose. The desk would be the only place you can't see the view.

Admins, then. Been there, done that.

I took a lot of temp jobs when we first came here. Temping in the day, waitressing at night, paying out half my earnings to sitters, but I made it work, and I was always there with a bowl of oatmeal and a smile when Carly woke up.

Things got better once my Etsy store took off, even better when we got the Upper West Side apartment-and-parrot-sitting gig.

"I'm here to...see the board." I shift my Smuckers purse. "Did they already start? I meant to get here earlier, but the subway."

"They'll be out in a bit for the official start." The black-haired secretary comes around the desk. She has a Princess Leia hairdo that I definitely approve of, and her name is April according to the sign on her desk. "Who is this little guy?"

"Smuckers," I say.

I take the wee prince out to receive his rightful petting, snap on a leash, and set him on the floor. "Did the meeting start? I thought it wasn't starting until two."

"Looks like some sort of pre-meeting," she says, scratching Smuckers's head. "Are you doing a charitable giving pitch? To the board?" she adds when I seem confused.

I suppose it's natural to think it, being that I'm dressed as a librarian with a flair for dirges and dogs. "No, I'm actually *on* the board."

April gives me the side-eye.

"I'm the new member," I add. "In place of Bernadette. Technically, Smuckers is."

April glances again between Smuckers and me, still not sure whether to believe me.

Not that I'm a mind reader.

Though my impressions are usually right.

Don't be jealous. If you spent enough time being hated by everyone with access to Twitter, Facebook, and TMZ, you, too, could end up with the ability to instantly process the tiniest of movements, one of the few perks of going through the hell that I went through, and a talent I seem to share with the common housefly.

I feel Henry coming toward me well before I see him. My housefly-like room monitoring abilities don't extend to people I can't see, but apparently Henry is a special case; the sensation of him nearing prickles over my skin.

I turn to find his cobalt blue eyes fixed tightly on me. He saunters toward me like the prince of Wall Street. And the prince of Manhattan. And the prince of sunshine and men's fashion and the coolly-striding-toward-you club.

My skin heats, and tiny Irishmen start up a jig in my belly.

The rest of them are flanking him on either side, but Henry outshines them, because he's Henry Freaking Locke.

"Vicky," he says. "And Smuckers. Right on time."

"Looks like you already started."

"Would we start without you?" He asks this in a friendly tone that makes the Irishmen jig even faster.

"Um...yes?" I say.

"That wasn't a meeting," Brett, aka the less glorious and way meaner copy of Henry, says.

"We'll be back in ten." Henry heads for the elevator, followed by his cufflinks and click-shoe entourage. Yeah, the board meeting definitely already started. First item on the agenda: exclude me.

"You're an *owner*."

I turn to find April looking at me anew.

"Well, technically it's Smuckers," I say.

She nods thoughtfully, seems to weigh her words. "You might ask for a full description of board privileges. Did you know we send cars to pick up all members?"

"No."

"There's a credit card attached to board membership that you can spend on meeting-related stuff. A projector, for example. Or a new case for the dog. Anything utilized in a board meeting would be reimbursed. You really don't know any of this?"

I shake my head.

"Have you sat on a board?"

"No," I confess.

"You'll like it here. Locke Worldwide is like family. Doing the right thing really *is* the right thing around here."

That's the Locke motto, and I find it sweet yet eerie that she acts like it's true.

Ten minutes later I'm in the glass boardroom with its floor-to-ceiling windows looming over all the world. Henry introduces me around. He doesn't bother to introduce me to April, who sits in the corner with a laptop at the ready.

People sit down. I settle Smuckers onto my lap. Henry saunters around the table handing out sheets of paper—the agenda.

My belly tightens as he takes his seat across from me, beautiful and sleek in his gray suit.

"I've never sat on a board before," I say. "So I'm wondering, before we start, if there are things I should know. The lay of the land. Maybe, you know, some sort of greetings wagon thingy?"

Henry doesn't try to hide his annoyance. It lights up his face in a way that maybe pleases me too much. "A *greetings wagon thingy?*"

"You know, that bag neighbors hang on the doorknob to welcome somebody who just moved in to the neighborhood, and it explains things they should know about neighborhood amenities, like playgrounds, and there are pizza coupons and—"

"I know what *greetings wagon* means."

"Smuckers is a bit new at all of this."

He flicks his gaze to April, who nods quickly. "I'll set up a courier," she says.

I nod at April. It took guts to help me. It occurs to me that I could give her a raise. Or can I? I own fifty-one percent of the company so it seems like I should be able to. Yet not. Because while I steer fifty-one percent of this company according to my title as majority shareholder of the steering board, it doesn't feel like I'm in charge of it at all, any more than riding a bucking bull results in any kind of steering of it.

They go over financials first, and there are a series of motions on pension funds—switching up investment vehicles or something like that. At first I try to keep up, asking for things to be explained, a task that Henry always takes on with his icy blue gaze at me that sends shivers skittering over my skin.

"...the balance sheet is figure two in your packet. We're unhappy with an underperforming pension fund investment. Are you going to vote with us to make it right?"

"Smuckers concurs," I say. Like I even get any of it.

I was always good at school, but this must be how somebody who doesn't speak English feels when they're plopped down into an English-speaking school. All these new terms. Now and then April, who is apparently the type to pull for the underdog, brightens from over in her corner, like when she thinks I asked a good question.

Ninety minutes tick by. Two hours. I question what I'm doing here, but I remind myself how I don't let rich people push me around. How Henry had me detained, tried to bully me and pay me off.

Never again.

So I sit up. I get mentally tired of asking questions, but I ask them, then I vote however Henry votes.

Henry did, after all, make the company bigger and stronger, according to the reports I crammed on the way over. He's fiercely protective of it, too, which I suppose is admirable. As CEO, he handles day-to-day operations, but I get to have the final say on those operations as Kaleb once did.

So, in a way, I'm in charge. I'm steering the ship and he's my galley slave. The idea of him sweaty and shirtless, straining at the oars, comes to me unbidden. He works out. Maybe weights. No, he's too cool for that. Henry would go for something sporty, like soccer. Or probably a sport where you hit something. Maybe boxing. Or rugby, all rough and tumble.

"Vicky?" Henry's staring imperiously at me. "Does Smuckers have a vote?"

"Smuckers is with you," I say. "On this one, anyway." I say it like Smuckers might not always vote with him. Smuckers is an independent thinker.

Henry turns to the next page of the agenda, calm and suave, a Gucci menswear god without a care in the world.

They drone on to the next item. I make us take a break, blaming it on Smuckers having to go out, but it's really me. Ten minutes later, we're back at it.

The one woman in the meeting, Mandy, seems to be a financial person. Brett is all about business relationships. Henry is the vision and strategy guy, and Kaleb is the corporate bottom line and super-argumentative guy. Other people are heads of various business divisions.

They discuss questions at length, look at all the sides of things. They respect and admire and protect each other. They trust each other.

It makes me feel lonely.

Another hour claws by. I'm hungry. Tired. Starting to feel like I did in the police station, and not at all like I'm taking my power back. I look down at my nails, which I painted special for today, just wanting to do a good job. Just wanting to show I'm not this piece-of-shit scammer.

I brush a bit of Smuckers's fur off my dark dress. Really, I'm so tired of fighting.

CHAPTER 6

HENRY

DID Mom think she was leaving me with one last little piece of hell? Getting the final word in? I should be thanking her; there's nothing I like better than a fight. Especially a fight I'm going to win.

This company is my family and has been for a long time—long before my mother chose a scammer and a dog over her own son.

And there's nothing I won't do for my family.

I propose another mind-numbing financial move. I've noticed she's actually interested in construction stuff—it's the only time she's really tracking. So I keep the focus on the financials. This is business we could conclude in a tenth of the time, but I'm reading everything. I warned the group that I would.

It's working; I'm wearing her down. When she feels especially tired, she scratches the dog's head, as if that will perk her up, and she's doing that now, big brown eyes glazing over.

If she had a team backing her up, we'd know about it by now.

According to our PI, she has no business background, aside from selling ridiculous dog collars and things. My guess is that she got her hooks into my mom thinking she was an easy, small-change mark and only later realized what a big fish she had. And she got greedy, tried to take down this thing herself.

All alone. Messing with Henry Locke. Who does that?

Soon I'll go in for the kill. I watch her stretch subtly in her chair. It took guts, I'll give her that.

Now I'll destroy her. I'll strip her of everything. I find myself wondering if her neck will pinken when she realizes. Will she come at me with anger? At times she seems almost to despise me.

Will she get that loathing glow again? Will she show her claws?

Something wicked twists inside of me, and it's not entirely unpleasant.

Brett kicks my foot. Givens wants Tuesday's numbers. I blink and grab my tablet. I give him the numbers, then sneak another glance at her.

When I'm relatively sure she's not paying attention, I bring up the voting amendment, a densely worded bylaw change that will redistribute voting rights, favoring family and longstanding board members over newcomers—namely her. It's worded in a way I'm pretty sure she won't recognize, given her lack of business knowledge. Three lawyers signed off on it.

I present it in a rambling monotone.

Basically, she's about to vote to strip her own voting rights. Once she votes for that, we'll reorganize the company. Reorganize her and the dog right out the door.

I yawn. Sure enough, she yawns, too. "All in favor," I say. She turns her brown eyes to me. She's been doing that. Pretending she understands and then watching me for a cue how to vote. Smart enough not to vote against her own meal ticket, I suppose. I created a nonsense amendment to test the theory, and I warned the group ahead of time I'd do it.

Kaleb wasn't happy with the plan; he said it went too far. He always feels like I go too far until Locke needs to send a hard guy to the negotiating table, and then he's happy for me to go too far.

So he went along, because I haven't been wrong once, and I built the shit out of this company. Even with Kaleb acting like a giant boulder around my ankle, keeping us back from real progress, I built it.

Even through the crash and the real estate downturn, when other builders were wheedling out of paying subs, I found a way to pay people, to finish jobs the right way, to keep our Wall Street end happy.

No way will a small-time scammer get the best of us.

I finish rattling off the amendment where she agrees to have no more say in company business.

Vicky isn't paying attention, though Smuckers is the very picture of alertness, suddenly, eyes like black buttons, tongue hanging out, staring at me like he's spotted a squirrel riding on my head. I look away, not wanting to encourage his excitement.

"All in favor," I say. We start around the table. My heart speeds up like it always does when I go in for the coup.

Vicky's going to go for it. I feel almost sad for her.

Almost.

These shenanigans wouldn't fly in a publicly traded company. Then again, neither would a dog on the board. In a private family company, all bets are off.

Listlessly, I raise my hand. "Aye." We get a string of ayes.

She raises her hand. Her pretty lips part. Her chest rises slightly, and then she pauses, brows furrow. "Wait, I don't even know what this is."

I sigh and read it off. "All present in favor. Just waiting on you."

She cranes her head forward, eyes narrowed.

"Can I get a definition of reallocation of plebiscite by seniority?" Vicky asks.

My heart sinks. "What is this, a spelling bee?"

"I just don't understand it."

"It's a procedural motion to ensure continuing smooth operation. An agreement on forms of agreement. You're going to have to get used to voting on matters of procedure."

She watches Brett and Smuckers. "Specific definition, please," she says softly.

Mandy groans.

"It's procedural," I say, sliding a packet of printed bullshit across to her. "A matter of continuation."

She lifts her gaze back to me. She's a fish out of water. A fish on land, really, flopping around, visibly confused. But she keeps flopping, keeps fighting. She's a scrapper, really. "Reallocation of plebiscite?"

Everyone looks at me. She's asking the right question. "The rule gives precedence to experience."

"What's *plebiscite?*"

"Ballot."

Her chest rises again. Another intake of breath. I know exactly when it dawns on her, because that glow comes back in to her face. "Precedence to experience. As opposed to a…?"

She waits for me to fill it in. I sit back, as if bored. I'm anything but.

She fixes me with a wry smile that twists up some part of me. "Maybe as opposed to a fluffy little dog?" she finally supplies.

"Not how I was going to put it."

"Well, then." She sits up straight. "Smuckers has considered your amendment, and he's decided to vote no." She turns to Smuckers. "What is that, boy? Oh, I'm sorry, *nay.*" She glares at me now. "I can't believe you tried to strip him of his vote. Do you have no decency?"

"When it comes to protecting this company? No."

Her gaze intensifies. "Just no?"

"None at all," I say. "No decency whatsoever. Nada, if you will."

Her pretty lips part. It's shock. Maybe a little bit awe.

I give her an amused smile, adjusting my jacket sleeve over my cuff just so. The suit was tailored by a man who charges three hundred bucks an hour and is worth every penny.

"Uh," she says. "You think you're all that? You're not."

"Oh, I am," I say. "I very much am. And for the record, I will crush you in the end."

"Smuckers had this medication once," she says. "We tried to hide it in his food, and he spit it out. No matter what we did, he'd spit it out." She puts one finger on the paper with the new amendment we printed up and slides it back across the desk. "Smuckers doesn't like when people try to fool him. That's his message for you."

"I have a message for Smuckers." I put my finger on it and slide it back across to her. "Smuckers needs to know that we have a private investigator on this case. Smuckers might not have very nice food to eat if you ended up in prison."

Finally she looks scared.

Brett swoops in. "I think we can all walk away from this table happy. Maybe Henry was hasty with that ultimatum. I say we settle this. One-time offer from me personally." He writes the number—$4,500,000.00. "This offer expires in two minutes."

My heart pounds. This is sloppy. The *third* final ultimatum. But he's doing it as a personal thing. And if she takes it, okay. We've shown how close she can come to losing everything.

She looks at the paper.

She's all alone caring for that sister of hers. She's poor—we have her banking information; we know it for a fact. She has every reason in the world to take it. Yet she hesitates.

"This is our last offer," Brett says. "After this, we'll take the company from you, and you'll get nothing."

She raises her brown eyes to me. It's me she's really dealing with. I like that she knows that. "You know what Smuckers hates even more than being fooled?" she says.

My heart pounds. She almost lost everything to me, and now she's going to tell me a dog story?

"He hates being threatened," she says. "And bullied. He really, really hates it."

"Well he's going to have to get used to it," I hear myself saying. "He's used to bubbles and bows and sunny parks but he's in the jungle now. There are animals here who are faster and stronger and smarter than he is. Animals who will dominate him easily. Savagely, even."

"Then you don't know Smuckers very well."

"Oh, I know all about Smuckers, and I'd suggest he practice rolling over. Baring his belly for the superior predator." I lower my voice. "Begging sweetly for mercy."

The color heightens in her face. This shouldn't be fun.

But it is.

I keep going. "Smuckers may think he can request packets and bylaws and definitions and get up to speed, but he can't compete here. He doesn't have the skills."

"Smuckers thinks owning fifty-one percent is the best skill to have," she says.

My pulse quickens. "Then Smuckers should prepare to be destroyed."

Kaleb clears his throat. "I think this meeting has devolved to the point where we can adjourn."

"We still have issues to take up," I say.

"More plebiscites?" She shoots a hard gaze at me. "No, thanks. Though I do have one request. An assistant."

I wait. She can have whatever she wants. Does she not understand that? She could take an entire floor as her office if she wanted. "Do you have an assistant in mind? You can bring in anybody you want."

"I'd like somebody familiar with the company and the board. Maybe April?" She gazes over at April. It's a good choice.

"If April agrees." I wave a hand at April. Of course she'll agree. Being Vicky's assistant will be a cakewalk compared to what she's doing. "You can take her to HR and hash it out. Try it on a thirty-day trial basis if you like."

April nods.

Kaleb moves that we schedule the next meeting for a week out. All present agree.

Vicky scoops up Smuckers, nestles him back into her purse, and swings out of the room.

"We got this," I say to the rest of the board. Everyone drifts out except Brett. He backs into the door, closing it behind him. Blocking me from leaving.

"What?" I say.

"Are you looking to fight her or fuck her?"

CHAPTER 7

VICKY

I can't believe how close I came to signing it all away. Henry is smart. And he's willing to play dirty. It's sink or swim, now, and I need to swim.

I'm a little bit scared. Last time I tried to swim, I drowned.

But I'm in it now. The ultimatum has been offered and yanked away. The only alternative is running away with my tail between my legs. And what kind of example is that to Carly?

April agrees to become my assistant. I don't think it's out of any real loyalty to me—I don't have illusions of her being my ally now or handing me secret strategies. April is a Girl Scout whose allegiance belongs to Locke Worldwide. She seems to think that if I understood what they're all about, I'd love Locke Worldwide, too.

We visit different offices in the Oz-like glass building, gathering things for the packet, and then I take her out to a French bistro and grill her on how the board works and what the people are like. She's smart. Straightforward. I like her and her Princess Leia hair.

I give her the rest of the day off and head home with the

packet she put together for me. It's a sheath of bylaws as thick as my thumb, along with some smaller envelopes, one of which contains a credit card and activation instructions.

In another I discover a check for seventy-five thousand dollars, one month's pay for being on the board.

I stare at it a long time. April told me I was getting it, but I'm still shocked it was just sitting in there. I take it out and hold it up to the light, as if that will tell me something. Is this really the check? Like maybe it's a piece of paper announcing the coming of the check, mentally preparing me, so I don't keel over out of shock. It seems like there should be more fanfare around a check that large, like it should be brought in on a satin pillow amid a heraldry of trumpets.

But of course it's real. I don't waste any time, because I still feel like Henry could yank it all away from me at any moment. He's probably working on it right now, spinning plans and sharpening swords.

I get right on the bus and head down to my bank. I hand it over to the teller expecting her eyes to pop out of her head at all the zeroes. Or maybe she has to call somebody over. But she just puts it in. I've asked for $600 cash back. She asks if I want that in fifties. I nod, waiting for an alarm to blare or something.

Instead I get the cash.

I have the account number of Carly's meager little college fund. I load in fifty thousand plus a chunk of my Etsy savings. It's something for Carly that nobody can take away—not even Henry.

Maybe that sounds paranoid, but it's not paranoid if you went through what I did. Rich men have a different set of laws, and sometimes they can bend reality.

I take the cab home, feeling excited and scared. I have so much money still left, it boggles my mind. I'm thinking about the people I could help. Mostly I'm thinking about this makers space I belong to. It's a shared workshop in a shitty, run-down section of Brooklyn. They have kilns, blowtorches, soldering irons, circular saws, industrial sewing machines, that sort of thing, and struggling artisans like me rent space there.

My mind races with ideas for all the pieces I could buy from my friends there, how much that would help them out. Henry Locke couldn't take that money back, either.

I smile. I feel strangely alive.

It's not just the money or helping my friends at the makers space; it's something about sitting in that boardroom fighting Henry. Something got stirred up; I don't know what.

Carly gets home and asks how it went.

"It was amazing," I say.

"They were nice?"

"Complete assholes. Especially Henry, the leader of the pack. One of the biggest jackasses I ever met. He tried to fool me into voting against my own wishes, but I didn't."

I think back on his words. *Baring his belly for the superior predator. Begging for mercy.* And the way he smiled when he said it. It's the first time I noticed he has dimples, and they're lopsided—one deeper than the other. Like one dimple gets more excited.

"Uh! Such a jerk!" I say.

"But you didn't vote against yourself?"

"Hell no." I look her in the eye—I need her to hear me on this. "When people come at you, you have to stand up for yourself. Nobody will fight for you quite like you will fight for you."

I want it again.

I'm already thinking about the next board meeting. It's next Tuesday, and I plan to be ready.

I should be working on my line for my Saks meeting. I have five days left and need drawings for demure little hoops to go with the small necklace set. I should be thinking about soldering the mock-ups, but instead I pull out Locke Companies materials.

I pull out the credit card. April told me that it's for things we need for the meetings. *Anything used in a board meeting can go on the credit card* she said. *A new briefcase. A movie projector, a purse for Smuckers. If you use it in a meeting, it goes on the card.* I'm thinking of my friend Latrisha, a furniture artisan. I could use the credit card to commission a new carrying case for Smuckers.

But then I get an even better idea.

I walk Carly to school the next morning. We wave to the beginner mimes, hard at work building their sadly misshapen invisible wall. We do a bit of window-shopping at the Fluevog store—I've told Carly she gets two splurgy purchases with our new money.

I wave as she disappears up the school steps. I bundle Smuckers into his flowered carrier and hail a cab, giving the address for the cavernous makers space.

All kinds of people rent space there—tattooed woodworkers and potters, hipster upholsterers, and jewelry-making metal workers like me. It's open twenty-four hours, because so many of us have straight jobs during the day, the bread and butter job while we try and make it as artisans.

I find Latrisha at her corner station, sanding away at a mod chair. I go over. "Sad face," she whispers. "I brought cookies and everybody ate them all." We bring snacks a lot. Sometimes we bring wine. Then she notices Smuckers. "The baby!"

I take Smuckers out and soon a dozen people are around, petting him.

I leave him with his new fans and go around and commission things—a pottery bowl set, metalwork shoe rack, glass-blown things. I write checks on the spot. I tell people I came into an inheritance; they don't need the details. I'll use the stuff for future Christmas gifts. I just want to spread around my windfall.

People buying stuff makes such a huge difference to makers.

Finally I get back to Latrisha.

"What?" she asks, because I'm smiling so hugely.

"I have a commission for you," I say. "It's something a little offbeat. A beautiful piece of furniture. But I need it in a week."

"You're hiring me." She crosses her arms and raises an eyebrow. "You know I'm not cheap. Especially for a rush job."

"I don't expect this to be cheap. In fact, cost is no object." I pick Smuckers up off the floor. "I want a really special piece of furniture for Smuckers. I'm imagining a cross between a dog bed and a throne. And it can't be plain. I want flourishes. Scrollwork. Metal. Jewels. Whatever. Just make it wildly outrageous. Maybe four feet high or so. I want him to be really comfortable, but regal, elevated above everybody else."

"I think you're taking this new dog mom gig a little seriously. You can put a bowl on the floor and he'll be just as happy."

"It's not for my house—it's…a long story. Trust me, I want a dog throne, the most elaborate thing you can possibly make."

She tilts her head, peering at me as if through a haze.

I give Latrisha the big update. She already knew about Bernadette and the fake whisperer gig, of course, but not about the will or Henry or my first board meeting.

She stares at me for a long time after I finish my story. "I can't believe you're in charge of Cock Worldwide. They sound like asshats!"

"You don't even know." I tell her how they tried to trick me. I repeat the jungle things Henry said.

Latrisha frowns and puts her fists on her hips. "A dog throne, you say."

She starts designing, showing me ideas for freakishly elaborate millwork. We push it further and further. We get a pounded sterling guy involved. She has this vision for some sort of medallion for the seat back. "I'm seeing it the size of a coffee saucer. Like a coat of arms, except not."

I sit up. "It needs to be enamel!" This is my territory—I used to love working in enamel. I do a sketch of Smuckers's sweet little face with a sequined bow tie collar.

Latrisha bends over my pad. I tell her what it is.

"I freaking love that," she says. "What are you setting it in?"

Henry's face comes to me, and I'm thinking WWHH—What Would Henry Hate? "Pink alloy. Neon pink alloy. This huge Smuckers face medallion set in neon pink."

"Like candy."

"Like candy." Yeah, I'm spending way too much time on a medallion for the Smuckers throne, but I haven't had so much fun designing something new in forever. The jewelry I create is as subdued as my court clothes and not really fun, but this? I'm loving it, even though it was inspired by that jackass Henry Locke.

Henry is a breed of man I avoid like the plague, thanks to Denny.

The minute I sense a guy might have family money, I'm out.

I'm merciless on CupidZoom, passing over any man with an Ivy League college, any man who shows pictures of himself wearing a Tartan plaid scarf, or who likes two of the following list: sailing, downhill skiing, golf, plus anyone who uses the term *equestrian*, or has a pilot's license. If he likes Coldplay, or if the only rap music he likes is Eminem, he's out. And if there is a III at the end of his name? *Triple adios*, motherfucker.

Latrisha helped me make that list. A two-bottle-of-wine list right there.

Needless to say, my dating history veers toward cooks, musicians, and students on the ten-year plan. My longest-running boyfriend was a cook, a musician, *and* a student on the ten-year plan; he wrote songs for me that I hated, but I didn't have the heart to tell him.

Newsflash: acting like you're into a song that a guy is singing really soulfully while looking deeply into your eyes is harder than faking an orgasm.

So that one didn't work out.

"Are you going to put Smuckers's name on the medallion?"

"That's what I was thinking, but it might not be fun enough," I say, then I sketch out the words *Smuck U.*

"I love that too much," Latrisha says breathlessly. "With his little sweet face? It's like it means kiss you or fuck you or love you or hate you. What are you going to wear?"

"What do you mean?"

"You're part of Smuckers's entourage. Sort of like, the organ grinder and the monkey—they both get the little vests, right?"

"I hope I'm the organ grinder in this scenario," I say.

"Oh, def. Henry can be the monkey."

"An entourage. I didn't think of that. Or what I'm going to wear, jewelry-wise."

"Girl, you're a jewelry maker and you didn't think of the accessorizing component to all this? It needs to be just as fun as what we're doing for Smuckers."

For seven years I've funneled my creativity into earning respect. The idea of ultra-subtle class. I never go for wild provocation. But she's right.

I feel this shiver of excitement as I flip my blank book to a new page. I'm imagining bright colors. Gorgeous, playful imagery. Sassy, irreverent sayings. I start sketching. Designing this line is the jewelry-maker's version of playing hooky. And when I imagine his gaze landing on me and Smuckers in coordinating shit? The fun only doubles.

Henry wants to go? Oh, I will go.

CHAPTER 8

Henry

I push into Chantisserie. "Two. Booth." I set a hundred-dollar bill on the host stand.

Brett gives me a look. *You could be nice*—that's what the look says. But between his fake nice request and my very straightforward hundred-dollar bill, I know which one this guy would choose. Every time.

People are not that complicated.

The host peers over his glasses at us, then down at his book. "This way." He leads us to a booth by the window.

Brett orders two scotches on the rocks even though it's early afternoon.

"It's mood alteration o'clock somewhere," I say.

"The second one's for you." He pulls out his iPad and slides it over to me. "The good news is that they found the loophole you thought they would."

I nod. I felt sure our lawyers could find a way to twist the "qualified to serve as permitted by state law" clause to eject her

76

on grounds of incompetency. "And something like this would fall under private mediation, right?"

"That's what they say."

Our drinks come. "Shouldn't be hard to prove, considering half a dozen people have witnessed her channeling the thoughts of a dog. Where's the bad news?"

He reaches over and swipes the screen. "They have to file, then get on the schedule. It's going to be slow."

"So we grease some wheels."

"We can't pay to speed it up. It has to go by the book. We gotta do this Boy Scout or it might get challenged."

"How long?"

"Weeks. I don't know," he says. "They don't know."

I swirl the ice in my drink. This is bad. She refused the money, which means she thinks she can get more. The best way to do that is to make things bad enough that we pay. It's a hostage situation.

He looks at me, waiting to see what I say. They always expect me to have the answers, the battle plans. Usually I do. But working under the direction of an unpredictable scam artist who pretends to know a dog's thoughts?

"So we manage her."

A perverse thrill shudders through me as the idea takes hold. I take a swig of my drink. Set it down. Close my eyes. Breathe. I focus on the calm of it spreading through me.

When I open my eyes, Brett's watching me. Waiting.

"Never imagined I'd feel nostalgic for Kaleb's minimum profit-per-square-foot ball and chain around my ankle," I say.

He snorts. "What the hell! Right?"

Kaleb never understood the new economy. He never got the memo that you sometimes make a bigger profit by taking a loss up front. That once in a while it's worth it to make cool shit. You can't put a price on being known as a builder that makes cool shit.

No, it's all about profit margins to Kaleb. The man is so 1980s it sprains my brain.

"Manage her. Keep her busy. Keep her from screwing things up. Keep her...favorably disposed."

"Should be easy for you. She's not with anyone," Brett says.

I nod. According to our PI, she's led a quiet existence. No boyfriend.

Brett grins. "So you can play good cop and I'll play bad cop. I'll gather evidence and work the lawyers and keep the PI digging, and you just keep her on her back."

I look down at my fingers around the glass, remembering the way she stared at them.

"You're into it, right? One of New York's ten most eligible bachelors? You could do a very good good cop. You could keep her sated until we yank the firm."

I snort. *One of New York's ten most eligible bachelors* was a title given to me out of spite by a journalist ex. Trust me, nobody who gets a title like that is ever happy about it.

"Get her into the Henry fan club," Brett continues. "Take her out. Charm her. Romantic picnics in the park. Billionaire helicopter rides."

I try to imagine doing the whole picnic-blanket-and-chilled-champagne-in-the-park thing with her in a way that wouldn't be fake or cheesy, but I can't. All I can see is her adjusting her glasses, brown eyes peering at me hard, like, *really*? "No, that approach—it's not right for her."

"What, are you suddenly a grifter expert?"

"It's too generic for her. The picnic thing and all that, it says, *Look at me, I'm romancing you.*"

"Kind of the point."

"Vicky won't go for it," I say with a certainty that surprises even me. "This isn't a woman who wants a heart-shaped box of chocolates. She's—"

What I almost say is that she's too good for that.

God, she's a grifter looking for a payday. I push the scotch away. "I'll handle her, don't worry. She won't be giving any messed-up orders."

"There's the spirit," Brett says. "Now, what about the press? What if they find out that Smuckers is heading up the board? That little bit of news could screw up a lot of projects. The stadium? They want an excuse to say no."

"I won't let anything nix the stadium deal."

"Well, they're looking for an excuse to say no."

I swirl the ice in my glass, trying to think how to keep a lid on something like a toy dog controlling a billion-dollar corporation, trying not to think about Mom, because that leads nowhere good.

And then I get it. "We go public with the dog thing. Full disclosure."

He narrows his eyes. "Not entirely tracking here."

"What Mom did is so hosed up, who would believe it? So we make it look like a charity stunt. *Oh, no! Bernadette willed her empire to the dogs. Look! The damn dog is in control and giving money to dog charities. Oh, no! Wink-wink-nudge-nudge.*"

A smile spreads across Brett's face. "Like it's just a PR stunt."

"Exactly. What mother would leave a company to the dog and not her CEO son?" I manage to say this without emotion. "We write an over-the-top press release. We give a big cardboard check to some dog pound. And guess who gets to be in charge of choosing the charity?"

CHAPTER 9

VICKY

I TAKE Carly and Smuckers out to a sidewalk café where we order whatever we want without looking at the prices, and for dessert we get our favorite treat: ice cream with a stupid amount of candy in it.

"Everything's good now," Carly says, searching my face for confirmation.

"Def," I say, because I want that for her, even if I don't have it for myself.

I still get spooked when groups of people seem to be looking at me; I think they recognize me, and that they're silently condemning me. A built-in flinch reaction.

I remember being shocked a few months back when people were looking at Carly and me down on the subway platform, and that whole hunted, hated feeling rushed over me.

Then I looked over at Carly, and she was grinning at me. She put her hand on her hip, gave me a cocky look, and said, *This coat is so badass nobody can even believe it.*

And I wanted to cry from relief. And happiness. My beautiful sister with her bright red hair and orange faux-fur coat. People stare at her and she decides she looks amazing.

That night after she's asleep, I go to my old jewelry collection, sifting through the pieces I've collected over the years. I finger a charm bracelet, one of the few beloved things I still have from my childhood, and that's when the brainstorm hits.

I'm thinking high-end charms crossed with Valentine's candy hearts. I'm thinking fun animal faces and playful sayings. Smuckers's face with *Smuck U*. A cat with *meow, mofo*. An owl: *GrrOWL*.

I start sketching and scribbling, coming up with increasingly outrageous messages. I stay up all night designing and making reckless decisions. It's just a one-time outfit, so who cares?

I work up a bracelet and a necklace, all animal medallions the size of quarters set in neon pink alloy. The fact that Henry partly inspired it all adds to the crazy, fuck-you fire of it. But really, it's not solely inspired by him. It's the city and the battle of the jungle and droplets of water on windshields, the flashing perfume billboard out our window, bright desserts on a tray and me having some fun for once.

Somewhere around four in the morning I redesign everything to make it double sided, with the animal face on one side and white letters on the pink metal. I design sandal charms and hairpins, too. It's messed up and wild. I forgot how much I missed color.

I drop my sister off at school and head to the makers space. Almost nobody is around. I make medallion molds of different sizes and work out how the lettering will go. Everything feels new. It's a lot of work for a one-time outfit, but sometimes you make shit just to make it.

The place fills up. I work through lunch, and suddenly Carly's calling. It's already time to get her.

It's only when I stroll out of there into the hot afternoon that I realize things I've been making don't feel new at all.

They feel old. Like Vonda stuff. I don't know if I want to laugh or cry when I realize that.

My insane collection is ready two days later, matched perfectly to the large Smuck U medallion that adorns the back of Smuckers's throne.

I show Latrisha the bracelet and necklace set.

"You're really committing to the madness," she observes.

I inform her that there will also be a large zoinks medallion in my ponytail.

She's just looking at the necklace. "I kind of want one. Exactly like this."

I tell her I'll make her one. A few other artisans come around. By the end of the day I have orders for ten pieces. I'm thinking about putting it on Etsy. I force myself to go back to my serious collection—Saks is tomorrow—but when I open the box I keep it in, my heart seems to sigh. Not a good sigh. A sad sigh.

Even tucked into elegant black velvet, the pieces look sad. I'm selling safety. Invisibility. Being on trial. Jewelry for a girl who wants desperately to be trusted. Wants not to be hated.

And I realize I want more.

CHAPTER 10

VICKY

THE PREBUYERS FROWN. "This is completely different," a woman in mod stripes says. She's rail thin like so many in the fashion industry trenches. "You can't switch."

"The old stuff was about women hiding their true personalities, and that's not what I'm interested in anymore," I say. "Jewelry should express something." Even as I say it, I'm wondering if I'm committing too much to the cray. But I can't deal with the old collection. It's like I've developed an allergy to it overnight.

Her blue-haired partner, who looks like he's eighteen, is not happy. He closes the case and slides it across to me. "We worked up a whole new biz-casual strategy for the other, and that's not this."

"We had this designated for a specific niche," the woman says.

The main buyer comes in. They both look really nervous. "We might have to postpone this," the blue-haired buyer says. "This isn't the collection we were slotting. This new one...no offense."

The main buyer frowns. "Usually when somebody says no offense, there is some. This I gotta see."

"I brought one that wasn't requested," I explain, not wanting to throw the prebuyers under the bus. "I wasn't thinking. I'll go back through the channels."

She makes a come-hither motion with her finger.

I slide the case to the middle of the table and open it. She pulls out the necklace and studies the animal faces with their weird little messages.

"Hmm," she says, stopping on GrrrOwl.

I try my best not to slump or appear to crumble. Did I go overboard in all of my enthusiasm? Lose my judgment? Yes.

But it felt good while I was making it.

"What do you call it?"

"Smuck U," I say.

She looks confused.

I pull out the sandal medallion. "Inspired by my dog, Smuckers."

She tilts her head. "What's the thinking?"

I look up and down. She thinks I'm crazy already, so it can't get worse, right? I pull out the bracelet. "People have tried to push Smuckers around. Take things away from him. Smuckers wears bow ties, and he's cute and fluffy, but he is so done with people pushing him around. So done."

Everyone is looking at me now.

"Cuff bracelet. All metal is a pink alloy. This is what you wear when..." I pull out the choker and hold it up to my neck. "Well, it's what you wear whenever you feel like it. It's high-end, but not playing the high-end game." I pull out a bracelet and lay it flat. On the front of each medallion, the size of a quarter, is a fun painted animal face. On the back are the various messages. *Zoinks. Hell no. Hell yes. Smuck U.* "It's not about what the world tells you to be. It's about what makes you feel alive. This is for a woman who's so done with being pushed around."

Do I sound like a crackpot? Probably.

The buyer gazes at the prebuyers. Back at the Smuck U collection. Back at me. "I like it, but it doesn't work for us, and especially not...it's not what we had slotted."

I thank them for their time and get out of there, down the elevator, out onto the sunny sidewalk where I'm jostled by pedestrians and assaulted by the scent of diesel trucks and burned hot dogs.

I just blew the biggest meeting of the year.

I might be making sequined dog collars for the rest of my life.

And I feel...happy.

CHAPTER 11

HENRY

SHE'S late for the board meeting. Almost ten minutes late. I'm surprised. I keep watching the elevators across the vast empty space that, since this is Manhattan, costs more per square foot than a Bentley.

Brett rocks back in his chair and says, "Somebody didn't read the bylaws as well as she should've."

The bylaws stipulate that if you're fifteen minutes late without alerting anyone, the board votes your percentage. It's a rule that was originally created so meetings wouldn't get held up if our grandfather decided to grab a dozen glazed bear claws from Jolly's on the way in from Long Island.

"Let's do this." I pull up the motion to strip her of her votes and enter it into the agenda with a sense of disappointment.

I was looking forward to today. Perverse, I know. But I'm curious to see what's next in the pretty little scammer's playbook. Does she cram on the bylaws? Bide her time until she attains expertise in all things Locke, and then go in for the kill?

Or does she play bull in the china shop, making us suffer and squirm until we make her a better offer?

Does she cut in a lawyer? Somebody to read everything that comes up for vote? I definitely wouldn't blame her if she did that, considering what we pulled in that last meeting.

Mandy seconds the additional agenda item and moves that we consider it first.

Kaleb seconds the emotion.

At thirteen after, right as we're about to vote her off the island, the elevator doors open.

I sit up, heart pounding. *Saved by the bell*, I think, folding my hands in front of me, ready to give her the amused smile that seems to annoy the stuffing out of her. Ready for another one of her prim-but-strangely-hot librarian outfits.

But it's not her.

It's a pair of mimes, and they're carrying something large between them—a piece of wooden furniture with shiny detailing, like some kind of fancy high chair. They start across the floor with the thing hoisted between them.

Vicky steps out of the elevator after them with Smuckers on a leash.

Her hair is tauntingly confined in that polished ponytail. Her simple brown dress has a slim, shiny belt that matches the dark brown of her glasses. But it's not her outfit that gets me—it's her bright gaze, her flushed cheeks, just the energy of her.

It charges the air around her. It sends shivers across my skin.

I have the feeling that medieval warriors must've had, seeing the enemy pour over the hill, flags flying, armor glinting.

I go to my feet.

"What the hell?" Brett mutters. We're all standing now.

The mimes proceed toward us with whatever it is they carry, followed by Vicky and April. Smuckers trots along on the end of a leash. Wearing a blue bow tie.

A Locke-blue bow tie.

My pulse races.

Vicky cuts ahead of the mimes and opens the door for them. They're your classic mimes' mimes: white painted faces, striped socks, berets, black suspenders, the whole dorky deal. They enter bearing the strange piece of furniture, acting surprised and delighted to discover us.

What. The. Hell.

I watch in shock as they set the thing—some sort of a cross between a high chair and a throne—down at the end of the table. They make a huge production out of shifting chairs around to make room. They measure the space with an invisible measuring tape, gesturing dramatically to each other.

They're not really very good mimes; this adds to the insult of it.

Vicky seems engrossed with the operation. Smuckers pants excitedly in her arms.

"What is this?" I ask hoarsely.

Vicky turns to me, adjusting her glasses in her tantalizing I'm-looking-at-you way.

"Provisions and accommodations shall be made for board members attending meetings," she says.

Damn bylaws.

My pulse thunders, and it's not just annoyance.

Kaleb clears his throat. "This is irregular."

"It's ridiculous," Brett bites out. "Mimes aren't accommodations."

As if the mimes are the problem.

The mimes are beckoning Vicky and Smuckers over now. Vicky goes and hands Smuckers to the shorter of the two. Smuckers licks a bit of white paint off the one mime's face in the process of being installed on what I see now is some sort of custom throne, like a high chair with a blue satin cushion. The back of it has some sort of circle picture of Smuckers wearing a Locke-blue bow tie, like a royal portrait.

I swallow.

Smuckers wags his tiny tail as the mimes hook him to the chair via a velvet ribbon, also Locke blue, salute him, and exit.

Kaleb grumbles from the other end. Brett comes to stand next to me. "The hell? Tell me that's not a throne for the dog."

"Okay," I breathe. "How about an elevated, highly decorated dog bed?"

"Not funny."

No, it's not funny. It's scrappy. It's...I don't know what. I don't know how I feel about any of it. It's been a long time since I didn't know how to feel about something.

Vicky goes over to inspect.

"Seriously?" I say.

She turns to me.

I shove my hands in my pants pockets. "You want to explain this?"

"Isn't it self-explanatory?" she says. "Smuckers needs a place to sit, too. I mean, does it seem fair to you that every board member here has their own seat except Smuckers? Who ever heard of an individual who sits on the board of a major corporation having to sit on another person's lap?"

I go over and inspect the image of Smuckers's face in the chair-back portrait. "A bit redundant," I observe. "His portrait, when he's right here."

"Smuckers likes people to know who's in charge. Especially since there was some confusion about it at the last meeting," she adds.

My gaze drops to her lips. Dimly I'm aware of Kaleb suggesting we call this meeting to order. She's wearing some sort of a necklace—circles the size of quarters between bright pink metal beads. Smuckers's face is on some of the circles. Others have cats and foxes, and some have words, like *Meow* and *mofo*.

Of all the things she could've done with her time over the past week, she's spent her time making custom jewelry to match the

Smuckers throne. This is a move and a half, what she's doing here.

So outrageous.

"Do you like it?" Her voice is husky. She lifts it a few inches off her chest for me to see better.

My knuckle brushes her throat as I take hold of one of the colorful disks, and I can't focus for a moment, because the sense of her is overwhelming. My skin feels too tight for my body.

I turn a disk in my fingers. It's cool and heavy and exquisitely made. On one side is the face of Smuckers. On the other it says *Smuck U.*

I keep hold of it. I don't know what it is. I don't know what she is. My knuckles hover just above her chest, my fingers just under her chin.

"Pretty nice, huh?" she says.

My heart punches in my rib cage. It comes to me here that battling a person can be as intimate as fucking them.

"It's as good a thing as any to wear while I take you down," I whisper.

"You think you can take me and Smuckers down?" Those plump, kissable lips form into a smile. "'Cause in that badass throne? Look at him!"

I bite my tongue. I don't give a crap about Smuckers.

Mandy clears her throat. "Should we get to it?"

I let go of the necklace. I turn and pull out her chair for her.

"Thank you." She sits.

April has taken up her post as board secretary.

Kaleb clears his throat. "I didn't dedicate my life to Locke Worldwide for a dog on a throne to preside in the boardroom," he says unhelpfully.

I take my seat opposite Vicky. I meet her sparkling gaze. "Is Smuckers ready to proceed with the week's business?"

"Very much so," she says.

I shift in my chair and introduce today's central agenda item, the authorization of funds for a software switchover. Mandy has been pushing for that, and she has a presentation.

Mandy puts the PowerPoint on the screen. I should be watching that, but I can't stop staring at Vicky.

"Wait," Vicky says. She moves Smuckers's throne so that Smuckers can see the screen.

I exchange glances with Brett. From the way his phone is tilted, I can tell he's filming for the competency hearing.

Good.

No mediator in their right mind will think this is anything but harmful to the company.

Mandy goes on about deeper integration of our construction, development, and architectural businesses.

I watch Vicky follow along. She asks a few questions—rookie ones, but she's interested. I was right about the construction stuff. Numbers bore her, but timelines and construction methods don't. It makes sense, I suppose. She has that Etsy store. She's made this jewelry and some of this throne. She does on a small scale what we do on a large one.

It's too bad she's the enemy.

When Mandy's done, Vicky turns to Smuckers. "What do you think?"

"Smuckers's share of the company will increase with this," I say. "This makes Smuckers richer while delivering better service."

She winces.

"What?" I ask.

"Smuckers doesn't like the idea of new software. The learning curve—he's not into it."

I frown. "If we wanted to stay away from learning curves we'd still be adding and subtracting on abacuses."

She shrugs. "You're preaching to the choir, dude. I'm not the one to be convinced here." She widens her eyes and tips her head toward Smuckers.

"Smuckers can hear me just fine," I say.

She holds up a finger and turns to the dog as if listening intently.

Mandy sighs loudly. Brett keeps filming.

Vicky says, "Smuckers doesn't like how you're talking to me when he's the one making the decisions. He feels alienated."

"Does he," I say.

"You should make your arguments directly to Smuckers," she says. "If you want him on your side you need to work a little harder."

"We're not going to do that, Vicky."

She frowns, eyes dark and dazzling. "Smuckers isn't feeling favorable to the funding, that's the problem here."

"We need this funding," Kaleb says. "We could lose millions of dollars of business here."

She shrugs. "Then I'd suggest you tell Smuckers directly why he should cast a yes vote. Really talk to him. Make him feel included. Because, between you all and me and the Locke World-wide flagpoles, you're not treating him with the respect he feels is his due. You tried to defraud him in the last meeting, and now you're ignoring him. Can you blame him for being unhappy?"

Smuckers is standing on his dog bed, wagging his tail, sensing the energy in the room.

I've done battle many times in the corporate world. I know the language of battle, the feel and sound of it. I know the moves, the signals, the rules.

She tried to play our game last time and nearly lost. We played dirty. She's asserting her power now, being unreasonable. Forcing us to orbit around her. And something else.

It's as if she's operating out of some kind of disdain, and most of it seems pointed at me.

She disdains me. It's...electrifying.

"Dreoger starts on the fifteenth," Mandy says to me, jolting me out of my haze.

I nod. "Right." We need the software. We needed it yesterday.

"That right there," Vicky says. "When you talk like that without giving Smuckers any kind of background, he feels unhappy."

I fix her with a hard gaze and get to my feet. I'll take the bullet for my people any day of the week.

I go to Smuckers. Smuckers's tongue is a little bit out of his mouth, and the hair around his face is puffier than last week. This, too, is by design—it just makes the optics all the more hosed up. The grifter. Toying with us.

"Smuckers," I say, "if we were to convert over to this new software, it'll result in a tighter integration of our core services. And honestly, nobody is worried about the learning curve."

"Project teams have been researching it...Smuckers," Kaleb adds.

"That's not very persuasive," she says.

"Look, Smuckers," I say, going for it now. "We really need your vote on this. I know what you're thinking, that a services integration will result in higher initial bid costs, so yeah, our bids might not look competitive, but this up-front integration will cut out surprises. Construction and design would work together, instead of a design being handed over to construction to interpret."

I look over at her.

"Can you imagine how much time that wastes?" I add.

She plays with her ponytail, which is just long enough to hang over the front of her shoulder. It's curled on the end, and I'm thinking about what her hair might look like down.

I get up and unclip Smuckers, take him out, begin to pet him vigorously, holding Vicky's gaze all the while. I know what little dogs like this like. I grew up with dogs like this.

Dogs were the only companions my mother really ever chose for herself.

Until Vicky.

Why her? Did they take walks together? Did Vicky take Bernadette out for lunch at her precious Gramercy?

Smuckers is licking me, practically trying to burrow into me.

"When everyone collaborates at the front, Smuckers, projects run shorter, with fewer surprises. That's more valuable than lower up-front costs, don't you agree?" I scratch his ears.

My gaze meets hers. Everyone in the room is watching the dog, but she's watching me, lips plumped together in a slight frown, gaze hot. Laser-beam hot.

I say, "The tighter integration of business units will be incredible."

Smuckers's little legs pump happily.

"Is that a yes?" I ask him.

Her lips part in shock. Annoyance. Her throat turns a compelling shade of pink. I wonder idly if it ever goes red.

Still holding her gaze, I put my mouth to the side of his head. I give her my amused smile that seems to annoy her. "Who's your daddy?"

"Uh!" Vicky arrows up and stalks over to me. "Not you!"

I feel her breath on my cheek as she takes him from my arms. She puts Smuckers back into his bed and clips him back up. Smuckers yips in protest.

CHAPTER 12

VICKY

WHAT THE HELL!

I'm supposed to be the owner but somehow, Henry's in control. Completely unbalancing me. Why did I think I was up to this?

I fold my arms tight over my chest like that'll push down my confused emotions.

He's a suit-and-tie guy, the epitome of rich, entitled suit-and-tie guys, a man who has already tried to screw me out of something. A dirty player who thinks he's the king of the universe.

I tear my gaze from him, put my focus on Smuckers. "What's that? Okay then." I sigh. "While Smuckers appreciates your effort, Mr. Locke, you really just didn't do it for him in the end. Smuckers votes no."

"You're voting no?" Mandy says, glaring at me, then she turns to Henry, expecting him to do something. I supposedly run this company, but everybody is always looking at Henry for everything.

"Smuckers votes no," I say, needing to take some kind of control back. "Smuckers didn't find the argument compelling. At all."

Mandy stands. She's mad. Everybody's mad—their anger twirls my gut into a pretzel, but I stand there like I don't care. They tried to push me around and I'm done being pushed around.

Never again.

"Can you articulate an actual reason?" Mandy asks in a barely controlled monotone. "Other than your being a jerk?"

"Let's dial it back," Henry says coolly. I don't know whether he's talking to me or her. Maybe both. He's saying something about the software. A phased implementation, something.

I'm not hearing him past the rushing in my ears, the thickness in my throat.

The horrible girl, hated by all.

I'm back walking out of that police station, all the angry questions and cameras.

I'm in my bedroom, hated Vonda O'Neil, venturing onto Twitter and Facebook, wanting desperately to find somebody out there defending me, saying they believe me.

It would've meant so much.

The picture they'd always post of me that summer became iconic. It was one my mom took of me just before we'd gone out to dinner at Applebee's the summer before. I was fifteen, standing against the hickory tree by the rusty fence, grinning like I'd never stop. I'd gotten straight A's and that was our deal—straight A's gets an Applebee's dinner.

That was a good summer. It was just my mom and my sister and me, mostly—no skeevy boyfriends.

Mom was in a program at the time, and she had some kind of prescription that leveled her out. And I felt like, if I just kept being the best daughter ever, things would work out.

Staring out at the camera that night, I could've never imagined all of America would've ended up staring back at me, hating me just a year later.

Carly had encouraged me to wear her blue sweater today to go with my Smuck U stuff, but I'm glad I didn't. Why did I think of such a crazy plan?

I straighten. *Don't crumble. Hold your head up high.*

I take a deep breath. "I'm sorry," I say. "I can see why you'd be mad after being bullied and tricked. Or being threatened if you don't take a payout. Or being unfairly brought to the police station...oh wait—that's what *you guys* did to *me*."

Mandy rises. "This is impossible. This is not okay."

Henry simply crosses his legs. "It's a business problem with a business solution."

Mandy slams her folder back together and yanks her laptop cord out of the wall. She walks out with all of the stuff hanging in her arms.

Heart pounding, I make a production out of closing my notebook and repacking my bag. I can feel Henry's gaze on me. "We'll revisit this thing," he says.

I feel dizzy. I should give it all back. Hide in my turtle shell. Why did I think I could do this? *Zip zip snap.*

"Hold on," Henry says. "We have something else on the table."

I set my bag down. I sit. I fold my shaking hands in my lap. "What?"

"We do charitable giving through the Locke Foundation," he says. "I can't remember the last time we gave to an animal charity. With Smuckers on the board now, I think it might be a nice gesture for the foundation to fund up a needy local rescue or shelter. A substantial gift."

I sit up. *An animal shelter?*

Kaleb is instantly on board, suggesting a giant cardboard check.

"Love it," Brett says. "People are going to hear about Smuckers soon enough. Let's make it a fun news story."

"Right?" Henry turns to me. "You wouldn't be opposed to that, would you? Or, I'm sorry, Smuckers?"

"That's the last thing I expected," I say.

"Do you want to spearhead it?" Henry asks.

"Me?" I study Henry's face. "Is this a trick?"

"Does asking for your help to identify a charity to give a million dollars to seem like a trick to you?"

"A million dollars?"

"For our portion. Partners might want to contribute if there's enough buzz. We can have a ceremony and introduce Smuckers. Have fun with it. Turn what my mother did into something positive."

I'm still stuck on a million dollars. *A million dollars?*

"For our portion," he clarifies, like that's the unusual part. And not CAPS LOCK! A MILLION DOLLARS! "And you can direct it to a specific organization. You know, if you have opinions. Or we can have a consultant handle it—"

"No, I have opinions. There's this dog and cat rescue shelter my friend runs—they're really good. They just started a stray drop-off center and they could do so much."

"Let's schedule it up." Just like that. *Schedule it up.* He turns to April. "Get the details and coordinate our calendars on the ceremony. Make a list of who to reach out to and all that." Then he seems to remember she's my assistant, and he turns to me. "Good with you?"

I nod, feeling stunned. Why are they being so nice? But I don't forget my manners. "Thank you. They're going to be excited," I say. "That is generous."

"It's what the Locke Foundation is for."

April is smiling in the background, because she is all about the Locke Kool-Aid.

"You want to give your friend a call?" Henry asks. "We'll want to keep it under wraps until we orchestrate the PR angle, but we can float the donation as soon as they need it."

I get on the phone to Kimmy to deliver the good news. The board members file out while she squees into my ear. I promise her over and over that it's real, that they're getting that money.

By the time I pocket my phone, it's just Henry and me and Smuckers. Henry has Smuckers all leashed up.

"What?" he says.

"It's just really nice. For the memory of your mother. For animals in need. For my friend's organization." I feel drained. Confused.

"I want to make this work," he says. "There's no reason we all can't get what we want, right?" He takes a step toward me, extending a hand. "Truce?"

I'm overwhelmed by his nearness, his unexpected kindness, the intense masculine energy that seems to be concentrated in his hand—so much so that I feel shy to take it.

But it's there before me.

I pause, mouth dry. Slowly, I place my fingers inside his. His hand is smooth and heavy, and it closes over mine, swallowing it up completely. Heat shivers through me.

"You know what we need to do now?" he asks.

"What?"

"Make one of those ridiculous giant checks," he says.

"That doesn't seem like the kind of thing that would be in a CEO job description."

"It's in the CEO job description if the CEO says it is. I make the operational rules here." He lets my hand go.

I stand there reeling, trying to untangle the annoyance from the allure when he takes Smuckers's leash and heads across the tundra of blue elegance. Smuckers trots after him without so much as a glance back at me.

"Hey…" I start after them. "You can't just take Smuckers."

He gets into the elevator and claps a hand over the door, eyes sparkling. Henry can do anything he wants.

"Fine." I get in and I stab the lobby button a few times. *Stab stab stab.*

"The doors don't shut faster when you do that," he says.

"Shows what you know." I stab it again. The doors shut. "See?"

He rolls his eyes. And we're alone.

The air between us is thick and heavy.

He turns to me, gaze serious. "We'll whip out the check at the fabrication facility. It'll be good for you to see some of the operations beyond the office."

I nod.

Just then the doors open and two women come barreling in with a giant cart. "Oh, Mr. Locke!" the older one says. "We can take the next."

"Come on, there's room." He rests his fingers on my elbow and guides me back to the corner in order to make room for the huge cart. It's just a light pressure, fingertips to elbow, but the sizzle burns clear through me.

His eyes rivet to mine. Did he feel it, too? He removes his hand, and I think he did feel it, but no, he's helping to adjust the cart.

"Thank you," the other woman says, with a gaze of enchantment.

Henry nods and grabs the bar at the back of the elevator.

The thing stops again and a woman and two small boys get on.

I set my own hand on the bar back there, right near his. His suit sleeve grazes my bare arm. My body hums with his nearness, with the tickle of fine fabric.

"We've got the Prime-Valu people on four," the one woman says, unaware of the strange combustion in our corner. "That room projector bulb issue, but just to be safe…" She seems to wait for his blessing.

He smiles his dazzling smile, the one Carly showed me in pictures, pleased with his minion. "Excellent call."

The women rattle off some corporate jargon. It's clear that they just really want him to see they're doing a good job. Everybody loves Henry, magical CEO of the world.

I fix on the projector cord, neatly wound up at the side of the cart, trying not to feel him so keenly.

Latrisha, my furniture maker friend, once said that living, growing trees extend beyond the actual physical space they take up. Standing next to Henry, I think that it's true of people, too.

It's not just the body heat of him; his shining power seems to take over the little space. Maybe that's what won him that hot bachelor award, that the space around him seems to crackle with power. Even the elevator is all about Henry.

I should inch away, but the giant cart is taking up ninety percent of the space. And anyway, he'd assume it was because of him. Like I'm overwhelmed with him or something.

It's in the CEO job description if the CEO says it is. I make the rules.

So arrogant.

Around the twenty-fifth floor I'm wondering if it's a smell thing—he has this vague masculine scent with manly notes of cinnamon and something musky. I breathe it in, letting it fill my nooks and crannies.

Maybe that's what's affecting me. Maybe he's wearing some pheromone concoction. A zillion dollars an ounce, made from the tears of mighty lions.

He's watching the numbers, so I turn my head slightly, in service of my scientific inquiry, breathing him in, telling myself he won't notice. It's cinnamon and musk and something oceany. Deep mysterious ocean with huge surges of waves.

I catch one of the boys studying me. "Are you smelling him?" the boy asks. "You were smelling him!"

"No, I wasn't."

"You turned your face to him and your nostrils went in and out. That means you were smelling him."

I smile like I think he's cute and then I give the rest of the women a baffled look.

Everyone gets out. The door slides shut.

Roller coaster belly flip.

Henry pushes off the wall with the lazy grace of a large predator. He shifts so that he's leaning sideways, eyes like sea glass, gaze glued to my lips. He lowers his voice. "You were smelling me?"

I grip the bar. "Why would I be interested in smelling you?"

"I can think of a lot of reasons you'd be interested in smelling me." He gets that amused smile I hate so much. He seems to think it's funny.

My skin heats. "Name one."

"Hmm." His eyes drop to my neck. "I'm going to go with lust."

"Oh my god, you are so full of yourself."

"That's not a no."

"Seriously? Do you automatically assume every woman wants you?"

He watches me, curious.

"Seriously. You think everyone lives to scrape at your feet, scrambling for crumbs of your attention and approval? Trying to smell you? And if a girl is truly lucky, maybe you'll pick her?"

He tilts his head. Waits a beat.

"Well?" I demand.

"Oh, I'm sorry. Are you waiting for an answer? I thought that was a rhetorical question."

"Oh my god!"

He beams at me, and right then those lopsided dimples appear. The smile that tugs at my belly.

This is his genuine smile—I recognize it as such instinctively. It's the smile that cameras never capture, the one that's not part of the Powerful Prince Henry show. Real. And so human.

Was he teasing me with the smell thing?

The elevator stops. The door opens.

And he's on, folks. He's straightened up and giving the million-dollar smiles to the group of senior execs. He places his beautifully masculine hand on the elevator door to keep it open and he turns to me, waiting. Ladies first and all that.

He's greeting the men by name, joking with them as they file in. They treat him with deference, like he's a minor deity.

We head out through the fabulous lobby with Henry carrying Smuckers. He's macho enough to carry a little dog. All eyes are on him. He knows all names.

I may control fifty-one percent of the company, but the world is Henry's billion-dollar oyster.

And how does he remember so many names?

It's a crisp, sunny day, cool for September in New York. Magically, a limo is there. The driver opens the door.

Henry turns to me, eyes a lighter, brighter shade of blue out in the sunshine. "How do you feel about walking a bit?"

"I'd love a walk."

He puts Smuckers down, and we set out through the crowds.

I catch people staring at us and I get the old familiar stir of worry that I've been recognized in spite of my hair-color change —long curly red hair was one of the more remarkable features of Vonda O'Neil.

Then I realize it's Henry they're watching. Even outside! Young starchitect billionaire Henry Locke. Sure, they're looking at me, but only to see who he's with.

And then somebody snaps a picture of us.

My heart starts to pound. It's okay if someone takes my picture, but what if they put it online? I look very different with my glasses and dark hair, but it's not like I've gotten plastic surgery. Discreetly, I slide on my sunglasses. And then he looks over at me and I wonder if he noticed the cause and effect of that.

My thoughts are interrupted by a fight up ahead—two guys have gotten out of their cars. There's glass on the road. Fender bender. Voices are raised.

Henry grabs my arm and puts me on the other side of him and sweeps Smuckers up in his arms, all this without even breaking stride. He mumbles something about the menace of texting while driving, but I'm stuck on the weird chivalry of him.

The crowds thicken even more near the subway station, but he keeps Smuckers under control. Strangers usually can't hold Smuckers right. Henry gets Smuckers.

"You're good with him."

"We grew up with these dogs," he says flatly.

Just then I recognize the corner we're on. "Hey, we have to walk up the next street. Come on." I lead down the block and turn, and there it is. "Griffin Place."

"What?"

"Griffin Place, my fave building." I point at the statue halfway up, the crouched winged lion. "See? My sister, Carly, and I...it's just one of our favorites."

"Oh, the Reinhold building," he says.

"Right," I say. "You probably know all the names."

"Being a smirkitect, you know. It goes with the territory."

"The Reinhold," I say, trying it out, like finally learning the name of an old friend.

We're moving closer to it. "In all of Manhattan? You like the Reinhold best?" He sounds incredulous.

"What? It's great."

"Hmm." He seems to view it as an odd choice. Looking at it through an architect CEO's eyes, I suppose it is. The building isn't tall, it's not special in terms of fancy flourishes, it's not even old—it's the 1940s kind, all blocky gray stone and deep rectangular windows. But the griffin is cool. Brave protector friend, mouth open in a silent roar.

He slows across the street, in the middle of the block from it. "What about it?" Like he's trying to see it. He really wants to know.

"It's the griffin," I tell him.

"What is it about the griffin? A lot of buildings have them."

"I don't know," I say, but I do know.

"Aesthetically?"

"No." I feel his gaze on me, and I know I'm going to tell him. I want to. I don't know why. "Symbolically."

"What does this one symbolize?"

"A moment in time," I say. "When my sister and I first got here, we got lost. We took this bus and it was a disaster." I smile, like it wasn't any big deal, but it was terrifying. "She was crying, and I pointed this griffin out and made up this stupid story about him being our brave protector friend."

There's this silence where I wonder if I've said too much.

"Did he help? The griffin?"

"A lot," I say. "She stopped crying and we took pictures of him. I printed one out and put it in the kitchen. If nothing else, he scared the cockroaches back down into the drain."

"You came here after your parents died."

"*Somebody* has been busy investigating my background," I say.

"Surely you're not surprised we investigated. Considering."

I shrug. According to our fake identities, our parents died in a car crash, then I graduated high school at age seventeen and got custody of her.

All lies. Except the custody-at-seventeen part, though it was more like I *took* custody. Got my baby sister out of a dangerous situation and myself out of the blinding glare of national hatred.

We keep on walking. I take a last look back, remembering myself then. Traumatized, slouching through the crowds in my new brown hair and innocent court clothes, hand-in-hand with Carly, finally away from Mom's lechy boyfriend with his creepy stare that got creepier every time she passed out.

Away from Mom's growing desperation for money for the next fix.

I'm not sorry I took Carly out of there. She was so young and vulnerable. I saved her—I know that to my bones. But she saved me, too. She was a reason for me to keep fighting.

We stop at a Starbucks. I get a java chip Frappuccino and he gets a latte. We take a cab the rest of the way.

The fabrication facility is a giant warehouse on Front Street—the old kind with arched-top windows.

We enter a massive, well-lit, state-of-the-art space full of state-of-the-art machinery in bright, primary colors. The place hums with activity and guys in Locke-blue jumpers making giant things out of metal and wood.

"We make doors and windows, refurbish heating plants, that sort of thing," he says over the din. "Locke owns so much property, it stopped making sense to sub this stuff out."

I keep expecting Smuckers to react to the loud sounds, but Henry holds him tight and scratches his snout in a vigorous way, lulling him with an overload of attention.

Is it possible that's what Henry is doing with me? Is it working?

He knows people's names here, too. A few come up and pet Smuckers. We head to an elevator bank at the center of it all and take it up to the drafting floor. We cross a tundra of desks and people doing things on huge computer screens to get to a place with lots of long tables.

He hands Smuckers over and pulls out a piece of foamcore the size of a door. "I'll cut this down a little for the check." He takes it to a table that has lots of measure markings and slices off two hunks with a large box cutter. "I don't actually do this, typically, but I don't want to pull people off jobs that have been waiting in a queue." He pulls his phone out of his pocket and taps. Soon he's the proud parent of a giant printout of a check front. He spray glues the back of the check and we roll it onto the foamcore, working together to avoid bubbles and wrinkles.

Just like that, we have a giant blank check from Locke World-wide. It's signed, but there's no dollar amount or recipient.

"Maybe we should get an armored car for this."

He doesn't reply; he's setting the check aside to dry. He's careful, even a bit of a nerdy perfectionist. "Come here," he says.

I straighten. Was it a little sexy, how he said that?

He leads the way to a wide-open space full of architectural models; desks and cubicles line the perimeter. "We have a few exciting projects you should be in on," he says.

We end up at a table displaying a five-by-five block area covered with tiny buildings and roads and cars and tiny green trees and people.

He puts Smuckers down.

"I thought architects only made these on TV. I mean, don't you have computers for this nowadays?"

Henry kneels down, getting eye level with the thing. "Building is one of the most tactile things you can do. We're creating physical environments. Making them tiny first, holding them and situating them, it reveals new things about the buildings and the spatial relationships. You see what feels right on the ground."

He touches the tallest building.

"Where is this?"

"Nowhere yet. It's going to be along the Queens waterfront. The Ten—that's what we call it."

I figure out the blue is the East River. "Dude, I hate to tell you, but Queens is all built up along the river."

"There's a swath of factories there that are moving to a less expensive area. We'll knock them down and replace it with residential and green space."

"It looks nice."

He twists his lips.

"You don't think it looks nice?" I ask.

"It could be better, but it's good for what it is."

"If it could be better, why not make it better?"

"Too deep in the pipeline."

Smuckers takes this very inopportune opportunity to jump up

and grab at a bit of fabric that's dangling off the side. The entire model jerks, and a soda bottle at one end dumps all over a corner of it.

Henry's on it instantly, sopping it up.

Another guy rushes over to help.

They both look alarmed that the tiny buildings and tinier trees got wrecked. It's all very strange, because this is just a model. *It's a train set village, people!*

Then I realize Henry's really upset.

Henry and this guy talk about who's available to fix it up, and I get the feeling they want to quick-fix it, like there's an ogre who lives in the closet who will come out and wreck the place if the model is messed up. Honestly, the whole thing is weird. Is Henry not the CEO?

Everybody is on an RFI deadline, whatever that is.

He scowls in his surly way at the wrecked side of town. I'm glad I'm not the person who put the soda bottle there.

"Right. Okay." Henry's tone is that kind of fake calm where you know anger is just under the surface.

He gets this cool intensity sometimes. It's a disturbingly winning combination.

CHAPTER 13

VICKY

IF YOU TOLD me a month ago that I'd ever find myself in a workshop room deep in a fabrication facility owned by Cock Worldwide, crafting with Henry Locke, aka the top cock of Cock Worldwide, I would think, in a word, *not*.

It seems like a dream doesn't it? Not a dreamy dream so much as one of those weird jumble dreams. Like, Leonardo DiCaprio is your father and he sent you a letter but you can't find your mailbox. Who blew out all the candles?

Henry has a couple of junior guys bring the model into a small side room and set it on a table. He dismisses them, shakes off his beautiful suit jacket, and rolls up his sleeves. "This'll just take a minute."

"Do you need it for a presentation or something?"

"No, it just needs to be fixed," he mumbles, conducting an intensive inspection of the thing.

I stand on the other side of the table conducting my own intensive inspection of the tiny paper trees, or at least that's the effect I'm going for while conducting an intensive inspection of his very large and muscular forearms, which are perfect in every way, right down to his golden skin and the sparse smattering of hair.

Some kind of big and chunky euro car racer watch hugs his right wrist. His hand has that rough-hewn look, but it's not gnarled or anything, like a woodworking codger. If the world of men's hands is a three bears cabin, his are the "just right" ones with just enough scuff to them. Hands you can respect. Hands that would feel nice against your cheek.

I swallow and force my gaze away to the built-in shelving, loaded with crafter supplies like modeling clay and paper and squares of balsa wood and cutters of every kind and glue and paint.

"Are you sure this whole business isn't a front for guys who are closet crafters?" I ask.

He's pulling down green cardboard squares and craft paper and tubes of glue. "This'll just take a minute."

He presses some of the craft cardboard to a cutting surface and starts making tiny cuts with an X-Acto knife.

He pauses and frowns at the thing. The sweet little dent appears between his eyes. I definitely like the dent. Seeming lost in thought, he starts unclasping his watch and pulls it off with rough efficiency, setting it aside.

It's a hot thing he just did.

I remind myself that he's just another handsome rich guy with every reason to bring me down. He even told me so.

We will bury you.

You're supposed to listen when somebody tells you something like that. My ears are listening.

The problem is that my libido is more interested in the competency porn striptease he did with the watch back there.

I swallow. "So, what's the deal? Why the urgency?"

"The guy who makes our environmental elements, these tiny

trees? He's from my grandfather's era...shit." He grabs a new square. "It's just a long story."

Just a long story I want to hear. Why the CEO of a powerful company has dropped everything to fix some tiny trees on a model neighborhood. "Quite the perfectionist," I say.

"Something like that," he says in his clipped way. *Long story. Period.*

Fine. Whatever, I think.

He's got a tree base created. He holds it up to soda-flattened one.

"An earthquake and a hurricane at the same time," I say. "Not a lot of buildings will withstand that."

He doesn't think it's funny. "See those balsa dowels?" He points to the left of the shelving area. "Can you grab one?"

I get one and bring it over. He takes it and shaves a series of tiny curlicues off, and it comes to me that these are the branch thingys. He attempts to glue a tiny curlicue to the tree trunk by way of tweezers, a toothpick, and a dot of glue.

Man fingers are good for a lot of things. What are they not good for? Tiny gluing work.

He completely smears the trunk with glue, which he tries to get off with a Q-tip; he just ends up leaving fur on the trunk. "Crap."

"You could pretend it's Spanish moss," I say.

He tosses it away.

"You need help?"

"I got it. I used to do a lot of this as a boy. Brett and me both. We'd spend hours doing these models."

"When was the last time?"

"I got this. It's like riding a bike."

"Except you have large hands now," I say, and not in any way like I think it's hot.

He just tries to work at it.

"It's too bad you don't have somebody with you who has way

more recent experience gluing tiny things to tiny surfaces with her slim, womanly hands," I say. "It's really a shame that there isn't anybody like that here."

He starts on another. Messes it up.

"Dude. Let me help." I tie Smuckers to a chair.

"You think you're an expert because of your Etsy dog collar store? This is a little more intricate."

"I make jewelry of all kinds, not just dog stuff," I tell him.

"We know," he says.

"Come on. You make the trunks and shave the branch curlies and I'll do the gluing. And please, your technique? With the toothpick?"

He looks up finally. "You think you can?"

I consider telling him I'll only help him if he confesses why it's so damn important, but it's getting painful to watch him struggle. "I know I can."

He cuts another trunk and slides it to me. I shove a toothpick up the trunk, basically reaming out the trunk, and then I make a small pool of glue and dip in the branches with the tweezer, then touch it to the area.

"Oh. That's more efficient."

"Was that a compliment?" I brush it off, because the air is humming between us. "Gluing stuff is my jam, baby." I blow air on it.

He cuts out another trunk. We get up an assembly line. We repair a few buildings. We collaborate on a tiny stop sign.

It's…nice.

There's something about making things side-by-side that only crafty girls know about, a kind of sweet, silent bonding that other people don't experience.

Henry and I are achieving this bond. I like it in spite of myself. Or in spite of himself.

I glue a tiny curlicue to a tiny tree, feeling his eyes on me.

CHAPTER 14

HENRY

HERE'S the thing about business—you always make your moves from a place of control.

I never ask a question without knowing the answer first. I never show people what I want unless I'm assured of getting it.

And I never, *ever* operate from need.

Needing something is the surest way *not* to get something. I learned that lesson young.

Which is why it was a good thing those elevator doors opened.

I was enjoying her embarrassment too much. She really *was* smelling me. Her neck was so pink when I called her on it, her frown so pouty, it was all I could do not to press her to the wall and take that pretty little mouth like a rabid animal.

I cut out another trunk, focusing on getting my shit back together.

Part of Vicky's genius is that she doesn't add up as a scam

artist. She's fun, interesting, easy to be with, pretty. Gorgeous, really, much as she tries to hide it. She's creative. Tenacious.

A weaker man might fall for her, might not care she puts all that goodness to use as a grifter.

She stares down at her tiny tree, inspecting her handiwork. She sets it down and uses the tweezers to make a quick adjustment while the glue is still drying. The tip of her tongue edges out the side of her mouth as she concentrates, peeking just up over the very corner of her upper lip.

If I was a different man—a more gullible man—I might be turned on by that. I might be imagining the taste of that tongue, maybe even the soft rasp of it against my cock.

I get up and go to the window, to the familiar old view, force my mind far away, back to the long afternoons after school in this room with Brett and Renaldo. Dad would be on his jet somewhere and we'd have escaped from this or that bored French au pair and found Renaldo, gotten him to bring us up here. He was running a lot of the operations by then, but he was never too busy to teach us model making. Or he'd take us out to the sites and we'd watch the subs work, tag along while he lorded over the superintendents on building sites across the five boroughs.

Renaldo's eighty-five now. He can't move around or remember much, but coming to work means everything to him— more than all the golden parachutes Locke Worldwide can give him, so we have him on models. The trees we're making took him days. It would crush him to see them down. He's frail like that.

I miss those days of getting lost in making the structural bridges and the tiny models. It calms me. I might be a happier person if I could just design, but the company needs me.

I slide the new trunk over for Vicky and her tiny gluing technique. "That's a good one," she says brightly.

I give her a look, like I don't need her compliments on my model-making technique.

She looks back down, chastened.

I watch the rise of her chest, the shift of light on the dark fabric covering her breasts that I've spent a lot of time trying not to wonder about.

She forms a kind of kiss as she blows on the drying glue. Does she know she's doing that?

Of course she does. She's a grifter. I need to always remember that.

Again the pink tongue tip!

A lot of women lick their lips at me—the long gaze, the lick of the lips, they have their place. But the most lewd lip lick has nothing on the appearance of Vicky's pink tongue tip during intense concentration. Her and her witchy little smile and mad tree skills and pink tongue tip.

Hot damn.

She holds it up for me to see, twirling it, inspecting it. "What do you think?"

I'm not looking at the tree.

"Why did you leave Vermont?" I ask.

"What?"

"Two young girls. Their parents die. Why leave?" It seemed suspicious to me when I read it in the report. "Why not stay?"

She looks away. "Prescott's in the middle of nowhere. Very rural."

"If I wanted to know that, I would've looked on Google."

She casts her gaze down; thick lashes sweep over high cheekbones. I sense she's hiding something, and I'm glad. I want her to lie, and for it to be obvious. Something to counteract how nice it is to spend time with her. How much I admire her quiet focus. Her sense of humor.

"Surely you knew people there. You came to a strange city."

"I didn't...like it there." She glues a tiny curl to a new tree.

"Why?"

She says nothing for a long time. Eventually she speaks. "This thing happened when I was in high school, and people hated me. Really hated me. Not normal hate but a certain incident got me a high level of hate all through that area. I didn't do anything wrong, but..." She trails off. "It doesn't matter. It was one of those things."

Her story has the ring of truth, and I want to hear the whole thing, but I know instinctively that pressing for more will back her off. Is this where her tenaciousness came from? Is it why she chose to scam people out of their money? As a form of payback? There are times when she seems to have a grudge.

"It must have been...hard."

"Alone and hated is a different country," she says softly.

I watch, mesmerized, as she starts another round of gluing, positioning the branches at the angle of the good trees.

She's silent for a while. Then, "Being hated, it's like a burn. It keeps hurting long after. And little things that don't hurt other people sting like hell. Sometimes even sunshine hurts. I don't know why I'm telling you."

I know why. Because being in this workshop together feels out of time. A break in the storm.

I shouldn't be empathizing with her, shouldn't be feeling this strange connection to her—subterranean. Like an underground stream, rushing between us.

She shoves the finished tree into a piece of foamcore and sets it next to the rest of the newly minted trees.

"Should we redo this light pole?"

"Probably," I say.

She picks up the most torn, most damp one, strategizing.

I grab a flat of balsawood. "The long sticks are the hardest to cut. There's a trick to it." I grab a ruler and make two slim cuts, then work the piece off with my thumb.

Her bright eyes meet mine as I hand it over. It's here I notice that her eyes aren't just brown; they're brown with bits of green in the cracks, like tiny shards of beer glass from different colors of bottles.

"What?" she asks.

I tear my gaze away from hers, struggling to tamp down the thundering of my heart. *Grifter*, I remind myself. *Grifter grifter grifter.*

The reminder steels me. We set up the rest of it.

"This looks good." I kneel and inspect it from the ground the way I know Renaldo will.

She sets her hands on her hips. "You can't even tell."

I check it from another angle. "You can't."

"Are you going to tell me why it's so important to have it right?" She's been burning with curiosity about that.

"Nope," I say simply.

"What? You're just *not* going to tell me?"

"Hmm…" I press my lips together. "Nope."

Her lips part. "Just *nope?*"

I shrug.

"Oh screw off. You think you're so funny." She folds her arms. "*Henry*. All eyes upon Henry, prince of all he sees. He's New York's most eligible bastard! He knows all your names and oh my god, he's soooo funny."

"What did you just call me?" I ask, biting back a smile.

"You heard me."

I tweak a tree, trying not to enjoy our wrong friction and how much she doesn't give a shit.

When I look back up, her focus is on the model. Not on me—on the model. "You said it would look different if you got your way. If it wasn't so far into the pipeline. How would it be different?"

The question surprises me. She's serious. She really wants to know. "Have you ever noticed how a lot of new buildings create a dead zone around them? Hunks of metal and stone that stop everything?"

"Well, that's the point, right?"

"It shouldn't be," I say, bending a tree. "I want buildings that aren't a one-sided conversation. Buildings should never feel like walls. They should feel soft instead of hard."

I look up, expecting her eyes to be glazed over, but instead, they sparkle with curiosity. This little scammer in her librarian getup turns out to be the one woman interested in my shit. "I don't get it. How can you make a building like that?"

Of course, she's a maker just like I am. Making her ridiculous dog collars between grifts.

But suddenly I'm telling her. And suddenly she's asking for pictures.

I have my phone out. I show her my favorite building, the Pimlicon in Melbourne. "Look at how porous it is. It doesn't block anything, it doesn't impose its will." I show her the curved greenery transitions. "See how it invites and engages?"

She takes the phone, studies the Pimlicon. "Like a dance."

I go next to her. My skin hums with electricity. "Exactly. Something like this would create a sense of place that draws people. The Ten is good for what it is. Locke is going to deliver better than anyone else, but if I had total control I'd do something vastly superior. Look at the way these structural elements invite..." I pause, because the way she's staring at my face is unnerving.

She looks back down. "Why design it in the inferior way?"

"It's a Kaleb project, and he's protecting our profit. He has a minimum profit-per-square-foot dollar figure that...keeps things boring."

I feel her gaze trail across my chest, my hands, like a hot caress. Damn if it doesn't get me hard.

"And you want to make something cool," she says. "Screw the profit."

"Nah. I'm not running a charity. We can make more money my way."

Her gaze burns into mine. "Your *vastly superior* way."

Teasing words tinged with affection. Suddenly I'm seeing her for the first time—this beautiful, impossible woman who makes a dog throne to mess with me.

She's supposed to hate me, but she wants me.

And hell if I don't want her.

"Vastly superior." My voice sounds husky. "Were I to have total control." Gently, I close my fingers over hers and unwrap them from the phone. She seems mesmerized by my movements. Her breath hitches.

I slip it into my front pocket and slide my finger along her jawline. I can practically see the shivers sparking along her skin.

I press my knuckle under her chin, tip her face up to mine. Her gaze is incandescent, her breath shallow, like a caught animal.

The kiss lingers in the air between us.

I lower my face and take her lips in mine. I devour her sweet, hot mouth. I don't know anything anymore. Warning bells are clanging and I couldn't give a shit.

"Henry," she breathes into the kiss. "Oh my god," she breathes. She makes it all one husky, hot-as-hell word. *Omigod*. The word heats my lips. She hates that she wants me. I hate that I want her.

I pull back and cup her cheeks, ribbon smooth. "You want to walk away?" I kiss her vulnerable neck, keeping her bared to me.

She gasps as I kiss her again. I nip the edge of her mouth where her tongue sometimes appears.

My IQ has taken a high-speed elevator to the lower level parking garage where cavemen chisel away at their square wheels.

"You want to walk away?" I repeat. "You do it now." I kiss the little bump on her jawline just below her ear. I press my lips to the pulse below her jawline.

I taste the flutter of her heartbeat, taste the power of me reflected in her body.

She curls her hands around my waist.

Dimly I remember this whole thing was supposed to be about ensuring her compliance. Her good behavior.

I don't give a crap about her compliance. I don't want her good behavior. I want her bad behavior. I want her.

I grab her ponytail, holding tight. I can almost pretend to myself that this is me making her comply. I'll tilt and adjust her head whatever way I want.

I kiss her top lip and then her bottom lip. I take her mouth full-on, every kiss newer and wilder than the last. "Vicky," I whisper against her soft lips.

She pulls away, eyes all fire and challenge. "You see me walking away?"

In a flash I have her pressed to the brick wall between arched windows, hands sliding over her hips.

Her fingers are like claws, working my shirt out of the back of my pants.

My tongue presses at the seam of her lips. She lets me in with a soft moan.

Finally I get hold of her tongue, that little pink tongue tip. I give it a soft suck.

She groans lightly, pelvis pressing into mine as though her tongue and her pussy need to stay on the same vertical plane. The more I suck, the more she grinds into me.

She's lewd and delicious, and she makes a soft little sound.

I break the kiss and start undoing her buttons, pearly little buttons, one, two, three, enjoying her gaze on my hands, the shudder of her breath.

"So superior," she breathes.

Her eyes glitter. "When given complete control."

Our pull toward each other is wrong and strong.

I slow. I don't know when I started thinking *our*. Or *us*. We're not an *our* or an *us*.

The only *us* for me is Locke Worldwide.

I grew up with the Locke Worldwide logo toy cranes the way other kids grow up with Barbie or Superman. From the cradle I was told stories of the fair play and partnership that the firm was founded on.

And she's the biggest threat to the company. A scammer.

I pause. Shake myself out of my lust-filled haze. This is good. I'm *supposed* to be seducing her. Wrapping her around my little finger. It just can't be the other way around.

And it won't be.

Stay in control. Never operate out of a place of need.

I kiss her again.

I give her a smile.

CHAPTER 15

VICKY

HE IS KISSING ME.

Henry Locke is kissing me. My shoulder blades press against the rough wall. It feels good. He feels good. My breath sounds ragged inside our kiss. Hands wander over my skin.

And he kisses me. Beautifully. Cradling the back of my head. Like I matter.

I melt into him, into the feel of his strong hands and the texture of his voice. I know it's wrong, but I'm so deep into the pleasure of him I might need a series of decompression chambers to get out.

I don't know what's happening and I don't even care. He could ask anything and I'd say yes.

I never dreamed I could feel like this with a guy. Like he's waking up something in me that died a long time ago.

He starts undoing my buttons. He breaks the kiss, but he keeps going with the buttons.

My gaze falls to his fingers. Warmth blooms between my legs.

I want to kiss his fingers but I don't want him to stop. I love the way they feel. Feather-light brushes at my chest.

"So superior," I say.

"When given complete control," he says, all rumbly. It's hot when he says that.

And then he pauses, midbutton.

Like he just thought of somewhere he had to be, or maybe he left the stove on.

He kisses again. He pulls back.

And he smiles.

And all the warmth drains out of me. It's his fake smile. His billion-dollar camera smile. The smile he uses to charm and direct his minions.

He's seducing me.

"Oh my god. So not happening." I push him away.

He steps back, gaze on my face. "What?"

"*What?*" I echo. "Just another business problem with a business solution. And the solution is your magic peen? Is that it?"

I don't wait for an answer. I grab my purse and sweep Smuckers up into my arms. "You're not going to get your way by fooling me, and you're sure not going to get it like this. Smuckers and I are so out of here."

"Vicky—"

I put up a hand for him to talk to. It's a bit 2003, but everything is relative.

CHAPTER 16

HENRY

BRETT and I leave a late lunch meeting with some pension fund people. Only the most important people get lunch with the Locke cousins.

I do my best to impersonate a seasoned professional who is fully engaged in the discussion, but deep down, I'm still reliving that kiss, reeling from the way it tore through my body.

I tell myself the kiss was a good thing, that I'm expertly reeling her in. The good-cop charm thing is working, right?

Yeah. Working on me.

I want to explore every part of her. I want to taste her skin, to hear her come with my name on her lips. Fuck her down to her toes.

Know everything about her.

I keep going back over our conversation, wishing I'd learned more about what happened back where she came from.

What happened in that town? How did she survive so young

and on her own with a kid in a place like New York? How did she think up the Etsy thing? It was hugely resourceful.

Her Etsy bio suggests she also designs high-end human jewelry. Our PI thinks that's part of what brought her to the city. Dreams of a fashion career.

After lunch, Brett and I head out to the site of an Olympic-sized ice arena and hotel complex in south Brooklyn that's an important joint venture with our Canadian partners.

Brett and I still like to walk the sites when we can.

It'll be a good thing to do. A walk through a massive construction site will center me, get my brain off pink tongue tips and soft sighs.

It goes well for a bit. We talk over plans for making up a rain delay and go over some plumbing issues.

Then I see the griffin on the side of the truck of one of the concrete contractors. I snap a picture of it, imagining texting it to Vicky. Imagining her face when she sees it, wondering where she is.

Is she making dog collars? Where does she make them? Does she listen to music while she works? I want in on her dreams, her keeper bookshelf, her playlists, her comfort TV show, her hated foods. I want in on her.

I turn off the phone and shove it in my pocket.

Kaleb shows up with the Canadians. We put on the blue Locke hard hats and head on in.

Brett's side of the family was never interested in the Locke business—it was my dad and my grandfather who ran it.

But Brett got bitten by the building bug early, so he spent a lot of time with my dad and grandfather and me out on the sites when we were boys.

After things got busy, it was Renaldo we'd tag along with. Renaldo was the master builder, overseeing the superintendents who oversaw the projects.

We spent a lot of summers with hammers in our hands under the watchful eye of Renaldo.

While we're out on the site, the partners ask about the Smuckers stunt—that's the way they put it.

I catch Brett's eye. "It's been everything we could've imagined," I say. "A unique way to honor Bernadette's memory."

"We're having a ceremony where Smuckers endows a shelter," Brett says. "We'll normalize things after that."

They look over at me and I smile. "But Smuckers is in complete agreement with us as far as a project like this goes."

"Two paws up," Kaleb adds, and everybody laughs.

Kaleb and the partners take off. Brett and I hit the falafel stand a few blocks down. "I can't believe it's working this well," he says. "The Smuckers thing. It's brilliant. As long as you can keep her under control."

"It's brilliant as long as nobody talks," I say, avoiding the keeping-her-under-control part.

Again I'm back there. I thought I'd die when she broke off the kiss.

But with Vicky, I actually am interested.

How did I get back to Vicky?

I update Brett on my efforts to reach out to everybody who was at the will reading, reminding them to keep the real story about Smuckers and my mom to themselves. "One drunken conversation with the wrong person and we're seriously hosed."

Brett turns to me. I know he's thinking of my father even before he says it. "He'd roll around in his grave."

Meaning, if he knew what Mom did.

"He'd kick right out of his coffin," I growl.

We get our falafels and eat them side-by-side, leaning against the car, watching the workers. It never gets old. In some ways, Brett and I are still those boys who can't get enough of diggers and cranes.

When I finish my falafel, I fish out my phone. I just need to send the picture and be done with it.

"Who are you sending a Morrison truck to?"

"Vicky. She has a griffin thing."

He lays into his second falafel without comment.

"What?"

"Nothing."

"She's handled."

"Did I say anything?" he says.

"You were specifically silent," I say. "So, yeah."

He snorts.

I pause, thumbs poised, unsure what to say along with the griffin pic. I type *Thanks for the trees.* Then I change it to *Here's to griffins and mad forestry expertise,* then I delete it.

I type *Friend of yours?* Then erase it. Then, *Thinking about bow ties.* Then I change it to *This guy is asking where TF my bow tie is.*

Delete.

This is all very disturbing, because I happen to be a master of texting the just-right thing to a woman, no matter what the circumstance, from pre-hookup banter to post-hookup emojis.

I don't know what to text to Vicky. How can I not know?

But I do know. I really want to say, *I loved kissing you. I forgot what it was like to kiss somebody because it felt like the only thing in the world worth doing. I forgot what it was like to sit and make things with somebody who gives a shit how curlicues line up. I wish you were here.*

"Soooooo," Brett says. "How *is* operation good cop going? Operation hot cop?"

I bristle at the name. "Just concentrate on your part."

More specific silence.

I look up. "What?"

He nods at my phone. "Cat got your thumbs?"

"If I'm going to do a thing, I'm going to do it right."

"Okay, Uncle Andy," he jokes, meaning my dad.

"It's under control," I growl.

He falls silent, not loving the growl. Then, "You sure?"

I stare at the image. It's a cartoon version, but fierce, protective. "She has a griffin thing. From when she first got to town." I turn to him. "Did that PI ever say anything about any kind of bullying incident in her past?"

"No. Though bullying doesn't always get reported. Her background is a little sparse. Her internet footprint is small for somebody her age."

"Something big happened back in Prescott," I say. "Somebody really did a number on her. Turned a lot of the town against her, it sounds like."

"I can ask the PI about it."

"Do it," I say. "Somebody went after her, and I want to know who. I want to know what happened and I want to know who."

I can feel his eyes on me. "Is this part of operation good cop?"

"Just get me the details." I type *Someone says hi* and send it off.

CHAPTER 17

VICKY

TWO DAYS AFTER THE KISS, April calls to inform me that Smuckers and I are scheduled to come to a groundbreaking ceremony for a brain disorders research facility on Staten Island.

I put on my favorite outfit, a maroon pencil skirt with a dusky gray sweater. I pause over the pearly buttons, remembering the way his fingers worked them, trembling just a little, as if he really wanted me. It was the hottest thing I'd ever experienced.

The hottest thing I'd ever experienced was a man undoing my sweater *as if* he wanted me.

I sink to the bed. Despair and resentment twist through me, bright and sharp. Smuckers watches me alertly from his nest of blankets.

It seemed so real for a while, but he's one of the best. One word from him and buildings shoot up to the sky and women fall to their knees. There's a reason for that.

What am I doing?

Wearing that exact same sweater style for him again, that's what.

I flop back on the bed and scroll to Henry's griffin text, like I have a dozen times before. Like that's proof he was thinking about me.

He was really thinking about his company, wasn't he? He tried a few underhanded things and now he's going with seduction.

He wants the company back, and why not? It should've been his. He deserves it back. He's not like Denny.

I put the phone to my chest and stare at the water-stained ceiling.

And I make a decision. This thing has to end.

Carly wanders in and shakes her head at my outfit. "That's what you're wearing?"

"I have something to tell you," I say. "I'm signing the company over to Henry."

"*Ex-cuuuuuse?*" she says, outraged and dramatic.

"It's not mine. It's not right."

"It belongs to poor Smuckers."

"Come on," I say. "It's Henry's birthright. I'm going to have Smuckers sign it over."

"But...all the money!"

"It's not ours."

"He tried to trick you," Carly says. "He tried to bully you. He had you detained!"

"And now all that ends."

"So a rich, entitled asshole who thinks he can get his way all the time gets his way?"

The memory of the kiss washes over me. I would've given him anything. It's dangerous. How far would he have gone? Seducing me out of sheer duty? "Decision made," I say.

Carly narrows her eyes. "Hooooold on. This is a pretty major financial decision."

I smile bitterly. "A multi-billion-dollar decision."

"Well, are you forgetting something, perhaps? A certain cooling off period that we promised each other to honor?"

"This is different."

"How? It's a major financial decision. It affects us both—that's our pact."

I sit up. *Shit.* "I can't—"

"We keep our word to each other," she says. "Right?"

Nobody has a nose for hypocrisy quite like a teen. I look over at the calendar. Twenty-one days. "I have to at least tell him. He's..." *trying to seduce it out of me.* "He's in misery."

"Oh, no, no, no, no, noooo!" Carly can see she's got me and she's enjoying it. "Making a commitment is a promise. If you're good for your word, saying you'll do a thing is like doing a thing. *Same as,*" she adds. "We keep our word, us two. And Henry and the rest of the Worldwide Cocks, what with their do-the-right-thing bullshit and then they try to trick you? Please—"

"Okay, okay." I hold up a hand. "But I'm giving it back."

"If you so decide after your cooling off period, then yes."

I look at her standing there, all on fire. "I don't know if I hate you or love you more right now."

She grins. "And you cannot verbally commit to it. No *I'm giving you your company back but I have to humor my sister.*"

I toss a balled-up sock at her.

"Bird," she says.

WHEN APRIL TOLD me a car was coming, I assumed it would be my own personal limo, as is the Locke Worldwide way, but when I step out onto the sidewalk with Smuckers in his fave riding purse, it's Henry standing there, holding the door open.

He pulls off his aviator glasses. My soul lights up like a switchboard.

"Good morning," he says. His brown suit fits perfectly over

his broad shoulders as if to say, *Oh, all of the places you will not go! But really, really want to!*

"Hi," I say, like I'm not awash in the Henry Locke magic. I slide into the limo, positioning Smuckers on the cock blocker side of me.

He sits next to me and hands over a java chip Frappuccino. Because of course he remembered. It's part of the seducer's job.

"Thank you." I sip. "So. A groundbreaking ceremony."

"It's one of the things you two'll be doing now." He pulls a small blue vest from a bag. It has the Locke Worldwide logo embroidered on the side of it.

"Oh my god." I put the cup in the holder and hold it up. "I don't know about this."

"Come on," Henry says. "A little team spirit."

"Poor Smuckers. He's officially on team Cock Worldwide."

Henry narrows his eyes. "What was that?"

"Cock Worldwide?" I study his eyes, get lost there for a second. "What? Are you honestly telling me you've never heard that?"

He gives me this look, like he thinks I'm joking. "Cock Worldwide. That's not a...*thing.*"

"You don't know?"

He looks uncertain. "Nobody calls us that."

I snort. "Yeah, nobody except everybody who stands on the ground looking up at the giant cranes. I get that the logo is supposed to look like a building between two bushes, but seriously? And just...the giant cranes? Erecting massive buildings?"

He looks at me, genuinely surprised. It comes to me that nobody wanted to tell him because they're too busy worshipping him.

"People wouldn't call us that," he says.

"It's cute that you don't even know."

"I think *somebody* has an overactive imagination."

"Oh, meaning me?" I say. "You think it's only me who calls it that?"

"Yeah, I do. Which reveals the direction of your thoughts."

"So arrogant," I say, as if his nearness isn't a tickle. As if my skin isn't pure shivery nerve endings when I get around him. "I'm not the one covering the city with massive phallic symbols emblazoned with my name. It's the direction of *your* thoughts we should be concerned about."

"Like a Rorschach ink-blot test," he teases. "Some people see cranes, the progress of a city, but you see something *quite different.*"

"Oh, *pull-ease.*" I snatch the vest from his hands and get Smuckers out of the purse. "You ready to be on team Cock Worldwide, buddy?" I put the vest on him. It fits perfectly.

"People wouldn't call us that."

"Think what you want. The world is your golden crib."

Henry reaches over and runs his finger over the cursive L in Locke, a move that brings his arm and hand dangerously close to my lap.

"The loop on that L looks like a C. You have to at least admit *that.*"

"Well...Cock Worldwide, huh." He seems to ponder. "If the name fits..."

"Oh my god!" I grab his hand. I'm just laughing now. "You are so bad!"

He grins at me, and there's a whoosh where the whole world stops. And I think he's going to kiss me. I know he's going to kiss me. And I want it.

God, how I want it.

I let go and sit back, cross my arms, take a shallow breath.

"What's going on?" he asks.

"Your fake seduction plan. You think I'm that stupid or just that desperate?"

"Look at me." Then, voice strained, "Vicky."

I don't look at him.

"I would never think you're stupid or desperate. They're the last things I'd think of you."

"I know what you're doing. And just...I want you to understand that you don't have to do it." This is as close as I can come to telling him I'm giving back the company without breaking the pact.

I don't have much, but I have my word.

He slides the back of his fingers across my cheek. My blood rushes hot through my veins. I shut my eyes.

Hard skin brushes soft, featherlight. Smooth and slow. His touch is so gentle, I think my heart might crack.

His voice, when it comes, is a whisper. "Kiss me, Vicky."

"I can't."

"Kiss me." His voice is low and urgent. "Be with me."

My heart stutters.

He skims down below my jawline now, sliding against my skin with the back of one finger, slow, slow and scorchingly tender.

"You want to."

"You are so..." I pause, breathless.

His finger travels downward, putting pressure on the top button, popping it. He finds more skin to slide down, pausing at the center of my chest, a whisper of a presence above my pounding heart.

"You are so..." I try again.

I don't have it in me to think up a playful insult. Heat swells heavy between my legs.

He leans in. Lips to my ear. His face is a soft rustle on my hair.

My breath comes faster.

"You're going to kiss me," he says. "Maybe not today, but you'll come to me. I can wait."

"Such an operator," I say, gaze falling to his hand at my chest.

He moves down, unbuttons another button. "You like watching my hands, don't you?" He undoes another button.

"Are you just undoing my buttons now? Yes," I say.

"And you're into it."

"And the arrogance just doesn't quit, folks." I'm going for light quip here, but my voice is rough with desire.

"You like my hands, I think." He undoes another button, revealing the top of my camisole. "You're going to like them even better when they're between your legs."

Dark lust arrows through me. "Oh my god," I say, as though I think it's funny. It's not.

"I'll get you off, baby. I'll take such good care of you. I'll take you slow and deep. I'll print every inch of your skin. Nothing— nothing about it will be fake."

"So entitled," I breathe, finally mustering up the strength to shove away his hand.

He pins me with his gaze. "I'll wait. I can bide my time."

"Well, you're going to have to wind your watch to infinity."

A baffled light appears in his eyes. Like a baffled light of wonder. That's probably fake, too. Fake fake fake. I'm not interested in his fake seduction.

I pull out my phone. "So what is this groundbreaking thing?"

He takes a ragged breath. Like he's so overwhelmed he can't talk for a bit.

I roll my eyes. "Seriously?" But inside, where he can't see, I'm shaking with need for him.

In a rough voice, he tells me about the facility, and how getting a reputation in high-tech research could lead to some important jobs.

CHAPTER 18

VICKY

THE GROUNDBREAKING TURNS out to be a lot of people in their Sunday best standing on bare dirt inside a fenced-in lot that takes up nearly an entire block.

And cameras. Lots of cameras.

I put Smuckers on his long retractable leash and let him run around and receive petting from his minions. I smile and laugh and discreetly lower my sunglasses.

But I can't help wonder what Henry had planned. What if I had said yes? Would we be at a hotel right now instead of here? Butterflies whirl in my belly every time I look over at him.

Brett comes over and presents Smuckers with a plastic squeaky shovel in Locke blue and everybody's taking pictures of him running around with it in his mouth.

Then the people involved with the facility get a silver shovel with a blue handle and they all take turns digging bits of dirt out of the ground.

When it's Henry's turn, he takes off his suit jacket, rolls up his shirtsleeves, and digs up a massive shovelful of earth, heaving it aside. Everybody's clapping, and he's standing in the sunshine with his wicked, billion-dollar Henry Locke smile. He jams the shovel into the dirt and grabs his suit coat, slings it over his shoulder.

When the applause dies down, he shoots a sly glance my way. He pretends to wind his watch.

He's mouthing a word. *Infinity.*

My face flares hot. But I just shake my head. Like I'm immune.

Brett has his own shtick. He holds Smuckers in his arms as if they're wielding the shovel together. Afterward, people close in and pet Smuckers. I realize that Henry never pets Smuckers just for the pleasure of it.

"You guys got him a little Locke shovel," I say once we're back in the limo. "Nice optics."

"I meant what I said," he says. "I'm waiting."

"For me to come and kiss you," I say.

"And then all bets are off, Vicky."

My mouth goes dry. "I heard you the first time." I try to think how to change the mood. I want to kiss him. Right now. In this place. "Do you not like dogs?"

He frowns. "I like dogs."

"I don't think you do. The only time you ever pet Smuckers is...for a purpose. You want to make him paddle his legs or calm down or something. You never just pet him out of fun."

"He's just a dog, Vicky." He doesn't deny it, and I feel a little sorry for him right then.

"You hardly ever even say his name."

"Smuckers is just a dog." He glances over at me. "Is that better?"

"A dog your mother left her company to."

"You think I'm jealous of a dog? Please, Vicky. If I wanted to wear my hair in a marshmallow Afro and live in a woman's purse, I think I could find a way to arrange it. This is New York, after all. There is probably a dominatrix out there who'd make it happen."

I cross my arms. "You know what I find weird? People aren't freaking out about Smuckers's control of the company very much. They all seem to think it's a PR stunt."

"A lot of people see it as a PR stunt. Connected to his dog shelter gift."

"And you're letting them think that."

"We are."

"Why not tell people the truth?" I ask. "Unless...I don't know..."

He says, "Unless we have more evil plans to get rid of you?"

I say nothing. Because, yeah, does he have yet another trick up his sleeve? I wish I could just tell him—don't worry, *you'll get it back.*

But how can I expect Carly to keep her word if I don't keep mine?

"You know how many people we employ?" Luckily he answers the question for himself. "Directly, we employ three hundred forty thousand people across ten offices worldwide. When you count vendors and subcontractors, it's double that. Those are real people with real lives and families and homes, people who depend on the health of this firm to make house payments and put food on the table. Do I want to announce that a Maltese is in charge of all that?"

I wait. I know a rhetorical question when I hear one.

"No. I'm not going to rock the company with that kind of announcement. I'm showing them that things remain consistent after Bernadette's death. I want them feeling strong, steady, capable leadership."

"Okay." I make myself not look at his hands. I try not to think too hard about him caring about people. Or turning out so different from Denny.

We have a late lunch at a sidewalk café in Soho. It feels like a date. He asks me a lot of questions about my life and my jewelry biz. He seems really interested in the makers studio, and I swell with pride talking about it, because it's such an awesome space and an amazing group of people.

Then I remember he's not my boyfriend. He's not even my friend. He's an entitled wealthy man who thinks I'm going to come to him and beg him to take me.

I keep my distance.

I tamp out every spark that lights between us. Sometimes I feel like Smoky the Bear, stomping sparks left and right. Too many to stomp out.

Day after day.

Biding my time.

The worst are those moments when he lets down his guard, when he stops being beloved playboy Henry Locke. When it feels real.

It's a mindfuck when it feels real.

Here is the last guy you should ever trust or want. He's fooling you. Fake seducing you. And you want him anyway!

The mindfuck of hanging out with Henry twists and contorts into confusing new shapes every hour over the following days.

The man is on this kick of showing me every aspect of the company. "You need to understand things to vote out of a place of knowledge," he says.

This involves Smuckers and me getting picked up in a limo and taken to a different part of New York or New Jersey and meeting people and learning new things that a giant company does.

Building turns out to be a small part of the Locke activities. Every one of those companies that got listed off in the will reading has its own little empire of activity.

Henry does work in the car and discusses corporate things on the phone with the people we meet. He's good at what he does. He really cares. Is this his new method of seduction?

On one outing we tour a nearly finished building that has a zero carbon footprint—it's heated and cooled through underground circulating water. Super green. Henry's excited.

It's infectious.

On another outing, we tour a mammoth prefab facility in New Jersey where they make parts of buildings so they don't have to build everything on site. He's just as excited about that. Also infectious.

"How do you know everyone's names?" I ask on one of our many limo rides.

"I make a point of it."

"But how? You know so many names."

"If something's important, you find a way to do it," he says.

Bird, I mumble.

He gets that amused smile that always annoys me. "What was that?"

I want to grab his lapels and yank him to me and say *fuck you*, lip to lips, and then kiss him.

But I know where that leads.

Instead, I lock my hands together in my lap and turn away.

The worst thing is the family feeling throughout Locke Worldwide. Like they really are one big happy family with Henry Locke as the strong, fierce leader, a man who'd go to the ends of the earth for his people.

It makes him twice as hot, how he fights for his people. How protective he is.

At times, tooling around the five boroughs with Henry, touring sites, meeting employees, learning new things at Locke HQ, I get this feeling like I'm part of that team, part of the family that Henry fights for and protects.

It's intoxicating.

And so predictable. So pathetic.

It doesn't take a team of psychoanalysts to understand why that would be wildly attractive to me, considering it's been me alone for so long, looking after Carly on my own. Even back home, nobody was protecting us. Nobody was fighting for us.

Sometimes when we're talking about the company I use the word *we*. As if I'm part of the Locke family. *So cool that we're opening an office in Raleigh. How are we doing on our stadium proposal? Wow, our development team is kicking the shit out of those assholes at Dartford & Sons!*

I constantly have to remind myself I'm not in the family.

We ride around in elevators and limos and other enclosed spaces and it's exciting. Sometimes our gazes lock and the earth seems to still.

My vibrator gets a workout at night.

I'm a week through the twenty-one-day cooling off period and I just want to touch him. Even just his arm. He's irresistible as catnip. Irresistible as a super-charged magnet. Or maybe irresistible as a black hole, the kind that sucks in spaceships and girls who just want to be loved and trusted.

None of his affection is real, that's the thing I need to remember. He's had PIs on me, after all. He thinks I'm a scammer.

I'm something far worse. I'm Vonda O'Neil.

Again I remember that picture of me, smiling out at the world so hopefully, repeated a million times across Twitter and Facebook with captions like *I'm a lying whore.*

Sometimes, right before I go out the door in the morning to meet the car, I give myself a little pep talk. I remind myself that I don't need team Locke.

I control a giant company and have access to all the money I could ever want. I ride around in limos with literally the sexiest man in New York, but somehow I'm still that hungry girl looking in from the outside, nose pressed to the bakery window, wanting just anything.

A crumb.

Henry is like the hottest and most charming vacuum cleaner salesman who ever came to your door. And you invite him in and you let him show you the vacuum, how well it cleans and how all of the attachments work. And you see that he loves this vacuum, and his love for the vacuum makes him insanely desirable. And you guys laugh and have fun cleaning the carpet. And it's nice.

And you keep telling yourself it's not about you—he just wants to sell you that vacuum cleaner. That is his only motive! Except it's getting harder and harder to remember that.

Maybe sometimes, when he's expertly changing that nozzle with his amazingly capable hands...or when he's smiling at something you said, and you're looking into his gorgeous blue eyes and getting that floaty feeling in your chest, those times you start to believe, that even though he came to sell you that thing, maybe he has started to like you.

Then you hate yourself for being gullible, because hello! He's New York's most eligible bastard and you're not even in the top million bachelorettes.

In fact, you're barely an *eligible* bachelorette for any bachelor, unless the bachelor in question is a poetry-scribbling parking lot attendant with self-esteem issues or a junior pastry chef with eight roommates and a video game obsession, or a cook/musician/student, not that that sums up my last three years of dating.

ONE OF THE hardest things about hanging out with Henry is how he has this knack for reaching into me and hauling the pure Vonda out of me. Sometimes provoking it out of me. Sometimes enchanting it out of me with his questions and his jokes and his endless interest in my opinions.

"I know what you're doing," I finally tell him at lunch after another afternoon of finding out about the awesomeness of Locke Worldwide, another afternoon of witnessing him play the part of the fierce protector, admired by all. We've left Smuckers behind today.

"Beyond the supposedly fake seduction?" He cracks a popadam in half and hands me the big piece, because it turns out we're both heavy into popadams.

I take it, remembering what he said about his hands. *So good between your legs. You'll come to me. I'll get you off. I'll print every inch of your skin.*

Needless to say, my vibrator has been getting quite the workout in recent days.

He studies my face, expression unreadable. He does that sometimes. Like he wants to know me. To figure me out. Again and again I tell myself it isn't real, but it feels so good.

And I want to kiss him. I want to press GO on us. I want to stab that button so hard he flies to me. I want him to print every inch of my skin. I'm not sure what that means in his mind, but I want it.

"You know what I'm doing?" he asks. "What would that be?"

"You want me to love Locke like you do," I continue in a breezy tone. "You can't trick it out of my evil clutches, you can't seduce me, so you're doing the next best thing. Trying to humanize it."

"Don't count out the part where I seduce you. That's still going to happen."

"Uh," I say, belly tightening. "You probably think all women would just die for your magic peen."

"Not all of them." Casually he cracks another piece of popadam. "Just the ones I've slept with."

Gulp.

"And for the record, my seduction of you isn't goal oriented. I'd seduce you if all you had was a dog bow tie Etsy store. Though, really, I should turn you in for animal cruelty. Because those bow ties you put Smuckers in? No."

"He likes his little bow ties."

"Trust me," Henry says. "He doesn't like the little bow ties."

"I think you're just jealous."

His eyes sparkle. "That's what you think?"

"Maybe I'll make one for you."

"My neck has a lot of girth." He lowers his voice. "You'd need a lot of sequins."

I snort, but I don't look at him. I don't want to see that on-camera smile of his turned on me.

I say, "You're trying to make me see how important Locke is to all your family. Keeping me from killing it. You think I'll kill Locke, but you don't have to worry. Things are going to be *okay.*"

"I don't think you're going to kill it," he says in the voice he sometimes uses when he feels like his communication is important.

I want to believe him. His opinion has become important to me, stupid as that sounds.

I grab the last popadam. "Right now, I'm thinking about killing this. You mind?"

I look up to find him gazing at me in his infuriatingly hot way. What is he seeing? What is he thinking?

I snap off a bit. "Crackly," I say. My forced brightness is designed to cover the hopeless feeling.

It gets worse when he shows me his absolute favorite under-construction project, the Moreno Sky, a boutique hotel in Brooklyn that will be built in the crater of a half-crumbled-down building. It incorporates many urban ruin elements into the mod design.

He shows me support beams of reclaimed wood, the slabs of reclaimed concrete walls with graffiti from the 1970s. "This would've ended up in a landfill."

I run my finger over the words *Keep on Truckin'* in blue. "Did people say that?"

"Apparently."

I can see why he likes it. The place incorporates a lot of the forward-thinking design principles from that building in Melbourne he's so wild about. You can see it in the way the structure is mostly greenery and engaging public/private spaces at the bottom and the way the building takes on mass as it rises.

He shows me more of the construction site, how they're folding old into new. "This is cool as hell," I say.

He hands me a hard hat. "We're not even in the building yet."

"Kaleb must hate it," I say.

"I practically had to give up my firstborn to make this happen," he says. "Running this place, I don't get to design and build that much anymore, or really getting my hands dirty on any level." He says this last in a wistful tone. Like he misses it. "You have to see from the top. Come on."

We climb a circular concrete stairway to the main floor, what will be the future lobby. Right now it's a noisy, unfinished space full of men and women doing different jobs—the trades, he calls them.

One side is a two-story wall covered in plastic. When the place is finished, it'll be a curtainwall, which is apparently a wall of windows.

He shows me more old timber and twisted rebar that was heading into a landfill but that Henry feels could be incorporated into lobby furniture—he needs to *get the bandwidth to figure it out somehow.*

That's how he puts it. I love his lingo sometimes.

We head to the "freight elevator" which doesn't look like any elevator I ever rode or ever would want to ride.

Henry punches a button that's attached to a metal coil thing. There's a screech and a rumble and our cage arrives. "Come on."

We step in and it hoists us up through a seemingly endless concrete column that would be utterly dark if not for a sputtering makeshift utility light clamped to the side.

Fear spikes through me during the long flickers when I think the light might go out—I wasn't prepared for how much like the well this would be—not the cage part, but how dark it is and the way we're closed in by dark gray walls and you can see light way up high.

I move a little closer to Henry. I was so scared in that well for so long. Scared of dying. Scared to call for help. Scared it was Denny and his friends out there, looking for me, scared that they'd get to me first, but wanting so bad to get out. Scared of the sounds. But mostly I was scared of the dark. I would sit in a little ball. I would tell myself if I got really small, even the darkness couldn't find me.

The elevator is taking forever, and I inch closer still, enjoying Henry's nearness, his strength. I tell myself he's just the vacuum cleaner salesman, not here to make me feel safe.

His fake currency still spends.

"Vicky," he says.

I brace myself. Does he notice I'm being a freak? "What?"

"Are you going to smell me again?"

I smile. "It's just a little rickety."

"I forget you're not used to this. Totally safe." He puts his arm around me. "Okay?"

I don't know whether the *okay* is about his arm around me or the safety statement. "Okay," I say.

"I wouldn't put you in here if I didn't know it was safe. I wouldn't do that."

I nod. It's not the elevator now, it's him, doing strange things to my body. Him being protective. Like I'm one of his people.

"But if you want to smell me, you can."

I don't want to smell him. I don't want the warm weight of his arm to feel so good. I want him to stop making me feel alive and happy. I want to not perk up in some soul-deep way when our gazes find each other from across a crowded room. I want him to not seem to admire the Vonda in me.

I want that not to feel amazing.

I lean in closer, stealing what doesn't belong to me. My head isn't exactly on his shoulder—it's difficult to do that when you're wearing a hard hat. But it's close.

He brushes a lock of hair over my shoulder. His knuckles graze my jawline. His touch is featherlight. Barely there.

But the energy of it hums over my skin, spreading outward in a burn, like fingers of heat warming cold, remote parts of me.

I fight the urge to turn my face to his hand.

"You look hot in the hat," he says.

"You're just saying that."

But when I do turn my head, his eyes are dark. Serious.

His voice lowers to a rumble. "I'm not just saying that, Vicky."

Oh, I want to kiss him. And, if anything, an elevator shaft that looks like a well should be reminding me why I have an allergy to rich, powerful men. It's not.

His eyes drop to my lips. My heart pounds.

The elevator grinds to a stop.

I'm shaking when we step out into wide open space, twelve stories over Brooklyn. And it's not about fear.

Open blue sky soars above us and massive pillars of concrete surround us, stretching upward. Chains with links bigger than my head are coiled in piles, and there are stacks of wood and massive metal things like strange Legos.

I stroll to the far side, near a squared-off column. There's a brightly spray-painted scribble on the concrete surface. Not from the 1970s, but new. Everything up here is new. Raw.

I toe the orange scribble like it's more fascinating than the royal babies of England, but really I need to be apart from him, because I'm reeling from the goodness of his arm on my shoulder. The forbiddenness of ever falling for him. Of thinking he's falling for me.

He comes up next to me.

I act like the operation of tracing the squiggle with my toe is of urgent importance. "Somebody went Jackson Pollack with the spray paint up here."

"That's actually a message. It's there to show the electricians the alarm conduit placement."

"How can you even read it?" I ask.

He kneels next to me, and his dark suit jacket stretches over his thick, solid arms as he points to different parts. "This is orientation. Right here is just a measurement. The fact that it's orange means any kind of telecom, but this'll be an alarm, of course."

Of course, I think. *Such a construction nerd.*

I stand, biting back the urge to run my hands over his shoulders, to get in on the tautness of fine fabric over solid man muscles.

He twists and looks up at me, chin stubble glinting in the light. My heart is in my throat.

I force my gaze back to the scribbles. "The colors tell you?"

"Just like you see down on the street."

"You're all secretly communicating with each other?"

He stands. "Yellow's natural gas. Red's electric. Blue is water."

His nearness affects me like a drug. My eyes fall to his lips, and I shiver.

"You cold?"

I'm not, but he's taking off his jacket and putting it over my shoulders now, cocooning my arms, and I like it very much. I like how warm and soft it is. I like how he adjusts it so precisely, like he cares greatly for my comfort.

I tell myself the idea he cares about me is an illusion. Wishful, magical, ridiculous thinking.

Ancient people thought the stars formed pictures of archers and bears and gigantic spoons, but can we be honest for a moment? They're just stars. They don't form pictures, no matter how many stupid diagrams you make. Like the stupidest dot-to-dot puzzles ever.

That's what I'm doing with Henry's affection. Making pictures that aren't there. Elaborate diagrams of him wanting me. But it feels so real.

He holds the lapels of the jacket snugly shut, his breath gusting warm on my forehead. "I'm so glad you could see this."

His tender gaze sizzles over my skin. Like he's really looking at me. And then he smiles.

His eyes sparkle. Uneven dimples appear. It's his Henry smile. The real Henry smile.

I reach my hands out from my coat cocoon and grab his soft, warm shirtfront, pulling him to me.

I kiss him.

Boom. He deepens the kiss. My kiss was soft, but his is rough and wild. With his other hand, he cradles my cheek, fingertips trembling with energy where they touch my skin.

"Vicky," he rumbles. He walks me backward into a massive concrete pillar.

My hard hat falls down over my eyes.

"No, no, no," he rasps, yanking it clear off my head and tossing it over his shoulder.

Because he wants to see me.

Somewhere behind us there's a *splock*, and a softer *splock* as the hard hat comes to rest. I can barely hear it over the hurricane of my pulse whooshing in my ears.

And I want him so bad, I'm shaking.

He fists my ponytail. My breath hitches as he slides the backs of his fingers up my throat, up to the tender underside of my chin. His touch sears me.

"Henry," I say, trembling down to my toes.

"I love watching my name on your lips." His voice is ragged.

Silently, I mouth his name: *Henry.* And then again, *Hen—*

He doesn't let me finish; my lips are still open when he kisses me, a desperate, open-mouthed kiss with the fury of a thousand senselessly whirling stars.

He shoves his hand into my hair, cradling the back of my head, pressing me back against the cool concrete post.

I can feel the shape of him against my belly, huge and hard. I want to wrap myself around him, to dissolve around him. To obliterate myself on him.

His breath is ragged as he bends to get our lips level. I reach behind him, fitting hungry hands around his warm, solid back, digging in with my fingers a little.

He makes a growly sound as he rains kisses over my cheek, my neck, before taking my lips once again.

The cool breeze caresses my exposed legs, but underneath my clothes, sweat trickles down my spine.

The entire building seems to sway in time with my thundering pulse, in time with Henry, pressing himself to me.

Somewhere down on the street, trucks and cars rumble by and honking horns are answered by other honking horns.

He's still wearing his own hard hat. It's sexy.

His breath turns erratic as he runs his hands over the sides of my hips, up and down. "You and your *skirts*," he says, like my *skirts* are a point of awesomeness.

Without warning, he grips my ass—clenches it hard—fingers like steely vise grips. He jerks me against his rock-hard erection and I gasp to feel the size of him through our clothes. "You feel that?" he snarls, notching himself to me, pulsing against me. "That's how you have me every day. Damn! You already feel good."

"Oh my god, yes," I breathe. He presses me harder. His weight feels amazing. I gasp as he kisses my cheek, my neck. Every time he moves, the pressure between my legs changes and my ache builds.

I'm pulling up his shirt, freeing it from his pants and belt. Finally I get to his warm abs. I press my hands there. I'm a thief now, taking what's not mine. Consuming his belly, rough smattering of hair over muscle.

I don't care if it's not real anymore. It's real enough.

"I've imagined this for so long," he says, pulling away, panting.

I shiver as he skims his fingertips over my sweater-clad breasts. "These fuzzy sweaters."

"Take it off me," I say. "Let me watch you unbutton it. Like before. How you started to before."

"Have you been thinking about it?" he asks. "You been beating off to it?"

"Yes," I breathe.

His fingers tremble as he unbuttons the pearl buttons of the sweater. I love that he's trembling.

"Pull up your skirt, then," he says.

I hunch over and pull it up, turning it inside out, gathering it up.

He pushes a hard-cut thigh between my legs. "Ride it. Move. I'm gonna need you good and wet."

"I don't know how much more wet I can…"

"Ride it," he growls. He gyrates his hips, getting up the rhythm. I match his movement, moving while he undoes me. It's a little embarrassing, but it feels so good.

"Harder," he whispers in my ear. "If you want me to undo these dainty buttons, you gotta do your part." He nudges my legs wider. "Ride."

I do it. Satisfied, he returns his attention to the buttons.

"I look at these buttons sometimes…damn," he pants. Like he's lost his ability to make sense. He kisses my forehead. "You watching me down there?" His fingers are soft spiders at my midriff, undoing the third-to-last button. The second-to-last button. "Unwrapping you. You watching?"

"I'm watching," I say.

"Is this what I'm doing when you beat off? Don't bother trying to tell me you don't." He knows it is. He flicks the last button. My sweater falls open.

His thigh between my legs is blunt waves of pleasure. He fists the center of my cami, uses it to pull me into a faster rhythm. "I love how you move on me." He skims his palms up the front of me, sliding over the white fabric, calluses catching and snagging. "Like this?" he says. "Is this what I do to you next?"

"Next," I pant, "you do whatever you want to me."

His chuckle is a rumble in my ear. He curls his fingers around the tops of the bra cups and jerks down. I gasp at the violence of the movement. My breasts pop free with a jiggle.

"Jesus, you're hot," he says. He throws off his hard hat and kisses me roughly, then pulls away, panting.

"Watch my hands, kitten, watch what I do to you." He presses his hands over my breasts, rough and warm. "So hot. My cum would look so good right here. All over these pretty tits. You look so prim and proper, it makes me want to corrupt you. It makes me want to unravel you. There are so many layers to you, and I'm going to fuck them all."

The layers comment sends momentary alarm through me, but then he plucks my nipple, and the zing of it flares bright white inside me.

"So entitled." My breath speeds. The city spreads out below us like another world, another time, dizzying and slightly unreal.

"Why aren't you riding?"

"I need something else there now," I say. "But isn't this a little bit exposed up here?"

"Nobody sees you but me," he says.

I think it might be true on a level he doesn't mean. I don't know how to feel about that. He slides the pads of his fingers over my lips. Lust runs thick between us.

"Open."

I gaze up at him, knuckles grazing his steely abs.

"Wetness is not going to be a problem," I say.

"Baby." The word feathers my cheek. "You're not the only one beating off to things these hands might do." He slides a thumb over my bottom lip, pulling it down. "Open."

I open and he slips two fingers between my lips, into my

mouth. "Suck. Get them nice and wet. These are the fingers that are going to fuck your pussy."

Heat rushes through me as I palm his bulge, as I suck his fingers, as I run my tongue over them. He slides them in and out, watching me.

"This is how you're going to suck my cock when the time comes. Except you're going to squeeze the root and give me a little teeth on the bottom. Try it."

It's so Henry to give me a tutorial on sucking his cock. I wrap my hand around his fingers and give him a little graze with my bottom teeth.

"Oh yeah. Perfect."

He pulls out his fingers and anoints my nipples. They pebble in the cool breeze coming off the water.

"Only I see you."

He pulls aside my panties with rough efficiency and curses, low and rumbly, when he finds me waxed and wet.

"Fuuuck," he groans. "What have you been hiding under these librarian skirts?"

"Not books," I say.

His fingertips brush my sensitive clit, sending a jolt of pleasure through me, making me gasp.

A dimple appears on his cheek and I kiss it. It goes away, but then it appears again and I kiss it.

"What are you doing?"

"Being so into you I can barely think," I say.

He pulls away, panting, eyes wild, beard stubble sparkling. "Oh, yeah?"

Suddenly I feel bare to him. Not just physically, but soul-deep bare. As if his fingers are everywhere inside me. "Yeah."

He slips rough, thick fingers deeper between the folds of my sex. My head tips backwards onto the hard pillar, eyes drifting closed.

"Oh, yeah," I say as he slides them against my clit with the perfect motion. He changes his angle, and this new sensation swirls through me, making me senseless and lightheaded.

"Do the nipple pluck thing," I whisper.

He breathes out a shaky *fuuuuck*. "You are so...*everything*." He does the nipple pluck thing and I cry out. It's rougher than I expected. Better than I expected.

He exhales a shaky breath and kisses my cheek and then my ear. His teeth graze my earlobe, sending wicked lightning all through me. He plucks my nipple again, softer this time.

It's like he's learning me. Exposing my secrets. Stripping me bare for the first time.

His fingers send rippling heat up through my core.

His strokes go long and strong. He slides two fingers in. I suck in a short, sharp breath.

"I gotcha, baby."

I crash over the edge. White-hot pleasure. Naked and alive.

"I gotcha, baby." He pins me to a pillar high above the city, raining kisses over my face. I'm lost. I'm found. I clutch his arms, kissing him back.

"Damn," he says again. As though the whole thing surprised him.

I feel shaky all over. And fresh and new.

I don't care what's real or not.

I'm all-in.

I drop to my knees, gazing up at him. I fit my hand over his bulge and give it a small squeeze.

"Jesus." He tunnels both hands into my hair, half ripping it out of the ponytail holder.

With shaking hands I undo his belt. He takes over, quickly undoing it. "Leave it to the professionals," he says.

And then he touches my chin. I think he's about to explode, but he touches my chin. Like he kind of can't believe I'm in front of him.

I love his eyes on me. I love the sunshine of his gaze. I usually prefer the shadows, but Henry's breaking all the rules.

I pull him out; he's big, broad, and club-like, pink at the tip. Soft as silk.

Watching him from underneath my lashes, I give him a lick.

He stutters out a breath. "Do you know how hot that is?"

So I do it again. I really will give him anything.

I turn my attention to his cock in earnest. I take him into my mouth, squeezing him at the root. A pained sound escapes him. Fingers close over my head. He starts to thrust gently into me, guiding my head but not forcing it.

A triangle of his belly is exposed and it pulses in and out, like he's breathing double time.

I squeeze the warm, velvety base of him. I take him deep.

His fingertips pulse and curl at my scalp with every thrust, like his excruciating pleasure is coming out his fingers. I sneak a look at him standing over me, broken and beautiful.

And then I give him a little teeth, just a graze at the bottom. "Holy shit," he says.

He clamps his hand onto my head and takes over the motion, fucking my face, coming with a strangled cry.

After he pulls out, he kneels in front of me. "Holy shit," he whispers.

"Yeah," I say.

He traces my lips with his finger. "It was more. How you were was more than I imagined. You're always more."

I put my camisole's bra cups back over my breasts. He starts buttoning up my buttons. Clumsily.

"The professionals," I say, taking over.

He stands, tucking in his shirt. "Gotta get you cleaned up." We get ourselves together and drift over to the elevator.

CHAPTER 19

VICKY

I STAB THE MAKESHIFT BUTTON, feeling dazed. *Stab stab.*

"Hey," he says.

A grinding sound comes from below. Like the elevator didn't get the message.

Stab stab stab.

"Don't do that," he catches my wrist. "You'll burn out the winch starter."

"Somebody is quite the micromanager," I say.

He kisses my fingers.

The little cage arrives with a strange whirring sound and I get in, and then he gets in and hits the down button. The elevator lurches and begins to lower. It sounds funny. Different than before.

Just then, a motor below makes a grinding, screeching sound.

"Shit," he says.

"What is that?" I ask.

"We're okay," he says, but the cage we're in grinds to a stop. The motor falls silent. The light flickers out.

We're in the darkness. Deep in a well.

"No!" I whisper, turning and clutching the cage side. "No…"

"We're okay. There're safety cables all up and down this." A light flashes on—Henry's phone. He's talking to somebody, trying to work out what floor we're near.

I slide to the cold, corrugated floor, arms around my legs, back against the chain-link cage. I'm in that well again, that well where I spent three lonely, terrified days.

Breathe. Breathe.

You're not there.

"Vicky?"

Breathe. Breathe.

He squats next to me. Gently, he settles his hardhat onto my head.

"Okay, that just makes me think we're going to crash head-first," I say. "Or something is going to crash on top of us."

"None of the above," he says, adjusting it to fit my head. "I'm only putting it on you because I know I'd lose points off the manliness portion of the New York's Most Eligible Bastard competition if people knew I was hogging the only hardhat in a situation like this."

I nod.

"Here's my thinking." He settles in next to me. "We know I can win the swimsuit part of the Most Eligible Bastard competition. And I have the name memorization bit nailed. But as you can imagine, the manliness portion is extremely important to me."

Hammers and voices ring up from below.

"You can smell me if you want."

"I'm so not smelling you."

He checks his phone, then puts it down in a way that lights the area in front of us. That helps, too. "My guys are down there working on the machinery. It's a simple winch starter issue…"

"A winch starter issue," I say. "Like what? Tell me."

"You want to hear about the winch issue?"

"Did I burn it out like you said I would? Wait, don't answer that. Just tell me about winches." I hate how tiny and scared my voice is. I really just need him to be talking. "Start at the beginning. The history of winches."

"Are you being sarcastic?"

I press my fingers to my forehead, feeling so messed up and hating the silence. "I'm being sarcastic, but also I want you to."

He seems thoughtful in the silence. He takes my hand, warm and cozy in his. "I have something better to tell. My secret."

"You have a secret?"

"How I do the names."

I look up at the outline of his head in the dark. "How?"

"I took a class in memorization techniques. You can't say anything. I don't ever want our employees to feel like a number."

"You took a class? That's commitment."

"It means a lot to people, and as the company grew, it got harder and harder. So I took the class. I know it sounds a little intense, but people...they see me in a certain way, and I don't like to let them down."

"Wow," I say. "You make it look so easy. You make it look so easy to be you."

He huffs out a quiet little laugh. Shifts my hand in his. "Anyway, everybody gets a special visualization location. If somebody is named Mike, I imagine him on a stage singing with a microphone. Clarence is in an orchestra playing a clarinet. Dirk is in dirt."

"What about Fernando?"

"Are you serious? ABBA."

"Like it's so obvious."

"Isn't it?"

"What did you use for me?"

"I'm not telling." I hear the smile in his voice.

I widen my eyes. "Come on."

"Nope. Sorry."

Playfully, I shove at his shoulder. I kiss his cheek. I nip his earlobe. "Please," I beg.

"Nope."

"Hmmph. Well I've got one for *you*, Henry. For the name Henry. And you won't like it."

He says nothing.

"You won't like it. Not. At. All," I add. Then it hits me. "There are thousands of employees! You remember all their names?"

"Only the local ones."

"That's more than a thousand," I say. "That's...intense."

"Once I started it, I felt like I had to keep it up." A thread of weariness winds through his words. He makes it look easy to be him. Doesn't mean it is.

More hammering from below. "How long until we're out?"

"I don't know. Between ten minutes and an hour."

"Uh." I pull into myself more tightly, my limbs finding the old familiar grooves with each other. I feel like I'm falling, falling, back into that well.

"Are you claustrophobic?"

I pull my legs tighter. I should answer, but I want him to talk, not me.

"You seemed okay in the many elevators we've been traveling," he says.

"It's because this shaft feels like a well. The unfinished sides, the light above."

"Oh." A beat, then, "Do you have...history with a well?"

"I fell in one," I say. "When I was younger. They didn't find me for a pretty long time, and I was just terrified out of my mind."

"How long?"

I'm about to say three days, but that's the kind of thing that gets reported in the news. "Long enough," I say. "I felt like I'd fallen off the face of the earth. But most of all, it was terrifying. I was scared of the dark to start with. And you don't know how dark the bottom of a well is—you have no idea. I thought I'd never get out. People couldn't find me. And there are slugs, and it's just…" I shudder. "It was a long time in there."

He slides his arm around my shoulders. "This isn't a well."

"I know," I say. "But I kind of don't know."

He pulls me close. I find myself leaning into him.

"It would be scary," he says. "Alone. Not sure if you'd be found."

"Yeah," I say. *Not sure if you'd be found by the right people, anyway.*

He pulls his phone out and whips off a quick text, then clicks off. A few moments later, the shaft is flooded with light from the bottom.

"Oh," I say.

"Is that better? Less well-like?"

"Thanks. It is better."

"You got out of that well, Vicky."

"I got out. And grew up to be a dog whisperer slash captain of industry," I add. He says nothing. It's a stupid joke. "I'm sorry. I'm just messed up right now."

Bangs and drills sound from below.

"It's hard to be powerless like that."

"It's more about the fear," I say. "Did you ever have that fear of footsteps in the dark? And then you get to the warmth and light of safety and it's such a relief. But in the well, it was like the footsteps never stopped. Hour after hour, the terror kept grinding on. It took everything out of me. Fear is exhausting. Little-known fact."

"How long were you in it?"

"Can we talk about something else?"

"I'm sorry that happened to you," he says.

"Something. Else."

He sighs. "You know that model we fixed together? With the trees? And I wouldn't tell you why it was important to fix it?"

"Yeah."

"Okay, well, now I'm telling you. There's this guy, Renaldo, he's the one who made it. He eighty-five, one of the oldest guys in all of Locke. He helped my grandfather and father build the company, and he definitely has enough money to retire, but building is his life. Those models take him forever to make, but Brett and I feel like it keeps him alive. And if he saw the thing destroyed...he'd be crushed."

"You seemed mad."

"Well, who's leaving their bevs all over the model? Right? Anyway, he was kind of an uncle to Brett and me. As my dad got too busy to deal with us, Renaldo was the one who'd take us around, make us learn the ropes with the trades. Brett and I would go and do our homework at that place, and if we finished in time, Renaldo would give us little assignments. Make a five-inch bridge out of ten toothpicks and a piece of string, stuff like that. And there would be a test, like the bridge would have to extend between blocks spaced five inches apart and be able to support a stack of ten quarters."

"A bridge made out of just a piece of string and toothpicks? How is that possible?"

"You'd be surprised what you can make from a piece of string and toothpicks. It's excellent building material."

"Maybe this is the part where you reassure me that even though it's excellent building material, you went on to use more durable materials in the construction of things like freight elevators in boutique hotels."

He turns to me there in the strangely lit shaft. "This thing's solid steel, baby."

I suppress a smile, because of course it sounds slightly sexy. "So you keep Renaldo on staff. That's sweet."

"He gave us an amazing education. He's a master builder —literally."

It comes to me that he didn't mention his mother. As if she wasn't in the picture. "Did your mom help out with the company?"

"No." He pulls out his phone. I don't press him on it. I'm not exactly the mother relationship queen myself.

"I want to tell you something and have you hear me on it. Trust me on it." I need to tell him without violating my pact with Carly.

"Yeah?" He slides his hand along mine.

"Your mother handed over the company to Smuckers." That's not violating our pact, right? It's a true fact. Light beams up from below, peeking through slits in the metal. "Things...tend to work themselves out. When something belongs to somebody, it tends to find them."

"What does that mean?" He watches my face with intense interest. "Is Smuckers giving back the company? Is there something in the will that reverts it?"

I shake my head. "*Things work out*, don't you find?"

"You can't say more?"

"I can swear to you that I never had my sights on Locke. I know you have no reason to trust me," I say. "I know what the evidence makes it look like. What it makes me look like. I'm not that terrible person. It's not what everyone thinks."

My throat feels thick. It's like the emotion of the last eight years is rushing up all at once, choking me.

"I want you to believe." The words rush out of me. "I need you to believe in spite of the evidence."

"Hey." He pulls me onto his lap, holds me tightly. "I believe you."

Emotion lurches through me. I'm stunned. Reeling. His arms pull tight around me. "I believe you. I trust you." He kisses my cheek. "I see you."

I swallow. I close my fingers around his arm. His breath warms my cheek.

And he believes me.

Contrary to all evidence, he believes me. The world seems full of possibility. Like what's happening between us could be real. Like maybe things work out for Vonda, too. Like string and toothpicks can make a bridge.

Clanks and voices ring out from below.

"Show me one of those bridges," I say. "I want to see."

He's got his phone and he's swiping the screen. "Brett sent me this last year. This is before." He shows me a picture of a tiny bridge with string running as tension wires under the arch of toothpicks. He swipes. "After." It's a sad little pile of quarters and toothpick bits.

"Awwww," I say.

"Wait, I might have one of the old successful ones." He's flipping through his photo cloud when the elevator lurches back to life.

I grab onto his arm as it begins an excruciatingly slow descent.

"Hold up," he says. "Don't think I'm letting you out before finding a successful one." He finally gets it, hands me the phone.

It's the bridge—string and toothpicks supporting quarters, but the shot gets his face, and that's what I love. He's maybe eleven, crouching behind the table with a shit-eating grin on his face and those dimples in full force. Happy. Proud.

Eventually, we reach the bottom and the cage door opens to a group of guys in hardhats. They help me out first, all apologies. Henry goes to inspect the motor with them.

I wander over to the reclaimed junk he wants to incorporate into furniture like it's something I super need to check out.

I'm afraid to think it's real, but I do. My heart pounds like a happy drum. I smile. I shove at the pile with my foot and smile like a madwoman.

I feel him near. I don't know why I always feel him.

I say, "They used to make everything so ornate. Even the most lowly electrical thing was ornately designed. Buildings had pretty flourishes they didn't need. Why don't they do it anymore?"

"We still do," he says. "Just in a different way."

I pick up a piece of grate with a vine pattern.

"How cool would it be incorporated into a table or seating?" he says.

I kneel and pick up a metal circle the size of a dinner plate with elaborate edge pattern, trying to get my head straight. It has numbers and a bird logo pounded into it. A patina of scuffs from across the ages.

I toss it onto the pile and pick up a block of weathered timber with old nails in it and a shiny metal plate the size of a playing card stuck to the side. "I know how to get this made into furniture. More awesome than you can imagine."

It's Latrisha I'm thinking of. This is her jam.

"Tell me."

His eyes lock onto mine and I'm back on that roof, breath coming in shaky tremors, awash in the goodness of him. Still holding my gaze, he tosses it back into the pile. It's a sexy, confident, screw-it-all move that I love.

It's the kind of thing Vonda would love even more. It's weird to imagine that, against all odds, he senses that fun, wild Vonda part of me. He trusts her.

He doesn't know the most important details of my life or even my real name or hair color, but he knows my Vonda side. And he knows my maker's heart.

"You got a truck?"

He comes to me—slowly. My blood races as he nears. Is he going to kiss me? I would let him kiss me.

But instead of kissing me, he stops.

I look up at his gorgeous lips and sparkly golden-brown cheek stubble and enchantingly uneven dimples.

"Did you just ask Henry fucking Locke if he has a truck?"

~

AN HOUR LATER, we're rumbling over the Brooklyn Bridge in a heavy-duty diesel pick-up truck with the Locke Worldwide logo on the side.

It's loaded with the best stuff from the site, courtesy of the crew that Henry called over. He told me to point out the best bits, then he disappeared.

He was on the verge of losing the Most Eligible Bastard's manliness competition at that point for not helping to load...but then he came back in work clothes—a long-sleeved green T-shirt and jeans and boots and gloves—and he started loading with the guys.

He went for the heavy stuff, like the hunks of concrete. He sometimes grunted, muscles bulging like melons under the light fabric of the shirt. I tried not to stare too hard as he worked. Or when he'd wipe the dripping sweat off his forehead with his big freaking glove, sometimes leaving smears of dust.

Manliness portion of Most Eligible Bastard unlocked!

We're heading deep into Brooklyn, away from the trendy parts.

"And you're not telling where we're going."

"Take a left up here on Oakerton," I say.

He takes a left. On we go.

I look at the increasingly decrepit buildings from his point of view, wondering what he thinks. Was I wrong to bring him here? No matter how dirty he gets his hands, he's a billionaire, a man from another world. He wields a shovel, yes, but some of those shovels have giant bows on them.

I check my phone. I texted Latrisha during the loading, making sure she'd be around and she hasn't responded.

This is the kind of reclaimed shit she lives for.

We pull up at the Southfield makers space. There's actually street parking in this part of town, of the leave-your-vehicle-at-your-own-risk kind.

I suddenly dread taking him into the dank and half-ruined warehouse, with industrial lighting and power sources hanging from ropes and duct tape on things. There are plywood partitions between workspaces. Giant welding setups that aren't entirely legal. Home-cooked venting that is totally not code.

Even the grungiest Locke fabrication facility is a palace compared to this. Clean and spic and span.

And then there's the culture of the place.

It's not all well-behaved jewelry makers who just need a soldering setup, or fashion-forward furniture makers like Latrisha. There's a wild edge to a lot of the people, from the tattoo-and-leather Neo-Renaissance guys over in the blacksmith area to the facially pierced mosaic artisans to the crazy-ass pottery people and neon guys and everyone else. Will the scene be too outlandish?

"You have an alarm on this thing, right?" I say.

"I'm not worried," he says. "Who's going to steal a load of vintage construction debris?"

"Um, you're about to meet them," I say.

We hop out and walk up the fractured sidewalk to the entrance. I wince as I unlock the skull-design metal door, made by said blacksmith guys.

I lead us into the hulking space, like the inside of a Klingon warship. And of course the first thing we see are the potters and blacksmith guys in the lounge area couches around a table loaded with empty beer bottles and some kind of sculpture that might be made out of part of a tractor.

I smile and wave at them. "Lively today." I grab his hand and pull him in toward the more subdued side.

"What exactly is this place?" he asks.

"Southfield Place Makers Studio. It's a makers co-op." We pass the welders and the collective hardware area where tattooed urban beardsmen argue over the schedule for a circular saw. "You have to sign up for some of the larger tools," I explain. "They're shared." I lower my voice. "That guy doesn't always follow the rules, but things usually go really smoothly."

He doesn't reply.

My mood fizzles as we go deeper, because I don't see Latrisha's bright red hat over the plywood partition of her space. This was a bad idea.

"You do your jewelry here?"

"Well, I need venting for soldering. I think I'd get evicted from my apartment if I tried it there."

"Damn," he says.

Miserably, I lead him onward, past rows of messy workshop tables made of raw plywood. Why did I think he'd like this?

It's not just the scene here, it's him, too. He's dressed down, but he's a different species than we are, like he can't wash the rich off, no matter how hard he might try.

"It seems a bit low rent, I know," I say, "but it's a great deal and the tools here are really good."

He doesn't reply, seeming stunned by the decrepitude.

I keep going. If nothing else, he can see some of Latrisha's furniture and maybe hire her, and that would be great. Whatever else he thinks about this place, Latrisha's furniture is amazing.

"And it's not like we let just anyone in, much as it might look like that. People have to pay monthly and we can kick them out if they're assholes. I mean, it's hard to do this kind of stuff in the city; it's not like we all have sheds in our yard, or even yards, and when you look at the start-up capital for like, a woodworker or even someone like me—"

"Vicky," he says in his laughing way.

I turn and walk backward. "We all have lockers for our personal stuff over there," I say.

"Watch out." He grabs my arm just in time to keep me from backing into a couple rolling a cart.

He smiles down at me, and it's one of his fake smiles. And that's not okay. "What's wrong?" I ask.

"It's nothing."

"Tell me," I say.

He lets me go. "It's a wealthy guy complaint. Trust me, you don't want to hear it."

"I know it seems a little shabby."

"You think that's the problem?"

"Or...low rent."

"Vicky," he says. "You're seriously apologizing for the state of the place?" he says. "It's utterly amazing."

Shivers swirl over me. "You think so?"

"I know so."

"I worried you'd think it's...I don't know."

"One of the little-understood things about having my kind of money is the insulation. It can be great—you're insulated from tedious chores and time sucks, and I never have to talk to anybody who I specifically don't want to talk to; other people talk to those people for me. But I'm also insulated from something like this. I literally can't have this."

"You could if you wanted."

"Yeah, okay, technically I can, because it's a free country, but I'd almost have to come as somebody else. Like a poser. Look at me. I could buy an airplane hangar and fill it with the best tools money can buy before dinner. I'd have to take a space from somebody who actually needs it." He's silent a bit. "This place is awesome. And I can never be one of the people who belong here."

I'm stunned at how I misread him. He wasn't feeling judgy; he was feeling jealous. Billionaire Henry Locke can't have this. And he thinks it's awesome.

I grin and turn to him, walking backwards. "I wanted you to like it. It's one of my favorite places in the world."

His eyes sparkle. "I like it a whole lot."

Heat creeps over my neck, because I feel like he's talking about me.

He catches up to me and takes my hand. My heart skips a beat.

"Do you have a lot of collaboration?" he asks. "Do people walk around and see what each other is doing?"

"Yeah, people hook up on projects, but it's not as if we're walking around all *dude, please tell me about this awesome creation of yours!* That would be a little dorky."

"They hook up from the lounge," he says.

"More often than not," I say.

I see Latrisha's head pop up, and I think, *Yay!* She widens her eyes at me. I suppress a smile. I warned her I was bringing Henry, but she still looks a little stunned.

We get to her space, and I see she's cleaned it up. "Latrisha, this is Henry. Henry, this is Latrisha. She makes furniture out of reclaimed stuff and it's freaking amazing."

"Hey," he says, taking her hand. "So nice to meet you."

"Likewise." Latrisha's apron is full of pockets and her hair is wound in a braid on top of her head like a rope crown. She's trying to disguise her grin, and it makes her look a bit mad. "I've heard a lot about you."

"I think I might be familiar with one of your recent pieces, actually," Henry says, moving over to her workbench and picking up a remnant of the polished metal she used on Smuckers's throne. He goes on to slide his hand over a partly finished stool on her workbench. "I love this burnished effect. How did you get it?"

She explains her burnishing technique, which I realize would be good with the reclaimed posts and wood. She ends up showing him pictures. They discuss finishes so extensively, it seems like a joke at one point.

I go to my locker and grab work clothes to put on behind the changing curtain.

When I get back, she widens her eyes. Yeah, that's right; it's Henry Locke, hot Henry Locke, here in our space recognizing the awesomeness of her furniture. It makes me feel ten feet tall.

He wants to hire her to do the furnishings and they talk about that. And I know he's not hiring her to appease me. She really is one of the best, and Henry would see that.

Henry gets this world. It makes my heart swell.

We head out to the truck, the three of us, and pick through the wood chunks and start matching parts together. We haul a few things out onto the broken sidewalk. Latrisha's thinking tables and a lobby desk. Henry has measurements on his iPad.

I get the idea of having Bron, one of our smithy pals, heat and reshape small bits of the rebar to make design elements. Latrisha is talking about an entire lobby desk of chopped and polished construction timbers, fit back together like a puzzle with mostly triangular pieces. It's an awesome idea, and soon enough, Bron, another smithy friend, and Henry are unloading the truck.

People don't recognize Henry right off, though I have no doubt word will spread once somebody figures it out.

But right now, to everyone but Latrisha, he's one of us, full of energy and ideas.

Maybe his work clothes cost more than a month's rent, but he makes up for it with his passion, not to mention his construction expertise. He and Latrisha and Bron and I take to the collaboration of making a grand lobby desk from the reclaimed materials like we've been working together forever.

A few people drift over and throw out suggestions. He draws the appreciative gaze of most every woman who comes by, but he just keeps rolling with the group, gazing over at me, all sparkly, when things are popping.

Henry is so full of contradictions. He's a powerbroker into controlling everything, but he can do brainstorming and team-work like a pro.

More smithy guys come over a few hours later and, not coincidentally, beers come out. The smithy guys clink bottles so hard, I think the glass might break. I wince and catch Henry's eye and he's just laughing, like he knows what I'm thinking.

And then he goes off with them, the three of them with armfuls of rebar.

"Oh, how far we've come from the dog throne," Latrisha says to me, watching them disappear.

"What?"

"You've done a one-eighty. From wanting to mess with him to *quite* the opposite."

I can't keep the smile off my face.

"What happened to the asshole?"

"His company is his family and, yeah, he's a complete asshole to anyone who threatens it. Which he saw as me, I suppose—"

"If he really knew you, he would know you're the most trustworthy person on the planet."

I smile without meeting her eyes. Latrisha doesn't know I'm Vonda O'Neil, either. I'm lying about my entire identity. But that's not what she'd hate me for. She's my age, around twenty-four. She would remember Vonda's supposedly destructive lies. She could've forwarded the news stories and liked the Facebook memes.

Somebody made a video of strung-together clips of me on the Deerville courthouse steps that made it look like I was dancing up and down the courthouse steps. They spliced in a lot of imagery of pigs rolling in mud and set it to music with violent, misogynist lyrics.

It got millions of likes. Latrisha could have been one of them. I could still go type *Vonda pigs* in the Facebook search bar and find the seven-year-old video online, and I could search the likes for her name.

I've done it before with people, like teachers of Carly's, but I had to make myself stop that.

Would Latrisha be in there if I hovered over those likes? Would Henry? God, he'd hate me. They both would.

"We've come to a good place. It's complicated."

"Record scratch!" she says. "Did you sleep with him?"

"Weeeeeell…"

"Oh-em-eff-gee," she says.

"No, we didn't do it…" I pause, awash in memory of us on the rooftop. And the way his lips felt against my skin, his hands.

"But you've been doing each other."

"We have." I toss a bottle cap into the trash. "And it's amazing. He's amazing."

"I thought he didn't trust you. Like you're this weasely scammer who stole his company," she says. "What happened to that?"

"We've gotten to know each other—deep down, beneath all the bullshit of this situation. We click. It's amazing. And I'm giving the company back."

"Hold on—what?!"

"Don't tell him. I didn't actually tell him, but I implied it. Carly and I have that twenty-one-day waiting period thing and promising is the same…"

"Bernadette gave it to Smuckers and you because you two were her only friends in the universe. She wanted you to have it. That is your security. You and Carly. You would give that up?"

"It doesn't feel right to keep it."

"What part of going from scrabbling along to super wealthy doesn't feel right to you?"

"All of it. Carly and I were getting on fine. We have a great life just how it is. And the company was never ours."

"So, let me get this timeline straight." She sets a hand on my shoulder and her eyes bore into mine. "He's an asshole to you. He plays dirty tricks. It doesn't work. Then he decides to be charming. And we *know* the tales of him in the sack. I'm sorry. I know he's hot. He's smart and fun. But he's not one of us. He just wants that company."

I'm shaking my head.

"No, you listen." She tightens her grip. "He's spending time with you and he's all that. And suddenly you're handing over the company. You—who hate rich, entitled assholes until this one decides to wrap you around his worldwide cock."

Something twists deep in my belly. "I know how it looks."

"Is that or is that not the timeline?"

My pulse races. "I don't care."

"You need to start caring. This rich boy is playing you," she warns. "Your first instinct was not to trust him. You need to honor that."

"My instinct is to trust him now."

Warmth slides over me. I turn to see Henry coming toward me alongside Bron.

Latrisha swears a blue streak, but I'm not listening.

Henry's all sweaty and wearing his big gloves. They're carrying something they made out of the rebar. Henry smiles at me, and the smile hooks to something deep in my belly.

"Don't be a fool," Latrisha warns, voice hard as steel. "This guy is leading you by the vajeen."

CHAPTER 20

HENRY

OUR EYES LOCK and she smiles, and hell if that smile doesn't light up the raw, cavernous space. Her true habitat. Cool as shit.

Her pink work shirt stretches tight over her tits in a way that reminds me of the roof and gets my cock stirring. Though that would suggest my thoughts have left that roof. The way she felt.

They haven't.

Latrisha is so serious beside her.

I glance down at my watch and back up at Vicky. She rolls her eyes. We've developed our own code, way beyond spray-painted scribbles on the ground. The way we click blows my mind.

Her strange promise in the elevator has me hopeful for the first time in weeks. She asked me to trust her. I do.

Screw it. I do.

More than trust her—she's making me feel things I haven't felt in years.

And I trust her on that strange promise. Things will be restored. Made right with the company.

Was there a side letter from Bernadette? Something binding her to silence? More messing with me from the grave?

I go right up to her and kiss her. Latrisha doesn't seem to approve of the PDA, but I do.

We get to work. I find myself watching Vicky when she's not looking. Waiting for her to smile. I watch for her face to light up when she likes an idea. When she doesn't like something, she tips her head and narrows her eyes, like she's not quite seeing it. Not getting the person's vision. So diplomatic.

My favorite is when our eyes meet and she straightens her glasses in that sexy, I'm-looking-at-you way that she uses to put an underline under our silent agreement.

My phone pings. Brett.

Can u talk?

I can. I don't want to. Being here is like a vacation from myself. The Henry Locke extravaganza. But I see that he's called a bunch of times.

I get up and wander to the lounge area, which is the one genuinely shabby part of the place, and call him.

"I've been trying to call for the last hour," Brett says. "Our PI got back."

The PI. "Right."

"Listen to this—it's fake. Extremely professional, extremely expensive, extremely fake identities."

I stop and turn. "Does he have proof of this?"

"He's getting it. It's involving bribes at a federal level. There are no photographs of the two of them online prior to seven years ago. He thinks she might be connected. The ID is mob-level good. This is a five-alarm fire."

"Mob? No. She's not connected. She's not a con. I'm telling you," I say.

"Has our guy ever been wrong on a case?" Brett asks. "Has he? No. Never. Pull your head out of your ass. She posed as a pet whisperer and bilked an old lady."

"She's giving the company back."

"Oh, she told you that?"

"In so many words."

"She's giving back the company. But did she do it? Did she draw up papers?"

"I think there's more to the will. I don't know. She's not in it for the money."

"Are you kidding me? Wait. You're sleeping with her."

"No, I'm telling you what is."

"Dude. You don't even know her name!"

"There could be lots of reasons an ID might be false," I say. "She could be running from somebody."

"Yeah, that's it," he says, voice dripping with sarcasm.

"Screw off," I say. "It's under control."

"Is this part of good cop? Is she there or something?"

"Let him keep digging," I say. I'm thinking about the way she talked about being hated. Bullied. Was that connected to the well? Did somebody put her in a well? Or worse? Is she so frightened of somebody that she had to change her name to get away from them? "Go for it. Find out everything about her."

There's a silence on the line. My about-face feels off to him. More than that, he doesn't like that I'm not telling him my thoughts. There was a time when I'd tell him everything.

"Okay," he says finally. "And I made ressies at El Capitan for six tomorrow."

"What?"

"Dude," Brett says. "Scanlund fundraiser? The Jacabowskis?"

I close my eyes.

Real life had to intrude at some point.

Mike Scanlund is a city council politician we're backing for assorted reasons. Black tie fundraiser. We're taking the Jacabowski sisters, who are high up in that campaign. The two of them and Brett and I frequently tag team on each other's issues at fundraisers.

"Can I sit there or are you going to hog the whole thing?"

I look up, and there she is.

"I'm going to hog the whole thing," I say.

She puts her hands on her hips, and before I can stop myself, I'm surging up and pulling her into my lap. She screams and laughs and loops her arm around my neck, and the way we fit, it's like she's been sitting on my lap forever, as if our bodies know just how to mold into each other.

I close my eyes, enjoying her. Wishing I could stay here and forget about Brett and all his bullshit. There has to be some explanation. I should just tell her what I know and ask her.

But what if...

"That front desk," she says. "Once the pieces are together? And with the burnishing? Right?"

"We rocked it," I say, trying to push out the shred of doubt burning at the back of my mind. I trust her. But trustworthy people get in bad situations. They get in over their heads.

"What?" she asks.

"Nothing," I say. "But you know, this place would be so much better if it had better shared spaces."

"What do you mean?"

"This is the only viable couch," I say.

"Yeah, well..." She frowns over at the junky couch across from us. The two ratty chairs.

I tease her about it being so *Road Warrior* and she hits me and I catch her wrists. I want to never let her go.

"Not just a nicer lounge area, but it needs larger and more functional collaboration spaces. The way we all had to crowd into Latrisha's area? No. You could double the workspace if you expanded to the upper level. There could be cots, sleeping rental by the hour, Japanese-hotel style. Hire a manager to oversee the tools and double as a barista and referee, and the stuff you'd sell would pay their hourly and you'd have somebody quasi-managing." I make suggestions about how they could get creative with events and partnerships, to figure out the right scale to make it sustain itself as a nonprofit. Anything to get my thoughts off the hell of that doubt.

She seems more amazed with every ensuing idea. It makes me feel prouder than all the year's groundbreakings combined. "That's brilliant," she says.

"I know."

She snorts.

I tuck a stray hair behind her ear. She's not a threat.

"Seriously," she says, "I don't know how you see it. It just comes together in your mind."

"It's not magic." I put my lips to her ear. "Have you *seen* the other couch?"

"Shut it." She laughs.

I let my lips hover there a split second too long.

She gets a serious look in her darkly fringed eyes. "You okay?"

"Yeah."

"Shit." She slides her hand over my forearm, to where I was burned at the forge end of the space. "You should put something on this."

I put my hand over hers. I don't care about the burn; it's the spark of our chemistry that's torching me. Everything is so fresh and real with her, with her glasses half down her nose and her devil-may-care hair and pink monkey-face T-shirt. She's beautiful to me like this. So different than anyone I ever date. Unguarded. Natural.

She gets a text. "Hold on." She shifts in my lap and taps out an answer.

My fingers press into her upper arm, her left hip. Memorizing the feel of her.

Her chest rises and falls, nipples pressing through worn fabric. A T-shirt and jeans is practical for this place, but it feels more right for her than the librarian shit. So why the reserved outfits? She makes her money in an Etsy store, or she did up until last month. She can wear anything she wants.

It's not like she's transformed completely, of course. She still wears her brown glasses. And the ponytail I so badly want to undo is still there.

I slide my hand over the glossy hair.

She tucks away her phone and gives me a fun, vixeny look and that little half-smile that I want to kiss right off her face. And I do.

She sighs. "I don't want to return to the real world."

Exactly. The current between us feels ancient, like a soul-deep déjà vu.

"But Carly'll be done with rehearsal soon."

A couple of guys I didn't meet walk by and she nods at them. I find myself pressing my hands over her thighs, letting them know she's mine.

She twists and looks at me. "What did you just do?"

"What?"

"Did you go caveman just now with the glare at those guys and the handsy thing?"

"Maybe."

She laughs. "You can't do that!"

"What can't I do?"

She narrows her eyes. "Behave."

I lean into her ear, whisper, "Or what?"

She narrows her eyes. "I dunno. Maybe I'll have all the Cock Worldwide cranes repainted with the face of Smuckers instead of that logo. How would you like that?"

Something in me goes still. She *could* do that. One phone call and she could.

Locke's most valuable asset is stability. A change like that would literally threaten thousands of people who depend on me. And she could do it. She has all the power.

One phone call.

Thousands of people. My responsibility.

The ID is mob-level good. This is a five-alarm fire.

I feel queasy.

She's searching my eyes. We've been laughing at the exact same things all month. If I weren't me, I'd think the crane thing was funny, too.

She tries a smile. "A cartoon picture of Smuckers's round little marshmallow head? Maybe not, huh?"

Do I really know her? Really?

I give her my breezy smile, the one that always fools the cameras, and I reach for my phone. I'm moving away from her.

"Kidding," she says. "Really."

I'm scrolling through my phone, like I might find a feel-less-screwed-up app there. They need to make an app like that.

"Come on, you think I'd do that?"

"I'm kind of a freak about that logo."

"Wait. You think I'd do that?"

A silence. I've let her closer to me than any woman ever. The fake dog whisperer who inherited my birthright.

Have I been reckless?

In my gut I trust her. Automatic. But my head is ringing with what Brett said. Our own PI doubts her. I don't know her real name.

Thousands of people depend on my leadership.

They deserve better from me.

"Oh my god. You seriously think I'd do that?"

"I don't know, that's all."

Her mouth falls open. Stunned. Hurt. "How can you not know? Like I'm an enemy of the company suddenly? Like I'm outside..." She goes pale. "Oh my god." Her phone's ringing, but her gaze is on me. "Because, of course, you still wonder if I'm a scammer."

"It's not like I'm standing here *wondering*..."

"I told you things would be right. I *swore* to you. I meant it. Oh my god—I'm so stupid." She pulls out her phone and answers. I can tell it's her sister from her tone. "I'm coming."

For once I don't know what to do. "Let me give you a ride, at least. Let's talk."

"I've had enough of your talk." She's texting.

"What are you doing?"

"Calling a Lyft," she snaps. "There's one two minutes away." She puts away her phone and heads to the other side of the place where Latrisha is.

"Vicky." I go along. "I'll give you a ride."

"Not happening."

Latrisha is there. Glaring at me. They exchange glances that probably contain girl communication about what a jackass I am.

Vicky grabs her purse, spins around, shoves past me, and walks toward the red exit sign.

I follow.

She turns at the door, looks me in the eye. "I'm asking you to not follow."

The way she asks, it's important to her. I fold my arms, teeth grinding. There are things I need to say, but I don't know what.

She pushes open the door and heads out into the night.

She doesn't want me following, but there's no way I'm not watching from the door, not when she's wandering around that gloomy sidewalk. She clutches her purse, forlorn under a streetlight.

I'm Henry Locke. People depend on me. I protect my people.

No matter what the cost.

A black car rolls onto the lot. She slips in and they drive off.

My heart curls into a cinder.

Dizzy, I wander out to my truck and start unloading the last pieces—a concrete block that weighs a ton and some massive wood slabs. I bring them in, one by one, to Latrisha's workstation.

I can't shake the memory of her wounded expression.

What have I done?

Latrisha eyes me as I muscle an unwieldy piece of debris into the corner. I say, "Why are the coolest looking hunks of rebar-wrapped concrete always the heaviest?"

"Somebody would help you with it."

"I want to do it." I get another load, and then another. I go back to her and peel off my gloves. She has paperwork for me to sign.

"I met her," she says when we're done, folding her copy.

"Who?"

"Bernadette. Your mother. She was mean about my hair."

I look toward the red-lighted exit sign, thinking about going for a night run later. Anything to run off this energy. "She had a hard time being nice."

"That's what you call it? Is that how she always was to people?"

"To people. Yeah." Not the dogs, though. Never the dogs.

"She was like that to Vicky. A complete bitch about her clothes."

"That's what you get when you sign up for Team Bernadette," I say.

"You think she signed up for Team Bernadette? Dude, your mom stalked her. She pursued her, manipulated her. Vicky did everything she could to avoid that woman, but she wheedled into her life and Vicky took pity on her and she made sure she was safe and all of that. And now here you are, screwing with her, too. Lay off."

I pause. "My mom pursued *Vicky*?"

"Your mother literally harassed her, demanding she talk to Smuckers after the fair."

I frown. "What fair?"

"The fair?" Latrisha continues. "Where she volunteered to fill in for the pet whisperer? Do you not even know this story? That's how they met. Vicky was there selling those bow ties, and the person who was being pet whisperer or whatever didn't show up. They had some booth or something. So Vicky volunteered to do it. They put this ridiculous outfit on her. And your mother comes along and Vicky's like, *Smuckers enjoys hearing you sing,* and your mother was convinced she had dog whisperer powers from then on."

Cold steals over my skin. *"That's* how it all started?"

"I can't believe you don't know. Did you care to even ask? Or were you too busy listening to Coldplay and shopping for tartan plaid scarves?"

"What are you talking about?" My mind reels. Dog whisperer booth. Were these the details Vicky had tried to give me? The ones I refused to listen to? "Singing," I say.

"Doesn't everyone sing in front of their pet? That's what Vicky said. And they'd run into each other by accident after that, and your mom would be all, *You have to tell me what Smuckers is thinking!* Offering her money and stuff. And Vicky would insist she wasn't a pet whisperer, insist there's no such thing. Your mom thought Vicky was withholding her psychic gift from her. Out of spite or something."

I nod. "Of course she would." Bernadette thought the whole world existed to spite her.

"Vicky and Carly would run into your mom a lot after that, mostly on this bench they'd pass every day going to Carly's school. They wondered if she was stalking them. Your mom would hit Vicky up for readings but she'd refuse. And then this one day your mother was all dizzy and faint. It was hot out..." Latrisha relates a story about Mom having a dizzy spell. Mom needing help up to her apartment. Feeling queasy.

Needless to say, I'm the one feeling queasy now. None of this sounds like a con.

It sounds like Vicky, though.

Latrisha tells me about how Vicky saw the dry water bowl,

how it made her worry. Of course Vicky would notice something like that and worry.

Fuck.

Latrisha tells me about the moldy bread out on the counter next to the butter. Was it all deliberate, Bernadette playing helpless to pull Vicky into her orbit? Probably.

Latrisha tells me about Vicky refusing money, so Bernadette hired Carly to walk the dog, as an end run around Vicky's objections. Classic Bernadette—if she can't pick off the strong animal in the herd, she goes for the weak one.

She goes on about how Vicky started playing dog whisperer when she thought it would help my mom. I walked in on her saying some pretty ridiculous stuff to her in that hospital room, but maybe it's what my mother needed to hear. How would I know? I hadn't spoken with her in years.

They all believed Bernadette was alone in the world. Bernadette would have encouraged that belief. She lived for drama.

My heart bangs out of my chest. Vicky told me she was a pet whisperer accidentally and I hadn't believed her. Who ends up as an accidental pet whisperer?

Vicky does.

Because she cares about people. Because she's a woman making her way alone in the world—without help, without protection—and she'd have empathy for another woman like that.

If anybody got scammed, it was Vicky.

She told me she'd make things right in the elevator. I heard the truth in her words.

And ignored it.

I text her nearly a dozen times. When she doesn't answer, I stop by her building. I pay somebody to let me in and make my way up six flights of stairs to her door. I've never been here, but I have her address from company records. I knock.

All I hear is a parrot squawking.

This is an apartment-sitting gig—she mentioned it once before. She made it sound nice. It's not. Judging from the building layout, those two are living in four hundred square feet at the most.

A real grifter would have figured out how to milk the company by now, or at least get credit on the promise of it. A real grifter would be living it up. A penthouse with a view. Meal services and maids. The mob? They would've made a move by now.

But more than that, I know her.

And I didn't listen to my heart.

Vicky and I had a relationship that ran deeper and more intimate than a lot of people I do big money deals with and I couldn't keep an open mind for her.

And it killed her.

I know. Because I know her.

I knock again. No answer.

"Vicky, are you in there? I messed up," I say. "I'm sorry." I knock again. I talk into the crack between the door and the frame.

It becomes pretty clear she's not home right around the time a neighbor threatens to call the police.

I stumble out of there wondering—miserably—*what the hell have I done?*

CHAPTER 21

HENRY

THE CHAMPAGNE IS FLOWING, but I'm hitting the scotch.

Unfortunately, no amount of drinking will kill enough brain cells to make me forget what an asshole I was.

There's a jazz trio on the other end of the lavishly decorated ballroom and Jana Jacabowski is trying to pull me away from the bar toward the dance floor.

"Not in the dancing mood," I say, setting my glass down for the man to refill.

Because all I can think about is the hurt on Vicky's face.

She never asked to play pet whisperer for my mother. She certainly never asked for that will to be changed. She thought she was getting money for taking Smuckers to some overpriced celebrity vet.

And I wouldn't trust her.

Of all the women I've been with, she's the only one who doesn't seem to care about the Locke fortune, the only one who bothered to look behind my name and wealth.

And what do I do? Treat her like a grifter.

My texts stopped delivering to her. Blocked. My calls go to voice mail, and I doubt she's been listening to those.

I stopped by the makers co-op. She wasn't there. I probably seemed desperate. I'm not embarrassed. I'll keep trying. I won't give up.

Jana Jacabowski waits. We had an arrangement to be seen here together and talk up each other's causes. She and her sister have been good allies for us.

Brett casts a warning look at me. "Brett'll dance," I say.

Brett puts on his most charming smile for her. What am I doing? Another dick move.

I snap out of it. The four of us have a deal. This is about the business. I down the scotch and take her out to the floor, moving on autopilot, dancing, chatting, spinning Jana around. She's a force for good in the city, a woman I respect. A dip for the cameras. She screams and laughs. Another spin.

I let Vicky down big-time. It doesn't mean I have to go on permanent asshole mode with people who need me.

Brett and Maddie Jacabowski spin by. I smile. If Vicky were here, she'd see right through that smile.

Jana and I do our time with the politicians. This is where she shines—the Jacabowski women are total movers.

A councilperson compliments me on the dog PR stunt. I laugh it off.

We discuss the Ten, the project everyone is excited about. "The Ten is transitional," I tell him. "It's forward-looking, yes, but I'm taking things much further now that I'm moving into leadership."

Translation: it's too late to make the Ten into the cool project it could be.

"Once you take over leadership from the dog?"

"Yeah, once I take over from the dog," I say smoothly.

"You guys actually did a stock transfer. That's ballsy."

"He really is in charge. He and his advocate." I wink. "We're doing our best to guide him. Smuckers would be putting fire hydrants all over Manhattan if he had his way."

Jana laughs. "The dog has more vision than some builders." I suppress a smile, enjoying her dig at Dartford & Sons, assholes of the building community.

Brett's there and we're posing for photographs. Somebody grabs Jana away and I use the opportunity to hit the bar again, but then I see Renaldo, hanging out on the fringes of the place with one of the retired city managers.

They're elderly guys who are still important for their wealth of knowledge, but they have zero power anymore. I go over, keep my back to the brightly colored dresses and black tuxedoes, so many peacocks peacocking it up.

Renaldo lumbers up from his seat and claps me on the back. "Henry!"

"He was telling me about the Ten," the man says.

Through my scotch-fuelled haze, I scramble to remember my picture for him—a fish. A whale.

"Jonah," I say, taking his hand, clapping mine over his.

The three of us take a seat at the edge of the place and talk development. Bonding. We talk about the Ten. I want another scotch, but I go for a club soda to avoid the famous Renaldo side-eye.

Jana Jacabowski waves from across the room—she's leaving with a friend. I sit back and relax.

"So what's really going on?" Renaldo asks me as soon as we're alone.

"I screwed up. I didn't go with my gut."

"Tell me," he says.

It's been ages since I went to Renaldo with something. He knows about Vicky and Smuckers, of course. I lay it all out. I tell him about humoring her until the competency hearing. I tell him about taking her around the company, and how incredible it's been. The bright, fun energy she brings. The goodness of working with her. I tell him about the makers space. "You would love it," I say. "Spending just that time with her without all the bullshit, that was amazing. We were amazing. She's special."

I tell him I'm more convinced than ever that she accidentally fell into this thing. Lay out everything about that.

Then I tell him about the joke she made and he winces. "Ouch. A dog face?"

"I didn't have to let it mess me up. Like I couldn't be strong for the firm and open-minded about her at the same time? I had to react."

He smiles into the distance.

"What?" I demand.

"She hit your button," he says. "Don't be so hard on yourself, Henry."

I watch him warily, bright brown eyes and skin like leather.

"Your mother was a crazy bitch. She dedicated her life to smashing every sand castle you managed to build. My picture of your childhood is you sitting on the front stoop of your mansion, clutching that bear of yours, crying your eyes out because she'd left. Yet again. Bernadette was a narcissistic gold digger who blamed you for everything. And your father didn't do shit to correct that."

"Don't," I say. "That's enough." He'd always kept opinions like that to himself.

"Yet you always wanted her love. You'd follow her around. Remember how she always called you Pokey?"

Pokey. Her nickname for me. "I never could keep up with her."

"Of course you couldn't. You were a child."

I shrug. "I'm glad for how she was. She taught me to be strong, to rely on myself."

"You've never been a liar, Henry. Don't start now."

I turn to him. It's been a while since Renaldo lowered the boom. "What?"

"Please." He mimics my shrug. "Like you don't care. You loved her and she broke your heart. These last few years, I know the Christmas gifts you'd send her would come back unopened. The cards returned, the calls unanswered. You never stopped trying to be a good son to her. You didn't want to be made strong. You wanted a relationship."

I frown.

He gives me a long look. "I watched you build this company, even with Kaleb blocking your best ideas. You sweat blood for this company. These people. Then your mother comes along and gives a strange woman absolute power over it. A woman who has zero reasons to care about it."

Who seems to actively hate rich guys, I think, but I don't say it. "Vicky's starting to care about it. She's starting to get what we're doing."

"Not the point." Renaldo crosses his legs, face grim. "She makes a joke about repainting the cranes in some ridiculous image? That's what your mother would do. Except she'd actually do it. You believed the worst because how else could it be?"

"I acted like she was my mother."

"Your button," he says.

"I need to apologize. I need to tell her..." Something. Everything.

"Do it, then."

"She won't see me. She won't answer my calls and texts."

"Think of something. You're Henry fucking Locke, for crissake."

That's how I end up in the waterfront workshop at three in the morning. I'm up in the third-floor model room. My tuxedo jacket is slung over a drafting table. I have an extra-large coffee at hand, but I barely need it.

I'm awake. Sobered up. Somebody was messing with my world, but it wasn't Vicky.

She won't answer my calls, but I can still talk to her—in a language she understands better than English. I work into the night and all through the morning.

CHAPTER 22

VICKY

I SIP coffee at our little table, trying to be quiet and not wake Carly, who's sleeping in her little curtained-off area with Smuckers.

"It never would've lasted anyway," I whisper.

Across the room, Buddy the parrot jerks his head, watches me with a shiny black eye.

I drop my head into my hands. Henry wanted to talk. What would he have said? But it doesn't matter.

Henry builds bridges from metal and stone, but trust is harder to build. Trust means crossing an invisible bridge made out of something you believe in. He wasn't ready to do that. Not for me. And why should he?

Why should he believe me when I said I'd make things right? But god, it felt good when he seemed to.

It felt like the world was new.

Nice fairy tale while it lasted. But he's just like everyone else. And maybe it was too much to ask.

Not like we could ever have a real relationship. He'd find out I'm Vonda and hate me. And if he let it slip, that would endanger Carly. Mom would find her.

I'll give him back his stupid company and that's it. That's all it ever could have been.

Carly comes out with her iPad, Smuckers at her heels.

"I thought you were sleeping," I chide.

"I sort of was."

"What's wrong?" I ask.

"Nothing," she says.

"What?" I press.

Her gaze goes to the black screen.

I grab it and tap it to wake it up and there's Henry, looking dazzling in a tuxedo. A beautiful woman on his arm. In another shot he's got her down in a dip, and they're both laughing.

I swallow. "What is this? Is this last night?" I look at the date. Yes. Last night.

Carly's behind me. "It means nothing. Rich guys have to go to a lot of those things," she says. "It's part of being rich."

I scrub my face, telling myself it's good. I told him to screw off in every way possible.

"I don't know how to feel about you knowing so much about the lifestyle of the rich and famous. It's a useless thing to study." I shut the thing off, but the image of Henry dancing with a gorgeous redhead is burned into my mind.

"That girl got a dance," Carly points out unhelpfully. "You got a company."

"Is it stupid-amount-of-candy-in-ice-cream time yet?" I ask.

She grins. "For breakfast? Don't bluff, I might take you up on it."

I get up and start her eggs. "Tonight."

On the way out, we discover the box in the lobby, addressed to me. It's the size of a coffee mug, but perfectly square, wrapped in Locke-blue paper.

"Uh," I say, shoving my key into the lock.

"Aren't you going to open it? Don't you want to see?"

"I already know what's in it. It's whatever rich guys think they can use to buy anything and anyone. I don't want it."

"Maybe it's something nice."

"I don't want it."

She grabs it. "Can I open it?" She shakes it. "Light as air."

"You need to toss that package."

"Without even looking inside?"

"Without even looking inside," I say, heading out.

Rich jackass, rich jackass, rich jackass, I tell myself, all the way to Carly's school. But it doesn't sink in. I need to get deprogrammed off Henry. There needs to be a service like that. I need to be strapped to a chair, and every time I see a picture of Henry I get shocked or doused with cold water.

But that just makes me think of that thing Henry said—*If I wanted to wear my hair in a marshmallow Afro and live in a woman's purse, I think I could find a dominatrix to make it happen.*

I smile.

I go to the makers space and of course everyone is asking where Henry is. Apparently he showed up looking for me. A few people have questions on the commission work. I give them April's number. April has instructions that I'm on vacation. She'll alert me to anything important.

It's on the third day that I turn officially pathetic. We were together for more than two weeks straight and I miss seeing his face. I miss the careful way he explained every last thing about his company. His dorky mnemonic devices for memorizing everyone's names. I miss the way we got to be finishing each other's sentences.

I won't see him. Can't.

Then comes the phase of jonesing so much for him that I start making jonesing bargains. I tell myself if I don't open the package, I might go online and look for new pictures of him, and that would be even worse. Right?

So it's entirely preventative.

Must. Open. Package!

I go find Carly. "You can open it."

She frowns. "You asked me to throw it away."

"Go get it."

She furrows her brows. "I'm sure the trash man's hauled it off by now."

"Yeah. Go get it."

Carly springs up and goes behind her little curtain. She comes back and sets it on the kitchenette table between us, practically rubbing her hands.

I slide it over to her. "You do it."

"I thought you'd never ask." She starts opening it, carefully. She was never a rip-open-the-present type. "A box," she teases, turning the box that was inside. "A really, really nice box of tag board. I wonder why he got you a box."

"Stop it! Stop screwing around."

She pulls up the lid, peers in. Her grin dissolves. She looks... stunned. Or is it a look of horror? For once I can't read my little sister's expression.

"What?" I ask.

"Oh my god." And then, as if that wasn't clear enough, "Oh. My. God!"

"What?"

"Wait. Close your eyes," she commands.

I sigh and comply.

"Now open them." I open my eyes.

My heart skips a beat.

There on the table between us stands a tiny, beautifully carved balsawood griffin. It's a perfect replica of Brave Protector Friend, the griffin that guards our favorite building. Our adopted friend and champion.

"He's beautiful," Carly says.

I pick it up and inspect it, turning it around and around, admiring how he captured the bold and grippy claws. The ornate detail of the wings.

"He got somebody to make our griffin friend."

"He made it himself," I say. "He got up there somehow and got some photos, and he carved it. This is all Henry—this vision. The passion of it. The way he knew."

"You're quite the expert."

Yeah, I think sadly.

"There's a card." She slides a tiny blue envelope across the table.

I take it and open it.

I should've trusted you. Let me fight for us.

CHAPTER 23

VICKY

I PUT on my favorite sweater—dark purple, so dark it's almost black, with black obsidian buttons down the front, and a black pencil skirt and a few white Smuckers hairs, unfortunately. I pick them off one by one in the back of the cab to Locke Worldwide HQ with Smuckers in his pleather purse. I need to see Henry. Partly it's to thank him for Brave Protector Friend. The note.

Mostly it's to see him. I've listened to his voice mails. Read his texts. In different ways they echo the small note in the griffin box.

The cabbie pulls up. I make my way through the grand lobby and up to the executive floor. It's unusually quiet. Henry isn't in his office. I head over to the admin area and find April.

She stands. "Hey!" She comes over and scratches Smuckers's little head. "We didn't expect you guys."

"Where is everyone?"

"Queens," she says in a tone, like, where else would they be? "The Ten?"

"Is something going on?"

"The emergency meeting?" Her face goes pale. "You don't know?"

"No."

"They carried on as if you knew. I assumed you didn't want to come—it's more detail than you usually get into. It's an emergency meeting."

I straighten up, unsure what to think. "Well, let's get a car."

Five minutes later, April and Smuckers and I are riding in the back of a speeding limo.

April has Smuckers in her lap. "It came up fast," April says. "The project is in jeopardy. It's bad."

"What happened?"

"Dartford & Sons. They're blowhards. Total asshole developers."

"So I've heard. What'd they do?"

She's absentmindedly playing tug with Smuckers. "Here's the thing with a development like the Ten—if Locke tells the neighbors about their plans before they've bought up all the properties, word will leak and a competitor will buy one key lot and hold it hostage. Dartford & Sons is notorious for that."

"So Dartford bought a lot in the middle of the Ten?"

"No—we just closed on the last property, so the Dartford brothers can't wreck it that way. Instead, they poisoned the neighbors against it. Acted like Locke has been doing things in secret. They'll get the councilperson to veto the project, make the land worthless, then try and get a racetrack through."

"Who wants a racetrack in their neighborhood?" I ask.

"Nobody, but the Dartford brothers'll bribe and lie their way into projects. They cross lines most people won't."

Sure enough, when we arrive at the community center, there's a red truck with the words Dartford & Sons on the side of it.

I pull open the door and we enter a cool lobby with a lot of bulletin boards and stacked chairs all around. A hallway leads left and another leads right. Down to the right is where we hear the yelling.

We enter the meeting room, which turns out to be a small gymnasium packed with so many people that they can't all fit on the chairs, so they crowd around the corners. We stand by the door, in the back of it all. I nestle Smuckers in my coat.

The people seem angry.

At Henry.

He's in front of them, sleeves rolled up, tie loosened. There's a PowerPoint image—an architectural drawing, all sketchy and with watercolor touches—on the screen behind him.

I recognize it as the artist's version of the Ten.

He's talking about it. How they're going to decontaminate the site. His vision for the walking bridge. Residences along the water. It's kind of amazing to see him in "on" mode—passionate about what he loves. Full of fire, even in the storm.

He spots me through the crowd, settles his gaze on me, and I feel warm all the way through.

He starts strolling with the mic, being the master orator that he is, a super hot Julius Caesar. He moves around the edge of the crowd, eyes fixed on me, like we're the only two people in the room.

Dizziness washes over me.

One of the angry neighbors gets up and starts criticizing how the walls go right to the sidewalk with no room for greenery.

Henry answers him, still coming at me. I straighten up, feeling like a virgin, bound and ready to be a sacrifice for the billionaire architect who can carve a griffin out of balsawood. Ready for him to ravage and tear me apart.

All in all, not a bad feeling.

He stops in front of me. My heart pounds. He lowers the microphone. Under his breath, he says, "Hi."

I swallow, overwhelmed by the effect he has on me, by how much I missed him. "Hi," I say.

He turns back to the room, addressing another objection, moving on like he's all about their conversation, but he's all about me. I know it when he stops, when he turns, eyes finding mine.

He defends the way the walls are, even though it's not what he ever wanted. It's Kaleb's stupid design, but Henry will defend it.

More angry people raise their voices.

"Those guys are Dartford plants," April whispers. "Planted in the audience to sink this project. They'll complain about the amount of greenery, which always rallies people. And they'll complain about the lack of public input—which they would actually get more of with Locke."

People are talking angrily over each other, rousing each other into a frenzy.

I'm starting to feel lightheaded; this is exactly how it was when everyone hated me. So much anger. "This is bad," I whisper.

"It is. Once those assholes have their *no* vote, they'll bribe some council people and put their racetrack in. But we can't say that, because it hasn't happened yet. Once it's done it's too late. They have *people*, let's just say."

The two Dartford brothers start criticizing Locke for bull-dozing their vision in, as if they're the white knights, riding in to save the neighborhood. It's all so wrong.

"Lies," April whispers. "Their motto should be *Where doing the wrong thing is the right thing.*"

Everyone wants a turn to yell, just like the days when my name was a trending topic on Twitter. I rub my sweaty palms on my skirt, feeling the urge to bolt.

I'm not back in Deerville.

Smuckers gets antsy. I pull him out of the purse and hold him as Brett gets up onto the stage and confronts the man. "One question—are you being paid by Dartford & Sons?"

The man deflects. Brett pushes. Brett doesn't have Henry's

charisma. More people are yelling. There are accusations now. April looks devastated.

"Why are they listening to those jerks?" I ask.

She doesn't answer for a while. I suspect she's actually on the verge of tears.

"There's no more *yes* in the room," she finally says. "Dartford & Sons are officially sinking the Ten." She shuts her eyes. "These neighbors are going to get screwed. And it's Henry's birthday next week, and all he'll get is the final dissolution..."

I'm not listening. Henry is looking over at me and Smuckers. I tilt my head, projecting sympathy, empathy. I see it right when it happens, when the Dartford guy traces the direction of his gaze.

"Oh, this is perfect," the blowhardiest of them all says. "Is this the dog? The new owner of Locke Worldwide?"

"No, no, no, no," April says under her breath. "Shit."

The blowhard Dartford guy is pushing through the crowd toward me, brashly and angrily, bearing a microphone.

I clutch Smuckers tight, pulse roaring in my ears. *What do you have to say for yourself, Vonda? Aren't you ashamed of yourself, Vonda?*

Everybody is looking at me now. My skin goes clammy. The hate is a hand, squeezing my lungs.

The Dartford guy stops in front of me with a smug expression. "Tell me," he says, addressing the crowd, "can you trust a company led by a dog?" He turns to me. "You're the dog's keeper? Don't you think this is a little reckless for a publicity stunt? To literally hand control of a company to a dog and his keeper? This dog legally controls the entire firm, does he not? This dog could sell the company for a dollar to a kid on the street. Is that a trustworthy move?"

He points the microphone at me, more formidable than a loaded gun.

I catch sight of Henry across the room, pushing through the people, trying to get to me. Rage in his eyes. He calls out, "Leave her alone."

"You have anything to say for yourself?" Dartford asks.

I stare at the mic. So familiar. This is a place I never wanted to be. Never again.

Never again.

Henry comes across, pushing through, shaking his head. *Keep quiet. Don't say anything.*

"Come on," Dartford chides. He's not looking at me, he's looking at everyone else. Because I'm not human. I don't have feelings. I'm Vonda.

I'm Vonda.

"The leader of the company has nothing to say?"

And right there, something kicks in. Something perverse.

Because I'm Vonda.

Without even thinking, I take the mic, hold it with a grip of steel. "Does the leader of the company have anything to say? You want to know? Well, how about it, Smuckers?"

I frown at Smuckers. Nod my head. "Oh, dear," I say. I turn to Dartford. "Smuckers says he is *so* sick of your shit. He can't *even*."

The room quiets for the first time since I got there.

"Very amusing," Dartford says, trying to take the microphone. I back away, daring him to go after a woman and a cute dog in front of all these people.

I nod as if Smuckers is talking and I'm listening. Out of the corner of my eye I see Henry's warning face. I pause halfway up the aisle. "Smuckers here thought he was going to a nice community meeting where we talk about making a neighborhood nicer, but instead, it's battle of the jerky titans. Please."

There are more murmurs. Chuckles.

"Very funny." The Dartford guy is coming for the mic.

I walk again. I feel Henry trying to catch my gaze, trying to shut me down. Too late.

"Is Smuckers in charge of this?" I look Henry in the eye. "Right now he is. This guy's right. A dog is literally in charge of a worldwide development and finance company. Here's the thing. Smuckers agrees with a lot of you about more green space, not less. He thinks so many buildings are just huge pieces of shit—new ones are the worst. Maybe they win awards, but seriously? Smuckers believes in human- and dog-centered design."

People laugh. Somebody yells "More fire hydrants!"

"Nobody's redesigning this project," Kaleb says. "That's not happening."

I turn to Kaleb. "Why can't we? Smuckers doesn't understand. Why can't it be nicer, like a garden?"

I feel Henry's gaze on me. Not thrilled.

"Because it took a year to design, and that phase is over," Kaleb protests.

"Smuckers doesn't understand. If people don't like it, why not make a new design? Right?"

A few people clap.

"We can't," Kaleb says.

The Dartford guys are laughing. I turn to them. Yeah, it's their turn. "But here's the thing. Smuckers hates racetracks. He thinks they're messy and noisy and bring a lot of traffic and are horrible in a residential area, and he knows you guys are going to put it in. I mean, seriously? A racetrack?"

"We're planning no such thing."

"Smuckers says that everyone in the building community knows you are. You tried to get one in on Brockton Greens, right? You have partners looking with you. Isn't that right?"

"I don't know what ridiculous rumors you've heard."

"Smuckers wants to know if you'd sign a thing right here swearing you wouldn't ever build a racetrack here."

Dartford glowers. He is not enjoying the feel of Smuckers's fluffy paw on his balls. "This is silly." He reaches for the mic.

I back away with my ear to Smuckers's mouth. "What is that, Smuckers? You think it's suspicious they won't sign a thing like that? I think so, too!" I finally catch Henry's wary gaze. "Henry,

Smuckers wants you to put up that slide of the neighborhood-facing structure."

"We're done with that slide," he says.

"Smuckers wants to see it again," I say.

"We've seen it," Henry says.

"Smuckers wants it put up." I raise my eyebrows. Does Henry really want Smuckers to pull rank?

No, as it turns out. Henry puts up the slide.

The Dartford guy protests. He doesn't want to revisit our project. He just wants the *no* vote.

"Let's make it amazing," I say. "More green, less building. We can do that, right, Henry?"

I can't read Henry's expression, but I know he doesn't like surprises. He doesn't like the feeling of being bossed. "We *can*," he says. "That's not really the question, though..."

"There are cost issues," Kaleb says. "With every square foot lost, the cost of the remaining goes up."

"So what if the cost goes up?" I say. "If it's cool. Let's see options. Something will have to go in to replace the factories that are moving out. What does it look like if it's something better?"

Again Henry catches my gaze. He shakes his head, a tiny movement most people probably don't catch. I put Smuckers's fuzzy muzzle up to my face, and Smuckers licks my cheek, and I smile at Henry. Because we're down this road now and there's no going back.

Henry grabs his laptop and gets up the picture he showed me —that's the one I want everyone to see.

I want them to hear him talk to the picture with the passion I heard. I think they would love him if they heard him like I did.

"How about this. We could integrate something like this," he begins. "This landscape is brown. Imagine it full of greenery and natural light." He shows them his favorite Australian building. "Look how the natural light flows. And this gathering space. We can do this. We can have this. We'd do benches along here.

Greenery." He goes on, getting excited, pulling people into his vision.

Kaleb stews. He'd rather lose the project than only make a few hundred thousand bucks. But Henry's on fire.

And sentiment is moving—I can feel it in the room.

There's a preliminary vote. People want Locke to develop the parcel. They want more meetings. They want Henry.

I want him, too.

I've set Smuckers down on his leash and take a breath, trying to come down from the panic I felt. Some teenaged girls are petting him. Brett and Kaleb are talking with Henry and he's nodding, hands shoved in his pockets.

He puts his suit jacket back on. All buttoned down. Perfect Henry.

Not looking at me.

Is he mad? He doesn't like being pushed around. Well, Bernadette was his mother.

When I glance over there next, he's coming across the room toward me, bypassing small groups of people, computer bag slung over his shoulder.

Brett stays behind. He looks angry.

Henry looks…beautiful.

My pulse races.

"Let's get out of here," he says when he reaches me, breathless. He takes Smuckers's leash and my hand. "Now."

"I can carry…"

"I got it." He's pulling me along, down the hall, toward the door, with Smuckers trotting alongside on the leash.

Somebody calls his name. I don't know if it's Locke people or neighborhood people. They want him back.

"I got your gift," I say. "It's the most beautiful thing anyone ever made for me."

He shoves open the door with strange force. My heart jumps. Is he going to yell at me, too?

I step out into the night, afraid to face him. Did I screw up again?

A strong hand grasps my arm. Henry spins me back to him. I'm flush up against him.

He gazes down at me, breath ragged, pulse banging beneath his strong jaw. He looks at me like he wants to say a million things, eyes full of tenderness. Wonder. People never look at me like that. But Henry does.

I brush my knuckle along the scruff of his beard, a whisper of a touch with enough electricity to light up the night.

I mouth his name: *Hen-ry.*

"Goddamn," he grates, dark and needy.

His lips come down on mine.

There's nothing tender about this kiss—he devours my mouth. His tongue sweeps lewdly across mine. A fist closes around my ponytail. He pushes into me, or maybe that's me, pushing into him, finding the way we fit, hot and perfect.

He pulls away. "The hell," he says. "How did I not believe you? How did I not trust you? All this time—god, I was an asshole."

"It was a lot to ask, that level of trust."

"Not when it's you."

My heart slams out of my chest.

Henry smooths back strands that escaped my ponytail, tucks them behind my ear.

"I didn't listen to what I knew about you. You're amazing and beautiful, and you take my breath away. And you said things will turn out. You gave me your word. It's good enough for me."

I press trembling fingers to his lips. "The circumstances are what they are."

"To hell with the circumstances."

I tighten my arms around him, press my forehead to his chest. "Thank you."

Smuckers waits patiently below us, panting. Just another day for Smuckers. He looks like he has to pee. "He has to pee," I say. "But not on flat pavement."

"So. Freaking. Romantic." Henry pulls Smuckers to a light pole. "Come on, boy." The light pole is way more Smuckers's peeing jam. "So romantic," he whispers.

"You're not mad?" I ask, circling my arms around from behind him. "About the meeting?"

He turns in my arms and rests his hands on my hips. "Mad?"

"From me doing the *Smuckers says* thing?"

"Baby, I have spent a lot of time on the wrong end of the *Smuckers says* thing. I have not enjoyed it. In fact, you could say I've pretty much hated it. Couldn't wait to be free of it."

I swallow.

"But seeing the Dartford brothers victimized by it?" He leans in. He brushes a kiss over my lips. "Priceless."

After Smuckers finishes fake covering up his pee with pretend dirt expertly kicked from his hind legs, we head over to the limo.

I slide in and Henry slides in after me, sitting right next to me. He shuts us into the small space and puts up the window.

"Here's something else I need to tell you," he says. "You made that joke, and I know you were being funny, and I reacted like an idiot."

"You care about the company—"

"No, I know you wouldn't do something like that, paint the cranes like that." He takes a strand of my hair.

I squeeze his hand. Would he say that if he knew I was Vonda? "Thank you."

The driver pulls out.

"Painting the cranes? That's a move my mother would make. And it sent me down a rabbit hole of fuckedupness that you said it."

I nod, easily imagining her doing something like that. Delighting in it. "I get why you cut her out of your life."

He straightens. "You think I cut her out of my life?"

"She was always talking like you did, like—"

"Vicky, she cut me out. She didn't want to see family. Her doormen had instructions to turn me away. You think I didn't try to see her? At least get her out of that shithole?"

"Right," I say, shocked at how stupid I was to have kept believing Bernadette's side of it. "I can't believe I didn't put that together. I mean, you're the most loyal person I've ever met. I should've realized."

"Bernadette talked a good game." He's so casual about it, that's what breaks my heart.

"I'm sorry."

"Oh, don't be," he says. "She knew how to have fun, how to make you feel like the only person in the world."

Even as he says it, I hear the *but*. I'm thinking about my own mom. "But it wouldn't last," I add.

Again he shrugs. Knowing him, he's starting to regret complaining right about now.

"And it's worse when that goodness is taken away," I say.

I want him to know I get it. He deserves something real, something that's not part of my fake identity.

He takes my hand, warm in his. He turns it over and traces the surface of my palm, as if to learn it.

Recklessly, I continue. "My mom was great when she was off drugs. But when she was on? Not pretty."

He stills. "She was on drugs?"

"Meth," I say. "And there were things she did when she was desperate for money, for another buy, the deepest betrayals."

I'm getting into dangerous territory—I'm not contradicting my fake identity, but I'm definitely off-roading from it. It was safer when we were enemies. Enemies hide things from each other. Now I just want to know everything about him, and I have this crazy idea that I could bare my heart to him, and it would all be okay.

Except it wouldn't.

Still, I continue. "Much as I had cause not to trust Mom, I'd always think things would be different the next time around. I always hoped."

He says nothing. Doesn't even flinch. He wants to hear. He wants to know things about me.

"The last betrayal was the biggest. You wouldn't even believe."

"And then your parents died," he says. "And you were alone with your sister."

My pulse quickens as he searches my face, as he fits our hands together, like fitting the pieces of my story together. He turns the knot we make over, so that mine rests on his.

"And you had to leave Prescott," he adds.

I lean into him, wanting to stop talking about my fake life.

"But you made it," he says.

"More or less." What the hell am I doing? "Hey," I lift my head. "April said it was almost your birthday. Happy early birthday."

"I don't celebrate my birthday," he says.

"Why?"

"I just don't."

He doesn't have to say why. I know. Bernadette. God knows how a woman like that did birthdays. "Okay."

He lifts my hand, still trapped in his, brushes a kiss over each knuckle, then looks into my eyes. "So, FYI, no birthdays. Now that you're in my life."

My heart flops upside down in my chest. The air stills. The cacophony of horns outside the window seems to fade. *Now that you're in my life?*

I feel stunned. Happy. He considers me to be in his life—not on the other side of enemy lines, but in his life. And he's in mine. Henry, with his fierce beauty and loyal heart and amazing vision for things, he's in mine.

I'm ecstatic for a fraction of a second, like I won some kind of lottery.

Until I remember why it could never work with us.

Vonda.

I never want to see hate in his eyes when he learns I'm Vonda. It would pierce me clear through to the bone.

He traces soft circles around my knuckles with a finger. I'm glad he has something to do, because things are turning too dangerous and too beautiful, all at once. And the air between us runs thick and wild. And I want him like mad.

Get away. You can't have him.

"But your birthday is soon?" I blurt.

"I want nothing to do with it. It's a thing with me."

"Fine. Your birthday is just another day," I say.

"Say it again," he turns to me, eyes hooded.

"Just. Another. Day."

Just another day—with one big difference, I decide.

I'll give him a present he'll never forget—the papers that transfer Smuckers's shares of Locke Worldwide to him. It's a few days short of the twenty-one-day cooling off period, but it's close, and the papers aren't technically telling him. I already hired a lawyer to do it. I told him to buy a ream of that thick parchment paper to print the stuff out on it so it would feel more impressively gift-like.

I want everything ready.

But I can't be in his life anymore. He's too high profile for me not to be revealed as Vonda.

It's not just about the hate in his eyes. It's remotely possible he'd believe me, but it wouldn't matter even if he did.

My getting outed as Vonda would hurt the people we most want to protect.

The publicity of Vonda would attract my mother's attention and she'd take Carly back in a heartbeat, use her to squeeze me. Maybe even Henry. Or just use Carly as a meth ticket somehow.

And Vonda O'Neil linked to Henry Locke? So toxic to the trust and stability of the Locke name. To his family he protects.

All those people with names he memorizes so carefully. He can't be linked to Vonda.

I need to stay away from him. Get out of his life and stay out. He'll love his birthday present. It'll make him so happy.

I visualize myself getting out of the limo. Walking to my door. Alone. It's not where this night is going, but things need to take a U-turn.

My heart hurts. I've never wanted to be real with somebody like I want to be real with Henry.

Smuckers fusses, and I use it as an excuse to free my hand from Henry's, like his fussing is this emergency that requires snout-smoothing caresses and a deep gaze into doggie eyes.

I try to think of some unromantic thing to talk about.

"One question," I say. "And you need to answer honestly. What is up with the Dartford brothers? Do they just sit around rubbing their hands and dreaming of building what people most don't want them to build?"

"And then laugh maniacally? Something like that."

"They were mad," I say. "I'm glad people could see they were jerks."

"It wasn't just showing them up as jerks," Henry says. "It was how you were. You have to understand, at these meetings, usually there's nobody on the side of the everyday people. I think they sense their powerlessness sometimes. Then you step in with the Smuckers thing, and it was brilliant. And you were on their side, and they knew it was genuine."

"They should've known you were on their side."

"Yeah, I'm still the developer. Whereas the way you blazed in, you were their ally. I think Brett and Kaleb are going to need months to recover. Shit. Kaleb's protests? We couldn't have staged it better if we tried. Like we'd written a script for him. It couldn't have been better. It really *was* like a dog is pushing everyone around, which I guess it was. It's the most bizarre thing I've seen in all my years in business. You and Smuckers did what we couldn't do in an hour of yelling—you made them open their minds and listen. You opened the door to a redesign of the Ten."

"That you thought of."

He brushes my neck with his knuckle. Hot blood courses through my veins. "God, Vicky," he says. "Battle of the jerky titans?"

"Umm..." My cheeks heat.

"You don't like rich, entitled guys. That's what I think."

I like one of them. A lot.

"I don't want to be that to you," he says. "Though I did try to trick you and make you sign everything away." He slides his finger over my cheek.

"And you got me arrested," I say.

"Detained. Still—I'm sorry about that," he says.

"Oh, you should be." I give him a fake angry look, like it's all a joke. Henry's made so many things new for me. He gave back some of the things that Denny stole from me.

His eyes are dark. He's not in a jokey mood.

"Well, to be fair," I rattle on, "I did put a dog throne in your boardroom and make you talk to Smuckers as if he were human."

"I hated it," he says. "But I kind of admired it, in a *what the hell!* way." He hooks a finger over the collar of my shirt. The sizzle of his touch spreads through me. "I didn't know what was up or down. When you did that."

Can't have you. Can't have you.

The air runs thick between us. "Brett seemed kind of angry tonight," I try.

"I don't care about Brett," Henry rumbles. We pass the glare of a shop-front spotlight and Henry's eyes flash hungrily. Focused on me and me alone.

I tear my gaze from his. We're near the park. "Where are we?"

He lowers his voice. "We're going to my place, Vicky."

"Just like that?"

"Just like that."

My heart is thudding so hard, I'm surprised the limo isn't vibrating. "Now who's being entitled?"

"Carly has a sleepover—April told me." His hand is back, taking mine like it's his.

"I don't know."

He pulls my hand to his mouth, kisses a knuckle. Still those hungry eyes. "You do." He takes my lips in a hard kiss.

"So entitled." My words sound breathless to my ears. My sex throbs. "You think you can get whatever you want?"

"Come home with me," he rumbles into my neck.

"I can't. It's not just my responsibility to Carly..."

"I'm tired of responsibilities," he says. "Let's forget them for a while. Be two people without any of it."

I rest my head back on the seat, gaze at him in the flashing dark and light. The feel of him looming slightly over me excites me. I want him to loom over me like that while I'm naked. I want him to pin my hands and devour me. I swallow. "Sounds to me like you're suggesting a dirty role play."

"The opposite," he says. "I'm suggesting us without the roles and responsibilities. We leave them in this car."

My mouth goes dry. Of all the offers in the world, he makes this one. My heart twists.

The shadow of a wicked smile plays at the corners of his lips in the dim light of the posh ride. Slowly, eyes pinning mine, he straightens his arms in front of him, shooting his cuffs.

He turns his watch hand palm up. My breath hitches as he releases the clasp with a snick. The watch falls into bracelet mode.

I swallow past the lump in my throat. "What are you doing?"

He slides a finger under the metal band and pulls it off his hand. Again that evil smile. He holds it out on his long, thick finger. I'm thinking about the way that finger felt inside me, back on that rooftop. Maybe he is, too.

He flings the watch onto the empty seat opposite us. It

bounces and comes to rest. Its hard body glints in the light. A symbol. A tease.

Maybe just this night, I think.

He rests a hand on my thigh, heavy and warm. His breath comes fast. "Now you," he says. "Leave something behind. It'll just be us."

I look down at my outfit, wishing I'd worn one of my necklaces. I would throw that on the seat for him. My sweater? But I have only a cami under it. A shoe? I hold out my hands. Not even wearing rings.

I set a hand on Smuckers's furry head. "Sorry, buddy, looks like you're spending the night in the car."

I feel a hand tighten around my ponytail. A voice deep and low. "This."

Shivers skitter down my spine. "You want my hair?"

"Shut," he gusts into my ear, "it."

I bite back a smile. Is the limo going a million miles an hour? It might be.

"Stay still." He pulls at the back of my head. He's working the band from my ponytail.

My breath comes out in shudders. He works it down the length of my hair, movements rough and clumsy. I like him being rough and clumsy with my hair. I like everything he's doing. I want to feel everything. I want to do this thing, us like two nobodies.

I feel when he gets it free. I wait for him to toss the ponytail holder onto the opposite seat, but instead he grabs a handful of my hair, seems to tighten his fist around it—not pulling it, just grabbing it.

It comes to me that he's never seen it down. I feel his nose at the back of my head. I hear him suck in a ragged breath.

My heart jumps into my throat.

"Put out your hand."

I do as he says, trying not to let it shake. He sets the tie in my palm with a shivery brush. I close my fist around it, holding it there for a moment, suspended in time.

Then I toss it to the seat.

It comes to rest next to the watch.

Avatars of the two of us, like dragonflies trapped in amber.

CHAPTER 24

VICKY

HENRY LIVES in a lavish prewar building on Central Park, all marble walls and chandeliers. A scary-looking bouncer-sized doorman in a brown uniform and brown hat opens the door for us.

We walk into the lobby, hand in hand. Leaving the world behind.

"Who's this?" the doorman says, grinning at Smuckers. Smuckers strains at his leash, tail a blur of wagging, because, *stranger petting!*

"It's Smuckers," I say, tightening my grip on Henry's hand.

Henry swears under his breath as the man kneels in front of Smuckers.

I slide my hand under Henry's suit jacket. He seems to vibrate under my touch.

Things turn out to be more exciting than Smuckers could've imagined—the man has a fist, and from inside that fist comes the smell of food. Finally the man opens his hand and sets down a bone-shaped treat, which Smuckers gobbles.

Well, who can pass up a bone-shaped treat?

"How's it going?" Henry asks him.

"Fine and dandy," the doorman says, ruffling Smuckers's hair. "Look at you, mister!" Smuckers is apoplectic with glee. He likes this doorman.

Henry drapes his arm around my neck and whispers in my ear. "Sorry."

I pull closer, slide a hand over his firm ass. "Will he have a problem," I whisper, "if we make out on the floor over there?"

"Come on, Smuck." Henry takes the leash. "See ya later, Alan," he says.

Alan salutes Smuckers and then us.

We head deeper into the maze of marble and chandeliers and elegant carpeting and get to the pair of elevators with golden doors. Henry hits Up, never taking his eyes from mine.

The elevator inspection license is posted between the two elevators, just like in our building, except in our building it's under smudgy Plexiglas. In this building it's in an ornate gold frame like it's a freaking Picasso.

"Some fancy action right here. If I'd've known, I would've put Smuckers in his silver bow tie."

Henry gives me this look like he doesn't give a crap. He's so past giving a crap. He yanks me flush to him, chest to chest, lips inches apart. His heart bangs against my rib cage. His cock bores into my belly—hard—like he wants to make me feel it.

"Yes," I breathe, immobilized by him in front of the elevator inspection certificate of the rich and famous.

His lips brush mine. It's a whisper of a kiss. A shimmer of sensation. Flesh nipping flesh. Teasing and electric.

I touch one of the buttons on his shirtfront. I slip my fingers under, seeking his warm body, pressing the back of my hand into the hard plane of his stomach. He lets out a little groan of surrender, then takes my upper lip in his teeth for a moment, catching, releasing.

I find his belly button. I slide my knuckle down his trail of soft hair into the elastic of his underwear.

A ding sounds from somewhere.

Henry's hands close over my shoulders as he kisses me. He maneuvers me sideways and backs me into the elevator without breaking the contact of our kiss. Smuckers is a blur at our feet.

Henry turns and stabs in a code, then backs me up to the wall, kissing me some more. He slides a hungry hand over my loose hair and then over the fuzziness of my sweater, over my breasts and shoulders, all the way down to my wrists, which he captures in his hands.

I'm a butterfly, pinned by his gaze, as he lifts my arms and presses them up against the dark velvet of the elevator wall panel. Again he kisses me, lips like plush pillows.

"I want you so bad I could die," I say.

He kisses me harder.

The doors slide closed. Smuckers is a small sentry below, waiting for the doors to open again. Or maybe he's trying to figure out the strange white shape he sees in the aged gold patina.

"Maybe you should stab some buttons a few times. Get this thing going."

"Nobody's stabbing any buttons," he growls into my neck.

I like the growl. I tunnel my fingers into his hair, grab two fistfuls, kiss his cheekbone, then his lips.

"You were supposed to leave your hands up there against the wall," he says.

"My hands are in a misbehaving mood," I mumble into the kiss.

The bar of his cock is finding the V of my legs under the wool of my skirt, pushing and pressing, just the good side of too much.

His breath sounds harsh. It heats my skin like a burn as he slides his hands over my hips.

Feverishly, he starts sliding my skirt up toward my waist. "These skirts." His hands tremble as he gathers it up, bunching. "You kill me all the time."

"Henry. We're in an elevator. What if somebody comes in?"

He pauses to cradle my chin with gentle fingers. His fingers are gentle but his gaze is pure savagery. Maybe he'll kill anybody who comes on. Maybe that's it.

His words feather over my lips. "You see me put in that code? That code takes this thing directly to the top floor, which is my floor. This is my front door we're in." He kisses me. "My doorway." He kisses me again, then pulls back to look into my eyes. "Mine."

In a heartbeat, the *nobody* game turns dangerous. *Mine.* He means me.

My shoulders press back flat against the velvety wall. My sex aches. Throbs. The third-floor light flicks off and the fourth-floor light flicks on, strange stars.

He kisses me. Melts me.

I'm a thief, and I've broken into somebody's beautiful home. I'm enjoying their furniture, helping myself to their food, wearing their soft clothes. It's wonderful, but it also hurts, because none of it can ever be mine.

Just one night.

He's back on the skirt project, making a logjam of thick fabric and lining, like ropes around my hips and thighs. "Uh," he says, stepping back, panting. "Get it off you."

I start to unhook the waist.

"No, no, hell no." He's shaking his head. "Keep it on. Just pull it up."

"You like when it's pulled up." My heart pounds. Even in this, he's so specific in his vision.

"Do it." He pants ferociously.

I can't resist.

I bend over and grip the hem, gazing at him from under my

lashes as I draw it up slowly, turning it inside out on myself. "You have to do it nice and *neat*," I say. "Or it doesn't get done at all." I say it all prim and proper, because that goes with the skirt fantasy he has.

There's a feral light in his eyes. The powerbroker billionaire of the century feels out of control.

Even before I have it all the way up, he falls to his knees in front of me. "Jesus, you're so hot." Strong fingers slide up to grab my fleshy butt cheeks as he presses his face to my panty-covered mound.

The elevator jolts to a stop. The doors slide open revealing a dark penthouse suite, moodily lit, city lights visible in the distance.

Smuckers escapes the elevator, leash dragging.

"Smuckers just…"

"Let him destroy the place." His words are hot against my throbbing sex. His tongue rasps over the fabric. "Let him set the whole planet on fire."

"Well, you have quite the low opinion of poor Smu—" My words die in my throat as rough fingers yank aside my soaked panties and invade my soaked folds, sliding, stroking.

Pleasure sparks through me. My knees turn to jelly.

"You are so wet." He's pushing my panties down my thighs, down my legs, pulling and mauling them off. "You kill me. You kill me with your secret hotness."

He grips my calf. "Up."

Shaking, I comply. He frees me from my panties, fingers and fabric a whisper against my ankle. He guides my leg over his shoulder, opening me to him. The air hits my heated core.

I grip the rail on either side of me, pulse racing. I have no right to be here.

I have no right to this man.

He kisses my bare mound, mauling it with his mouth, edging

his lips deeper between my folds. I let out a strangled cry when he hits my clit.

Confident hands press the flesh down there wider. I squirm and whimper as he swipes a tongue over the length of my seam.

He holds me tight. "Vicky, Vicky, Vicky," he breathes into my heat, licking me mercilessly. Rough whiskers abrade my inner thighs.

I feel wild. My blood rushes thick, like warm honey, throbbing through my veins.

"I have needed this," he breathes, "so damn long." His every word tickles my clit. "So damn long. I have needed this for so long."

Then his tongue is on me, soft and warm and long and flat.

My shoulder blades press against the wall as he strokes me higher, stoking a tidal surge of feeling into the tip of my bud.

Every lap of his tongue builds the feeling higher. His licks are relentless. Merciless. Brilliant and driven, like him.

He changes his tongue. It feels pointy and stabby now. "Please, Henry, please."

Harsh fingers grip my thighs. His tongue seems actually to curl against my bud.

"I didn't know a tongue could do so many...shapes."

He stops licking and looks up at me, dark hair wild, eyes glittering. He's the most beautiful thing I've ever seen.

"That's what you're getting out of all this?" he asks. "The wonderful world of the human tongue?"

"No! Please, go back!"

"I love how wet you are for me." He traces a drip of wetness on my thigh to where it disappears. He finds another.

I need him so bad, I'm shaking. "You have to go back." Sweat trickles down my spine. "Please."

"You're even hotter begging like this."

I grip the rail. "Please."

His mouth is near my clit again—I can tell by the heat of his breath. He holds me in place, traps me with his hands and mouth. I'm his prisoner.

Finally his mouth is back on me again. He feasts on me. I whimper and squirm.

Hot, determined fingers dig harder into my ass as he licks me into a frenzy. The world begins to dissolve around me.

When he sucks the bud of my clit into his mouth, my breath goes shallow. "Oh," I say. One short, sharp word.

He gives it another pull and the pleasure crashes over me, crashing and breaking over me like a wave. Explosions of surf and pleasure and white-hot light.

My head falls back against the wall panel. My breath saws in and out. He's stopped the licking but his mouth hovers there, like he can breathe in my ecstasy.

He moves up my body to stand in front of me. I'm shivering, shaking.

His hands cradle my cheeks as he rains kisses over my face. "We're going in there, baby, and I'm going to strip you naked and fuck the daylights out of you. I'm going to fuck you like there's no tomorrow. You good with that?" He kisses me again. Again.

His words drug my veins. Good drugs, wild and intoxicating. My mind is thinking *yes*, and then I'm whispering it. *Yes, yes, yes*, to the rhythm of his kisses.

He pulls back, studies my eyes.

I mouth his name. Long and slow, I mouth it. *Hen-ry*.

He exhales raggedly. His hands are on me. He's picking me up. I scream as I'm whirled around. He carries me through his place, past low lights. Past furnishings. Kitchen. Walls. Hall. Into a spacious bedroom.

He throws me down on the bed. I scoot back a little, and he crawls right over to me and grabs my legs, yanks me under him. "Where're you going?"

I like no past or future. I like no roles. He goes to work on the pearly buttons, fingers trembling. "I never feel like this," he says, suddenly serious. "I never feel this messed up. Your skirt was an engineering problem I should've understood, but I felt like...a bear. My hands like a bear."

"I liked it."

"I'm serious. You're all I could think about, all these weeks."

"Me, too," I say. "I watch you. I try not to want you," I say.

He growls with satisfaction when he hits my camisole. "You always have these under there?"

"Kind of," I say.

He yanks the cups down so they're under my breasts. "You need to be dealing with that skirt right about now. I need it off you." His voice is sluggish with lust and desperation.

I unhook and unzip my skirt as he tongues my breast. Then he makes me take the rest of my clothes off.

I'm naked under him, just like I imagined, but he's not playing his part. I'd imagined hot, arrogant Henry in his beautiful suit, crassly using me.

Instead he's skimming his hand over my skin, like he's learning me. Mapping me. Enjoying the *me* I hide under the court clothes. Enjoying Vonda.

It's too much. Too much vulnerability.

"Henry." I reach up.

He grabs my hands. Kisses a finger. Keeps them clasped in his. "Shh."

He runs two fingers under my breast, a whisper of a movement that nudges it up just slightly. "I love you right here." He slides his palm down over the curve of my belly. I quiver to his touch. "And right here."

Stop talking, I think.

Fingers roam over my hip, pressing, printing. "Here."

He nudges apart my legs. My heart jumps into my throat, knowing what's coming. He trails a lazy finger over my mound. I arch up when he makes contact with my clit. Steely eyes holding mine, he plays with my sensitive folds.

"You are so beautiful."

He's not just printing me, he's seeing into me. All the possibilities, the hidden things. Like the Moreno hotel. He sees beauty where everyone else sees rubble for a landfill.

I whimper. A strange sound to my ears—misery mixed with utter pleasure.

"I've got you, baby."

All this time I thought the worst thing that could happen would be me being exposed as Vonda.

I was wrong.

The worst thing that can happen is the possibility that he might love Vonda.

I rip my hands from his grip and pull him closer. "This is hardly fair. You with all the clothes." I reach down to his cock, grab the bulge, fitting my fingers around best as I can with his pants still on.

I know when I get it feeling right, because he growls. I pull, erasing everything he's doing. I bite his ear, taking back control.

"Not. Fair," I say.

"Fair is for judges." He rises up over me and undoes his belt, looking at me naked under him. He yanks it clear out of the belt loops, all hot and crass.

The tender mood is gone.

"I plan to be totally unfair with you. I'm going to exploit every advantage. I'm going to keep you naked underneath me and fuck you until you're screaming my name."

"Uh," I say.

He presses my hand to my sex. "Do yourself, baby. Get yourself ready."

"I want you to."

He gives me a stern look. Bossy, stern Henry hasn't quite left his CEO self behind. I'm feeling better now. I slide my fingers between my legs. He unbuttons his shirt, gaze heavy on my skin. I get up a rhythm.

He strips off his shirt, revealing a muscled chest. He tosses the thing aside, then rips off the rest of his clothes, gaze never leaving my fingers. "You don't know how hot you are."

"Come here," I say. I need him to cover me.

He's fumbling in his bedside drawer. A thrill sparkles through me. I turn on my side and slide my palm up his thigh, a smooth, massive pillar below his cock, which juts out hard, thick and veiny and beautiful in the moody shadows of the room.

Henry's cock is beautiful, just like him.

"Didn't you have a job you were supposed to be doing?" he growls.

"I have a different job now." I take hold and he groans. "A lateral move," I add.

He groans again as I slide my hand around steely hardness. "... gonna kill me," he mumbles.

I sit up and lick up the side. "There might be a graze of teeth involved." I swirl my tongue around the glistening head, salty and smooth.

With a strangled cry he has me on my back. He's tossing a condom wrapper. He's rolling a condom onto himself with quick, efficient movements, gaze never leaving mine.

"Fuck me," I say. My words sound breathless. My entire being feels like it's in suspension, waiting for him, craving him.

"You sure?" he asks, sliding his head to my clit with the help of his thumb, which gets me reeling, almost setting me off.

"I'm sure." I buck my hips, urging him on.

He presses me back down, pinning my hips to the bed as he glides himself around on me with perfectly tantalizing pressure.

He's rubbing my clit harder and more mercilessly, zeroing in on the most wildly tickly parts of me.

I make a little begging sound. I'm moving under him, rhythmically, like he's already fucking me.

I let out a breath as he pushes into my swollen sex, huge and thick.

"Holy shit," he says, voice full of wonder.

My blood races. Everything is spinning out of control. Being joined with him is too much truth, suddenly. Truth hiding a painful lie.

"Henry—"

He kisses the line of my jaw and starts to move inside me. "We don't have to think of anything," he says. "Just concentrate on me moving inside you. How hard you have me. What you do to me..." He seems to lose his train of thought here. "How unbelievably good..." He drives on, driving us upward, stoking the flame of us.

His skin glistens with sweat. Hard planes of muscle. A shiver of hair on his belly when I put my hand down there.

I'm on top awhile, then he's on top. Then it's me against the headboard. Every new thing seems to be the best idea ever.

"I want to memorize every sound you make," he says. His glistening biceps bulge as he moves over me. Hot, hard flesh. The smell of sweat. Breath sawing. "Everything is new with you. Every way I feel is new with you."

"Me, too," I whisper thickly.

"You're close," he says, and he begins to move slow and steady. He changes his angle, seems to swell inside me, stretching me. It's painful and good at the same time.

His eyes burn into mine. The intimacy of it sears.

Then he's hitting my clit, and I'm spinning away. "Henry, please! More." I grab his hair.

He goes harder. "Pull it, baby. Take what you need."

I cry out as an orgasm tears through me.

He presses his face to my shoulder, stilling, shuddering inside me, coming with a small guttural sound.

When we're done, when he's out of me, he cages me with his arms. "You are so unbelievable," he says.

I slide a finger down his cheek, then run it back up, down and up, loving the feel of his face, his whiskers. I think he likes when I touch his face almost as much as I do. Or maybe because I do.

"I was going to take more time," he says. "I had a plan."

I smile.

"I mean it. I want everything perfect for you."

"You were supposed to leave your CEO role behind, remember?"

"Sorry," he says.

"Don't be. You make me feel like one of your people. You're so beautiful with your people. They're so lucky."

"You are my people."

I swallow and press my finger to his lip, trace the pillow of it.

I'm his people.

My throat is so clogged up with emotion, I couldn't reply even if I wanted to.

He kisses me again, and I'm in heaven on the cool sheets below him.

CHAPTER 25

VICKY

I SHOWER while he makes phone calls about the Ten.

I dry off and put on one of his soft, beautifully made dress shirts. When I wander out of the bathroom, the smell of garlic and cheese hits my pleasure center full blast.

I find him cooking. Shirtless. Bare feet. Jeans hugging his hips just so.

"What are you making?"

He turns. His eyes go dark. "What are you wearing?"

I give him an innocent look. "This?"

He swears and turns back to the stove. "Alfredo sauce. And I'm at a critical point in this operation. There's wine breathing. Why don't you pour us a glass."

It's *breathing*. He's so nerdy about doing everything perfectly.

I pour two glasses and go back. Set his by the stove top.

"You have to add the cheese to the sauce so slowly," he says, adding a microscopic amount of cheese to the pound of melted

butter and heavy cream he's been stirring slowly and methodi-
cally. "So slowly."

"It smells amazing."

He adds another micro amount, and another, and another.
"Most people don't do it like this."

But Henry does.

I set down my wine and put my arms around him, making
contact with the muscles and hard planes of him.

"You are so going to ruin dinner."

I kiss his back. "I'm trying not to."

"Trying." I can hear the smile in his voice. "Trying is not
doing." He flicks off the stove, smashes a lid onto the pan and
turns. "Look at you," he says, advancing on me.

I back up. "Look at me what?"

He reaches out but I move just out of his grasp and turn. And
run. His place is huge and you can run in it. I make it to the living
room.

Rough hands grab me, turn me around to face him. He grabs
the shirt and rips it open, then pushes me down to the couch.

A condom appears. We fuck furiously, hands grasping, teeth
grazing. His hot weight pins me.

He pulls up my leg to get deeper.

I hold his hair, taking him, pain and pleasure mingling.

He smashes his sweaty forehead to my chest when he comes. I
stop pulling his hair and just kiss it, coming down from my
orgasm and enjoying his.

I kiss his hair as he comes. He's everything.

He flops over at my side.

He gets this serious look. "It was never like this." He slides a
hank of my hair through two fingers, with an expression like it's
the most amazing hair he's ever felt.

"Me, too," I say.

He seems to like that. He watches me with such warmth and

affection. It feeds my soul. "I'm glad," he says. "That was unbeliev-able. I wanted to do everything to you."

"You kind of did."

"Oh, hardly."

"Oh, *hardly*." I smile. "I love to feel you come inside me. I love how your body feels."

"I love how you breathe," he says. "Sometimes you just breathe and I want you."

I kiss him on the nose.

"And that biting thing…"

"Yeah?" I smile.

"Yeah," he says. "And that wet finger thing."

I narrow my eyes. "What wet finger thing?"

"You know. The touch."

I furrow my brow, trying to think what he means.

"When you lightly touched my asshole with your wet finger? It was…hot."

I frown. God, was I in that much of a fugue state? "I wasn't doing anything like that."

"You just touched it, really lightly."

I study his eyes, trying to figure out if he's joking or what. That's when Smuckers jumps up and runs over the back of the couch, looking down at us, tail wagging, tongue hanging out. "Oh…" I say.

"What? What's wrong?" He follows the direction of my gaze, and a look of horror comes over him.

Horror.

I snort and smash my face to his chest.

"So not funny," he says.

"It's a little funny," I say into the sweaty pillow of muscle on his chest.

"Go away, Smuckers!"

I'm just laughing. "I honestly don't know if that clinches your Most Eligible Bastard status or destroys it," I say.

"Don't even," he says, rolling on top of me, caging me.

I snort. "And to think I imagined you didn't like dogs."

"That has to be the last joke you make about that." He leans down, biceps bulging.

I frown. "The last? Isn't that a little extreme?"

He kisses my neck. "I mean it. Or I might retaliate in the most excruciating way."

"I might like it," I say. "But okay. Last joke."

CHAPTER 26

HENRY

IT'S after seven by the time we sit down to eat. I pour more wine and watch Vicky pick up her fork.

"You think the sauce survived?" she asks.

"I know it did." I set down the bottle and stand behind her, rest my hands over her shoulders. "I think you're going to be pleasantly surprised with this dish."

She looks up at me. "You just think you're Mr. Awesome."

"Kind of." I kiss her cheek.

"I'll be the judge of that." She swirls the noodles in the sauce. "The talent portion of Most Eligible Bastard contest," she jokes.

I lean in closer. "I do believe I aced the talent portion of the contest earlier tonight."

"Hmmm," she says. "Good point."

She slips the forkful of fettuccini between her pretty lips.

A sheen of pure wonder creeps into her gaze. "Oh my god," she says.

"What's that?"

She gazes back up at me, brown eyes sparkling. "Parmesan garlic taste freak-out."

I sit down. We eat. A lot. She actually has seconds, like the best date ever.

After dinner we take Smuckers out, strolling around in search of dessert. We decide on a bag of warm baklava from a food truck. We take it into Central Park and sit on a bench, feasting while we watch an extremely acrobatic man dance to a fiddle and a snare drum.

Vicky makes exactly zero jokes about what I'll refer to as The Smuckers Incident. In fact, she doesn't have to; all she has to do is look at Smuckers and then look at me with an utterly innocent expression, and the joke is in the air.

"Fuck off," I growl.

"What?" she laughs. "I can't look at you guys now? My two fave guys?"

"No, you can't," I snarl.

I'm not mad. It's fun. It's all fun with her, like the best kind of escape, the way it was at Southfield Studios, us hiding from the world and carving out our own zone of simple pleasure inside the larger, more complicated real world.

She leans against me. Whatever hesitation she had about us being together before seems gone.

What was it?

She's an enigma, but I don't mind. The more layers of her I peel away, the more I like her. The more I want her.

I put my arm around her. She snuggles closer and something in me warms.

It's strange sitting in the park with Vicky. And it strikes me as strange that it would strike me as strange...until it occurs to me that every activity in my life fits into one of two categories: seduction and business.

Sitting in the moonlit park fits into neither. It's just nice.

How did my life get so unbalanced? Even my beach house in the Hamptons—I use it to entertain clients or I don't use it at all.

It's not there for pleasure, and I certainly never take women up there—I don't like to give them the wrong idea, which is that our short-term hookups might not be short-term hookups.

"Hey," I say. "What are you and Carly doing for Labor Day weekend?"

"I don't know," she says. "Nothing special."

"You want to get out of the city? I have a beach place in the Hamptons."

She sits up, seeming alarmed.

I brush a strand of hair from her eyes. It's so sexy when she wears it down. "What is it?"

"Well..." She stares at a crushed Pepsi can, shining in the grass. "With everything so crazy..."

No, she means.

I almost don't comprehend it. She's taking the *one night, no roles* thing seriously. Treating this as a hookup. It defies my understanding of the universe, like water swirling the wrong way down the drain.

I spent most of my dating career enforcing hookup rules. I recognize it when I see it.

Three words: No. Fucking. Way.

I set my fingertips to her chin with the gentle touch that gets her hot. I brush a kiss onto her lips. "Why not extend it?" I say. "Vacation holiday. Who says we can't extend it? Nothing intruding."

Her pulse bangs in her throat. "Just for the record, things will be set right." She watches my eyes. It's important to her that I get that. It feels right to trust her on that.

"I'm not worried about that. I take you at your word. I'm not talking about the company, I'm talking about this." I lower my voice. "You know you want to. We're in this far. Let's keep it going. All the complications. Screw it all. Three more days."

This gets her thinking about it.

"We leave the whole spiderweb of our lives behind," I say. "We leave it here." I kiss her again. "Or, actually, in the limo."

"I can't leave Carly." She puts her hands in her lap. "Not for a weekend. I mean, she's sixteen. She would probably be fine. She'd love me to leave her with the place to herself but—"

"I didn't mean just you, I meant both of you," I say. "I'd love to meet her and have her up with us. The best beach is just a few blocks away. We have a full staff. She can have her own room. We could leave Friday, early."

I can tell she's thinking about it. "The traffic...."

"Right," I say. "If only I owned a strange machine with a propeller on the top of it that could fly right over cars and buildings. Oh, wait, I do."

She grins. "Tell me it's not blue."

"It's blue."

She studies my eyes, as though she's not sure whether to take me seriously. What's going on? Am I pushing things too fast?

She pulls out her phone, swipes around, then groans. "Carly has two day-long can't-miss dates to run lines with her girlfriend," she says. "They're trying to get leads in the fall production. I forgot they carved those out for this long weekend."

"Have her bring her girlfriend. Trust me, we have the space." I trace the shell of her ear. She's caving.

"Of course, they might not get much studying done. Two of the guys from One Direction have rented the place next to mine. They might be rehearsing for some kind of duet tour. It could be distracting."

Her jaw falls open. "Seriously?"

"Would I joke about something like One Direction?"

"This feels like blackmail," she says. "If I don't say yes and she finds out, she'll literally kill me."

"That would be terrible," I say.

CHAPTER 27

HENRY

CARLY HAS VICKY'S LAUGH, Vicky's eyes, and definitely Vicky's spirit.

But while Vicky has brown hair, Carly is a fiery redhead. It's amazing to see them together, to see Vicky in girl mode, laughing and pointing with Carly and her sarcastic friend Bess as I take off over the city.

Carly says soothing words to Smuckers, who's in his little case in the back and not loving the ride.

We land on the helipad at the estate garden house.

It's fun to see the three of them experience the grandeur of the place, which was built in the 1920s by one of the Vanderbilts. They make me love it all over again.

Vicky goes to help the girls settle while I give instructions to Francine, the head of the staff. "I know it's not what you're used to," I say to her.

"It's a breath of fresh air," she says.

"You know how messy teenaged girls are?"

"It's thrilling to see you have...friends here. We're all so pleased."

I'm about to protest that I bring friends here. But I don't.

The two of them stake out the bedroom on the very end of the south wing. We order in wine and soda and gourmet pizzas. They stay exactly ten minutes. It's hard to compete with the promise of two guys from One Direction.

Vicky and I drink wine and talk about everything—even a little business. She wants to make sure we got the software Mandy requested. She changed her mind about it soon after I started taking her on facility tours. I tell her it's in place.

Now and then the girls come through with reports that they heard music, and they carry on detailed analyses of whether it was recorded music or if it was the guys in jamming mode.

And as Vicky and I are fucking that night on the edge of the hot tub on the top veranda, and again as we have slow, lazy sex the next morning, I think to write One Direction a fan letter just for how completely they keep Bess and Carly glued to the other side of the mansion.

"You take good care of her," I say that afternoon. Vicky and I sit on the porch overlooking the expanse of lawn, which ends in a pool, a cluster of cabanas, and the beach, edged in sea grass, deep blue-green water beyond.

Perched under an umbrella at the edge of the actual beach, Bess and Carly are in full teen girl splendor mode, running lines and staking out the neighbors, and Smuckers is a streak of white, running all around the lawn. The umbrellas are Locke blue, a fact that Vicky makes fun of.

"We're all each other has," she says simply.

I try to get more about her earlier life, but she's vague, and eventually I find the conversation has circled around to her desire to know why I wear dark suits in the city and beige linen suits in the Hamptons.

Does she just hate to think about that time? I won't push her. I pushed her enough. And we're supposed to be away from it all.

The four of us walk along the beach for Saturday sunset, a ritual from when I have business visitors, who tend to enjoy the backyard view of the mansions, the lifestyles of the rich and famous, though they rarely admit it. Carly and Bess are no different, but they do admit it, pointing out different displays of excess. Vicky seems unimpressed, if not slightly hostile toward displays of wealth.

Between houses, the girls run ahead with Smuckers, kicking around in the surf.

"Back in your town, remember how you told me about being bullied?" I say.

Vicky gives me a blank look. "Sure."

"Was it somebody wealthy?"

Her brow furrows. "Why would you think that?"

"Just wondering. You're not impressed like a lot of people are. And, well, you did call me a rich, entitled jackass at one point."

She takes my hand. "You know I don't think that."

I keep my eyes on the horizon, feeling her gaze on my face. I wonder if that's why my mother chose her. I hate the question I'm about to ask, but it's been burning in me. "Did my mother seem...happy in those last years?"

She squeezes my hand. "Henry—"

"I just...didn't know her the last few years. I missed her." I never say that aloud.

"She seemed happy...in her way."

I nod.

"I wasn't sure how much you wanted to know about her. But, yes. She had her routines and Smuckers. She'd terrorize people in the neighborhood, like when they wanted to pet him, she'd act angry. That was kind of her jam."

I smile. It's a bittersweet feeling, more sweet than bitter now.

"She was such a character," I say. "I always imagined I could repair things. That somehow I'd break through and we'd have a heart-to-heart."

"I'm sorry," she says.

I make her tell me all the stories she can remember. We stand in the wet, sucking sand together, the ocean swashing around our ankles, watching Carly and Bess swim, and Vicky tells me little anecdotes. One after another.

We laugh about it. It feels good. No—it feels utterly amazing.

"I'm glad she had you around," I say.

She kisses me on the shoulder. "I'm glad I could be."

"Why do you think my mother chose you?"

"I don't know," she says.

"Maybe it's silly to keep wondering about it, but I do. Do you think my mother chose you because she sensed you have an allergy to guys like me? Did you two talk about that sort of thing?"

"Hmm."

"I know she ostensibly chose you on the basis of your being a dog whisperer, but she could've done a lot of messed-up things with that will. Yet she chose you."

"I really think it was about the dog," she says. "She loved that dog. Even the last words she said to me..." She stops, clearly regretting going down this road.

"It's okay, you can tell me," I say. "Please. Tell me. They were the last words she said. I want to know."

"Well, they were about the dog. Clutching at him, and she goes, *I love you, Pokey.*"

My heart stutters. "What did you say?"

"*I love you, Pokey.* I don't know why she called Smuckers that, you know, there at the end. I never heard her call him that, but it had to be Smuckers she was talking to. Smuckers is a little pokey, you have to admit."

I swallow past the lump in my throat.

"What is it?" she asks, looking up into my eyes.

"Thank you," I say.

"For what?"

I pull her to me, dizzy with the whooshing ocean and this beautiful woman and my bittersweet heart. "Just...all of it."

That night, Brett begins his texting assault. He has juicy information from the PI to share. I tell him I'm not interested—the last thing I want to do is to shatter the trust between us. Vicky will tell me things when she's ready.

Brett won't let up. Eventually I just block his ass. He'll be pissed, but I want this time away. My assistant will let me know if there's a corporate situation to deal with.

The competency hearing is scheduled, of course. But I've decided to call it off.

She's assured me things will be made right. I trust her to do the right thing. I trust us to figure out a way forward together. And whatever Vicky's hesitation is about us being together, I'll overcome it.

I'll call off the hearing when the mediators are back in the office on Tuesday, and then I'll tell her.

There's a fireworks show on Monday night. Carly and Bess go up to catch it at Cooper's Beach. I've arranged a candlelight dinner on the veranda.

Vicky is stretched out on the bench seat next to me, leaning back against me, feet splayed out to the side. She has on a pink skirt and gold sandals that look good with her yellow blouse. She's been wearing brighter colors, but this is really different, the result of shopping in town with the girls. She looks good in colors. It seems right for her. The jewelry she makes is colorful. Why not her clothes?

A boom sounds from up above, followed by some smaller ones. "I'm glad the fireworks are going off behind us," I say. "Because if they were right out there over the water? I'd have to arrest myself for multiple cliché violations."

"The foam on the waves is just as bright. It looks almost neon," she says, staring out at the water in the moonlight.

"It's the phosphorescence." I toss a piece of steak to Smuckers.

She pulls on my lapels like she does when she wants me to come close and kiss her. "Come here."

CHAPTER 28

VICKY

WE ARRIVE BACK LATE. Exhausted. Henry sleeps at my place, because I don't want to leave Carly.

I feel sheepish about the state of it, but at least it's clean. He seems to like it just fine. And who cares?

This thing is over, anyway. It's what I keep telling myself.

His birthday is on Friday. I need to be out of his life before then—that's the promise I've made to myself. And if he's sad, well, he'll get the papers to restore his company.

It's the right thing to do for Carly.

And it's the only way to keep Vonda's toxic PR from bringing him down. And the people of Locke who depend on him. It's the right thing for Vonda.

There's a board meeting scheduled for the morning—it's unclear who called it—Henry thinks Kaleb called it, because the agenda is about the timeline for the Ten, and maybe hiring an extra outside team to expedite the redesign, and there's something about utilities. Because buildings are apparently more complicated than just building a thing—you have to figure out how it hooks up to everything else.

We drop Carly at school and head to the office in the back of a limo with Smuckers in a flowered carrier on the seat beside us.

Henry pulls me onto his lap. "Have I told you how hot you are recently?"

I kiss his lower lip, then his upper lip. They're little suck-kisses, a technique I pioneered over the sex marathon that was Labor Day weekend. I kiss him again.

"It's been so long since I was just happy. Stupidly happy," I say. I pull back to find him watching me with his very serious Henry face, cobalt-blue eyes dark and serious. "Thank you."

"Does it make you a little sad?" he asks.

Like a wine connoisseur, he hears every note in my voice.

"Did I sound sad?" I tilt my head, like I have no idea why that could be.

"I'm happy, too," he says softly. "But nothing about my happiness feels stupid."

Something twists in my belly, spikes of joy and grief, sharp but good.

I'll always have this feeling to remember, I tell myself.

The car drops us at the front of Locke headquarters under the Locke-blue flags emblazoned with the Cock Worldwide logo.

We link hands and go in through one of the array of highly redundant doors—the double ones this time, held by a doorman. We cross the enchanted five-story-tall lobby dominated by the giant jagged rock with shimmery water cascading down it.

I'm wearing bright colors again—an orange flowered top with blue pants and sparkly heels, more spoils from one of the high-fashion pop-up shops in the Hamptons that Carly and Bess and I hit.

But the clothes weren't entirely their idea—I realized that, looking in the mirror this morning. The bright colors and sparkles are Vonda's style. It feels good, like I've busted out of some sort of shell. Or maybe like I'm home.

I'll always have that, too.

Henry cages me in his arms against the elevator wall as we ride up. The elevator has become one of my favorite kissing places, a stolen window of privacy.

And for just this moment, things feel like a fairy tale.

Henry growls when we reach the top floor. He's in a brown suit and a maroon tie with tiny black owls on it. Carly and Bess bought it for him as a thank-you gift. I knotted it for him this morning.

He grabs Smuckers's flowered carrier.

"You don't have to—"

"If you think I'm not man enough to carry a flowered dog carrier that looks like a purse, you haven't been paying attention, baby."

I snort and poke him in the side.

We get out and cross the expanse of corporate grandeur. People have already assembled in the glass boardroom chamber. I hate to be out of our magical private bubble, but I love seeing him back in his habitat, back in the place he so loves.

Smuckers rides happily in his flowered purse, the picture of dog cuteness in his Locke-blue sequined dog bow tie.

Henry grabs the handle of the glass door and holds it open for me, gazing down at me. The air between us crackles.

I practically glide in. I turn to say hi to the other board members.

And the world screeches to a halt.

He's beefier than I remember, with a thicker neck than back in Deerville.

I tell myself it can't be him. *It can't.*

But the blond hair is the same, and then he smiles that smug smile.

My hands go numb. An icy clawing steals up my back, up my neck. Saliva fills my mouth, like I'm really and truly going to puke.

It's my body, reacting to what my mind can't comprehend.

"Henry, Vicky." Brett stands, smiling like the cat that swallowed the flock of canaries. "I want you to meet our new leadership consultant, Denny Woodruff."

The room seems to tilt, or maybe that's my world, tipping on its axis with everything sliding off.

How is it possible?

"Leadership consultant?" Henry bites out, confused.

I'm not confused—not when I meet Brett's eyes. He knows exactly who Denny is. He knows exactly who I am. Vonda.

"Denny'll be working closely with us on board leadership and cohesiveness issues," Brett announces in a friendly, casual way that's everything fake. "I think this will be especially helpful to you, Vicky. To get you integrated, to get us working in tandem instead of at odds. You'll be working very closely with Denny. Every board meeting, Denny will be right there, helping you integrate productively."

My mouth goes dry.

"What is this?" Henry says. "Vicky doesn't need leadership consulting." He looks between me and Brett. "What's going on?" He sets Smuckers's carrying purse on the table.

"Kaleb and I agree this could really be good for the board," Brett says. "We made the move. It's within our rights to add a board consultant. We don't need a majority for that, just twenty-five percent. His salary is a matter of operations budget…" He's rattling off company jargon, bylaws jargon.

Denny's up and out of his chair, meanwhile.

My mouth goes dry as he nears; I feel too frightened even to move.

He goes around to Henry first. He takes his hand and pumps it up and down. "I've done a lot of work with the Percival

Group. I went to Yale with Dale Runson, who I think you know."

Denny's naming off names. I look over at April. She furrows her brows.

"Okay." Henry sounds annoyed.

I'm a little bit behind him. He doesn't see me backing away. He lets go and addresses Brett. "Let's take five. I need a sidebar here with you and Kaleb."

"Denny's a board consultant," Brett says. "The point here is to include him, even in sidebars." Brett looks at me. "*You* don't have a problem with this, do you, Vicky? Part of being a competent board member is to work well with others. If you don't think you can work with Denny…"

Denny smiles. "Vicky! I'm excited for the opportunity to work with you. I feel like we can accomplish a lot together." He's coming to me. I tell myself to stand firm, to not back up anymore, but I take a step back. Another.

Denny has his hand out. "I promise you—"

I back up, senses reeling. "Get away!" The words come out a whisper, like one of those dreams where you can't seem to make your voice work.

"I understand that they sprang it on you," Denny says, stopping in front of me, way too close. "But before long, it'll be old home week, I promise." He grabs my hand, making me touch him, making me shake it. I yank it, but he won't let go.

In a flash, a vicious hand clamps Denny's arm. Denny's head rocks forward as Henry yanks him backward, throws him up against the glass wall.

There's shock in Denny's eyes in the moment before Henry drives a fist into his face.

Denny staggers sideways. Smuckers barks madly. There's a crack in the glass like a lopsided star.

Henry turns to me. "You okay?"

"No!" I'm backing away, away from it all. Henry comes to me but I fling up a hand. I don't know what stops him in his tracks—the wild motion or maybe the look on my face.

I grab my purse and burst out the door, run across to the elevators. Henry calls to me, but I'm stab-stab-stabbing the button. I have to be away from them—all of them.

Henry's flying toward me just as the doors open. I get in and *stab stab stab* the doors shut—who says that doesn't work? I ride down to the lobby, alone. The ride seems to take forever; the air inside the little box is way too bright.

It seems like forever before I'm out on the street, out in the too-dreary, too-crowded morning that seemed so promising not fifteen minutes ago. I push upstream against the workers and tourists, edge through a line at a bagel breakfast sandwich truck and head around a corner, weaving through the crowd, heading toward the water.

Smuckers is still back there. Shit.

I duck into a dark doorway and text April to ask her to see to Smuckers. I don't know what to do or what to tell her. She'll figure it out.

I'm in some kind of a service doorway, a skinny stairway with an unmarked black door at the back of me.

To my right is a brick wall, the soot of a century making the red of the bricks nearly black in places.

To my left is an ornate wall, thick with a hundred coats of paint. Soaring just above that is a bistro window. People up there are cozy with coffee and pastries and papers. If I stood up, I'd be level with their shoes.

But I'm down here. Vonda.

I try to think what to do, glad they can't see me. Glad nobody can see me. I make myself small, wanting the world to just go away.

They know.

By now Henry knows. Brett probably followed him and told him.

I hug my knees, chin on my right kneecap. Denny'll blab. People will find out now. I try to think of some way to stay Vicky, to stay in the city, but the danger of Mom taking Carly back is too much. God, she'd find a way to extort the entire company, using Carly as leverage. And all the publicity.

Legs block my view of the street. Slacks. "Vicky."

My blood races.

"Leave me," I say.

"Not likely." He sits on the stoop next to me. "What happened?"

"You don't know?" I don't give him a chance to answer. "I just want to be alone."

"Can I be alone with you?"

I want to cry, because it's so Henry to say that.

"You know."

"Know what?"

"They didn't fill you in?"

"Baby, I just ran halfway down a skyscraper stairwell until I could get an elevator and then down two crowded blocks, pissing off about five dozen bumbling pedestrians trying to find you. I've been a little busy."

"How'd you know I'd go this way?"

"Who cares? What's going on?" His phone is going crazy. "That Denny guy back there. What was that?"

I shake my head. Everything feels so enormous.

More ringtones.

He pulls it out of his pocket. "Calls from the tower. Probably Brett. What happens when I answer? I've had him blocked all weekend. What happens when I unblock him? What am I going to see?"

I take his phone from his hands. "Uh," I say, pressing the cool, smooth screen to my forehead.

He waits. I'm trying not to cry.

"Well, that answers that," he says. "A forehead print. That's what I'll see."

I shake my head. "No joke," I whisper.

He puts his arm around me, pulls me into his warmth. His protection. I have this thought that everything from here on in is a stolen moment. I guess they all were.

"What's going on?"

"I didn't want you to know. I thought you'd never know."

"Know what?"

I shake my head. "The thing is, I knew if we stayed together, it would come out, and everything would be ruined. You'd need to do damage control and, god, you'd hate me."

"I couldn't hate you, Vicky."

"Maybe not," I say in a small voice. "But you could hate Vonda O'Neil. You could hate her. You probably already do."

He shifts, speaks closer into my ear. "*What* are you talking about?"

"Vonda O'Neil?" I pull away. "You don't remember liar Vonda O'Neil? The whole sordid scandal eight years back? Everyone remembers Vonda O'Neil."

He searches my face, expression remote. I see when he gets it, because it's like he's seeing me new. "Wait—"

"That's right," I say.

"You're Vonda O'Neil."

"Ding." I say it breezily, as though it costs me nothing. It costs me everything.

"And Denny Woodruff...that was—"

"Denny. The wronged victim, yeah. Falsely accused," I say. "The poor sweet boy with his bright future that was threatened by selfish, lying Vonda."

I watch Henry's eyes. My blood races as I wait for the removal of the arm, the retraction of affection, the blotting out of the stars that never made a real picture anyway.

He doesn't remove his arm, but I can practically see the gears in his mind turning. The gears in his memory.

"Remember? The trial? The world-famous mayo shirt?"

"Oh, right. The shirt was supposed to prove he'd kidnapped and...tried to assault you. You said it was semen, but it was mayo."

"Yup. It was mayo."

"That was you? Wait—the well. You ended up in a well."

"You didn't pay very good attention."

"I was in college."

"I *hid* in a well as part of my plot to destroy Denny's future. I pretended I fell in there. Three days I was in there. All the better to get media attention. It's what I wanted all along."

There's this long silence. "So this is what you're going to do?" he finally says. "Don't I get the real story?"

I ball my hands to keep them from trembling. Strangely, I don't want to tell him the real story. It's easier to let him think the worst. Because I so badly want him to believe—so badly. I gamble less of my heart if I don't tell.

"I thought you trusted me," he says.

I regard him with bleary eyes.

"Tell me."

I look at my kitten-heel shoes, maroon with a little sparkle. *It'll hurt too much when you don't believe me.*

"It's me," he says, voice so achingly tender. "Just you and me."

And I'm thinking of being in the elevator shaft with him, how amazing he was. And the little griffin he carved me. And the buildings he dreams of making. He's an idealist. In a world of people shooting at targets, he's shooting at the stars. He's making bridges from bits of string.

And suddenly I'm telling him.

I tell him about the high school party. Keg, bonfire, music, the usual. I'd wandered off, bored, not drunk enough to think my way drunker friends were funny.

That's when Denny abducted me. He was a few years older—a year out of high school. He sealed my mouth with his giant hand and dragged me into his trunk. To his hunting cabin. I woke up terrified, half naked, with Denny coming at me.

"Fuck," Henry bites out. "I shoulda killed him in there."

My fingers close over his arm. *He believes me?*

"Don't worry, I won't really kill him. *Maybe.* Then what?" He pulls me to him, more tightly.

"I always think it was my terror of him that made him ejaculate all over my shirt instead of getting to the final act. Like my terror turned him on."

I feel him tense. I pause. "Keep going," he says. "You're okay. We're okay."

I tell him how Denny stormed off, and I thought for sure he was going to come back with an ax to chop me up.

"Left you there."

"Yeah. And something in me kicked in, working at that knot. I freed myself even as his boots crunched the gravel outside. I grabbed my panties and my shoes and ran out the back, pounding feet over cutting branches. I barely felt it. I just had to get away."

"In bare feet. Through the woods."

"I hardly felt it until I fell into that well. It was deep, but I only sprained my right ankle and broke the toe of my left. It could've been worse, but the thing was filled with years of brush and leaves and dirt, and that cushioned my fall."

I tell him about hiding myself under the leaves at the bottom of the well when Denny looked in with a flashlight. I hid even when the first wave of searchers came through. That was damning for me in the trial, that they looked in the well and saw nobody. Why hide? But I was scared. I thought it was Denny and his friends, come to get me.

When things got quiet, I really did try to climb out, but I couldn't. Even without the pain of my injuries, I couldn't. The sides were slimy and high, and there was nothing to hold on to. And it was so dark.

I tell him how I buried myself in the debris at the bottom and hid. Terrified.

"That's why you stayed quiet."

"Three days I was in there." All the while I was becoming famous. Vonda O'Neil. Disappeared from a teen party in the woods, the stuff of fairy tales, but there were no bread crumbs. No bowls of porridge. No baby-bear beds.

I go on with my story. How I was in shock by the time they pulled me out—that's what the nurse told me. Half out of my mind. I told my story to the cops. Denny tried to rape me but he didn't, and I got away. After a quick visit to the hospital, I was released to my mom, with all my dirty clothes in a bag.

I was in such a state when they pulled me out, all I wanted was to be home, bundled up in bed with my things around me. I would've said anything to get warm and clean in my own bed.

"It was only later I remembered my shirt," I tell him. "I opened up the bag and found the crusty stain and I realized he'd, you know, the shirt. Mom is the one who kept back the shirt. I was sixteen. I wasn't thinking five moves ahead like she was."

I pause, amazed he's still with me, there on that dark stoop. The people of the Financial District file back and forth on the sidewalk a few yards in front of us.

They seem miles away.

"I thought we should bring it to the police, but she said we should keep it for the trial. She said we couldn't trust the police, that we needed to keep the evidence. The Woodruffs tried to pay me off. A half a million dollars. Five hundred thousand."

"That must've seemed like a lot of money to you. You passed up a lot of money."

"I wanted to stand up for other girls. I had evidence...I felt so sure..."

I suck in a breath, determined to get through the story calmly.

"I was so sure I'd be able to prove it with that shirt, you know?" I continue. "When it came back as mayonnaise, I thought the police lab was lying. Like the Woodruffs paid off the lab, and I demanded an independent analysis. Mayo again. By that time, I was this monster. Months later, I found the bank statement from my mom's account. Twenty thousand dollars deposited into it the day before we produced the shirt for testing."

"The Woodruffs," he says.

"It was a pretty common shirt from Savemart. I think they bought a duplicate and switched it. The mayo would've been the Woodruffs' idea. My mother would never have thought of something so devious and damning. The mayo is what made me look like I deliberately tried to frame him. Like a teen without sophisticated knowledge of forensic techniques tried to frame this rich boy. Everybody hated me. The world was this wall of hate."

"The betrayal you were talking about," he says. "That was your mom selling the shirt."

I nod. "There was nothing she wouldn't do. She was a good mom before Dad died. But after..." I shake my head. "But I just wanted justice. I wanted the world to know what kind of guy Denny is."

I look up at him, blood racing, waiting for questions, but all I see is affection. Concern.

"You believe me?"

"What? Of course."

I search his eyes. "Because of how I was in the elevator?"

"No, because of how you are period. Because I know who you are."

My belly flip-flops. "You didn't even know my name until now."

"A name isn't who a person is."

I put my forehead to his chest, smash my face to his chest. The relief I feel is nearly overwhelming. "Thank you."

"Don't thank me. After what you've been through? I don't

remember the specifics of the case, but I sure remember the Vonda O'Neil feeding frenzy. I remember that. And you were innocent all that time. God."

The world feels like it's raining, and the rain is a mixture of tears and pure water that's washing everything clear.

He believes me. He's with me. I want him to say it again. And again and again.

"That's when you came here?"

I sigh. "My mom took a year to burn through the money. She had a lot of bad boyfriends. She was going downhill. It got less and less safe for me and Carly as the money dwindled. I'd been secretly saving, though. And then I did an interview they paid me for, and that was a lot of money. That was what I used to move one night. I just took her and ran. I didn't want Carly to stay back there. It wasn't safe for either of us, but especially not Carly. I mean, it wasn't always so bad. Before my dad died, we were a normal family. A happy family."

He sets a hand on my arm. "I can't even imagine."

"You believe me," I say.

There's an angry edge to his voice. "Of course I do."

I feel like laughing.

"I don't know how you could doubt it," he says. "I mean, after all those hours we spent in that little workroom toiling side-by-side using toothpicks and glue to get tiny paper curlicues to stick to tiny paper tree trunks? When two people go through an experience like that together…"

I snort and scrub my face with my hands.

"Seriously, even if I hadn't been in that elevator shaft with you, where it was, let's face it, pretty obvious you're not somebody who would've gone into a well voluntarily—"

"I would never," I say.

"I know. And also, Denny? That's not a good guy there."

"You know him?"

"Jesus, the way he came at you? Don't need to taste much to know if it's cottage cheese."

"You punched him."

He gets up from the stoop, stands in front of me, reaches down, and pulls me up into his arms. "If I knew what I know now, I would've put him right through that glass."

CHAPTER 29

HENRY

WE WALK FOREVER. It seems important for her to move, like she needs to put physical distance between Denny and herself, and a car won't do.

She needs to grind it out. I get it.

I'm trying to keep my anger in check, because an angry guy isn't what Vicky needs now.

But honestly? I want to be rearranging Denny's face. My fingers curl with it. The battles I wage are usually about money and board-room maneuvering, but this one I want personal and painful.

It won't do anyone any good, I know. Still.

And Brett. What the hell was he thinking?

Of course I know what Brett was thinking. Our PI cracked through her fake identity, figured out she's Vonda. Brett thought that if he put Denny on the board, it would run her off and add fuel to the incompetency fire. He would've been recording it.

I know she's feeling better when she points out how

dazzlingly blue the sky looks against the yellow Reynard Electric building. "It hums with blueness," she says.

"Unbelievable," I say. But I'm looking at her. I'm looking at her like she's a gift. Vonda O'Neil. Strong as steel, with what she went through.

We grab chicken and rice from a halal cart and eat it on a bench at Marcy Place triangle park on the Lower East Side. We throw leftover bits of bread to the pigeons. She's still shivering, so I give her my jacket to wear. She wraps it around herself and snuggles into me on the bench there. I keep my arm tight around her. "I'm so sorry," I say into her hair.

"What did *you* do? You didn't invite him."

"I started those wheels in motion. Scheming with Brett."

"I don't blame you. In no universe would I blame you for that." She puts a finger to my lips when I start to protest.

We end up walking clear up the East Village and taking the East Side Line the rest of the way to my place. It's afternoon by the time we get up there.

I settle her into a chair out on the veranda overlooking the park. I drape a light blanket over her shoulders.

She smiles up at me. "Come here."

I set my hands on her shoulders and kiss her.

"I feel better," she says. "Thank you." Her neck is warm under my thumbs. She's so beautiful, she doesn't know. I slide my hands over her blanket-covered arms, warming her more.

I leave her out there and make her tea and bake cookies out of the premade cookie dough I keep in the refrigerator. "Cookies and tea," she says when I bring them. "Next thing I know I'll come over and you're knitting tea cozies."

"I think I'm man enough to knit a tea cozy," I say. Whatever that is.

She grins. "Oh, you're man enough to crochet a doily."

We watch the people in the park and talk about nothing.

Doing useless things with her feels more important than the most massive asset takeover.

She complains about me fattening her up, but we nearly finish the pan.

She drains the rest of the tea and straddles my lap, kissing me, her cocoon a tent around us. It's a slow, lazy kiss. The sunlight behind her tips the edges of her brown hair gold. She feeds me little bits of the last cookie and kisses me some more.

We need to talk about the Vonda situation, but now's not the time. There's been enough Vonda today.

She slides the pad of her pointer finger around my lips like she's memorizing the shape of them. "I like feeding you cookies," she says.

"That's convenient," I say. "Because I like your fingers in my mouth."

"Yeah?"

"Yeah," I whisper.

Her gaze turns mischievous. She removes her hand from my lips and trails it down her neck. My heart begins to pound, because I'm also man enough that every ounce of me is focused on the pink and succulent end of the path her fingers are tracing.

Slowly she slides it down her shirt and into the waistband of her blue pants.

I feel her eyes on me, but I can't tear my gaze from the shape her hand makes in her pants, between her legs.

I watch, mesmerized. It's so sexy, I just want to flip her over and consume her like wildfire, but I hold back. It's not what she needs.

She strokes off, thighs rocking above mine. My cock grows hard as granite. Even the weight of her on my lap is hot.

I slide my hand over hers—just lightly, just to be there with her, to feel what she does.

My breath gusts in and out. I can feel my nostrils flaring. I'm starving for her. I need to feel her naked against me, skin to skin, belly to belly, heat to heat.

I tear my eyes up to meet hers, beer-bottle brown, translucent in the daylight.

"Mmm," she says teasingly, lips curling.

"Vicky." My voice sounds strangled. Like it might be coming from somewhere else. "Vicky, Vicky, Vicky..."

Slowly, eyes still locked on mine, she draws out her hand, holds up two glistening fingers.

I grip her wrist and my lips are closing over her fingers. She yelps at the speed and violence of my grab. "What are you, a vampire?"

I suck every last bit of her off of them. She tastes sweet and dirty. She's trembling. Vibrating. I feel it where my skin meets hers.

I run my tongue along the underside of her fingers, giving her the wonderful world of the human tongue and the sparkle in her eyes tell me she's thinking that, too.

She yanks her hand from my mouth and runs sloppy fingers down my chin and down to my straining dick.

She cups me, squeezing. A shudder thrums through me. I'm about to burst out of my skin for her. I cannot get enough of this woman. I think I never will.

"Carry me," she says. "Hurry."

I don't need to be told twice. I palm her ass cheeks and sweep her up. She locks her arms and legs around me as I whirl her around and walk her in, stopping once at a wall just to press her there and kiss her.

I bring her into the bedroom and lay her down. I unbutton and unzip her, kissing silky soft skin. She wriggles under me, soft limbs in a nest of sheets and clothes and the blanket from the porch.

Her panting has a music to it. A high, shaky note, in and out. Her breath gets shakier when I touch her pussy. She grabs onto my hair, pulling as I do her, as I expertly match the speed she did herself with. She groans and pulls. "I won't last if you do that!"

I'm stunned at how bad I want her. I want to tell her, but I don't want to scare her.

There aren't words for it anyway.

Well, maybe there are.

I stand and pull off my own clothes with much less ceremony, looking her over, laid out for me. Her gaze looks drugged. She presses a foot to my belly while I take off my pants.

I roll on a condom. I crawl over her and worship her. She kisses my biceps as I press her hands over her head, as I settle between her legs, spread open for me.

Not for Henry Locke, Most Eligible Bachelor, but me.

She watches me with those brown eyes, watches me as I guide myself into her. I push low and deep into the hot grip of her body, trembling all the way in.

She lowers her eyelids, gone with pleasure. Her groan, when I'm fully inside her, is the sexiest thing I've ever heard.

She squeezes my ass as I move inside her, rocking gently into her. I change my angle until I hit that spot that makes her gasp, sweet and sharp, and then I stay there, moving at it, watching the way her eyes glaze over. Taking her clear over the edge with me.

Afterwards, I throw on a robe and go around to the veranda to fire up the hot tub.

"I didn't know this was over here," she says, coming up behind me and circling her arms around me. She's wearing one of my shirts. It makes me want to walk her right back into the bedroom. Maybe the wall.

"Little-known secret of my veranda."

She dips a toe in. "Mmm."

It's a cool, crisp day—the kind tailor-made for a veranda hot tub.

"Go on. Get in. I'll grab the beers."

She narrows her eyes. "I thought you weren't supposed to drink alcohol in these things."

"Maybe you can look into making a citizen's arrest later on," I say.

She grins. "I think I will look into that."

When I get back, she's in there, eyes closed, head tipped back. I hand her the beer and sink in next to her.

"I should get Smuckers," she says, sounding relaxed. "I really, really so should."

"April can handle Smuckers," I say. "Also, I don't think Smuckers would be fun in a hot tub."

"Not to mention how bad it would mess up his hairdo."

I'm in my living room later on, waiting for Vicky to come out and weigh in on where to go to dinner. We're planning on picking Carly up as soon as her rehearsal is done. We might even try to catch part of it. We did a lot of line running with her and Bess over the long weekend, and she had a great presence. I'm looking forward to seeing her in action. We make a plan to sneak in the back to catch the tail end of the rehearsal.

I grab my phone and I'm scrolling Instagram when the elevator doors open.

It's Brett.

I stand, teeth gritted so hard I'm shocked they don't break. I haven't contacted him. I'm too angry.

"Dude," he says, coming in.

"*Dude?*" I get in his face. "What the hell were you thinking? You knew who that was and you brought him in?"

"Of course I knew. But you're the one who stole the show. That punch? Stroke of genius. The ultimate good cop move."

"You bring him *in?*"

"We didn't even need him. I just got off the phone with Malcomb. Her lawyer contacted him about terminology questions for papers for signing off ownership for a dollar. I underestimated the powers of the Henry Locke dick."

"What are you talking about?"

"The company. She's giving it back. For a dollar. And you'll be happy to know that I smoothed everything over with Denny. We own a parcel of land up north that the Woodruffs want for something. Small price to pay for keeping him quiet about a dog and Vonda O'Neil on our board because please, that would be a disaster."

My mind reels. She's giving it back for a dollar?

"You deserve an Academy Award, brother. We don't even need the competency hearing now."

"That's not—"

My words die out as his face drains of color. He's looking over my shoulder.

"Competency hearing?"

I spin around and there she is, hair still wet, but she's dressed. Except for the naked pain shining in her eyes.

Her voice shakes. "Competency hearing? Operation *good cop*?"

"It's not what you think." I go to her.

"Get away from me!" She pushes me. "All that was an act?"

"Of course not!"

"What's operation good cop? Is that a thing?"

"It was," I begin. "A stupid thing."

"What's the competency hearing? Is that also a stupid thing? A *hearing*?"

I exchange glances with Brett.

The wounded look in her eyes kills me. "You were going to put me on trial? For competency?"

"That's not how it is."

"You said you trusted me."

"I do trust you. I was going to call it off."

"But it's still on. As of now." She searches my eyes. "Is it still on? As of this moment?"

My heart feels like it's cracking. "I was going to call it off."

"Please, just say. Is it still on? As of now?"

"Yes. Technically it's still on."

"Technically." She snorts. "And all this time, were you guys gathering evidence? To destroy me?" She holds up a hand when I take a step toward her. "Awesome performance. I guess that's one thing Brett and I can agree on. It was absolutely award winning. Bravo."

"I wasn't performing."

She grabs her purse and her jacket and heads to the elevator door, then stops.

I stop behind her, heart pounding. Is she reconsidering? Remembering what's between us?

"Vicky," I say.

Slowly she turns, but the warmth is gone from her eyes.

"Don't worry, I'll still give it back. I'll sign and deliver those papers I drew up. For half a million."

"Don't," I whisper, when I realize the significance of the number.

"That's my offer."

"Henry—" Brett starts to say something. I shut him up with a quick look. He widens his eyes. He wants me to take it. It's way cheaper than the millions we offered a few weeks back.

"This isn't you," I say. "You fight for things."

"I didn't get the half mill the last time around. So you'll pay it to me, and if you don't, the world will learn that Vonda O'Neil and Smuckers run your company."

"Vicky."

"It's Vonda," she says. "I'm Vonda O'Neil. And I have to say, keeping me on good behavior with the good cop act while you gather evidence for the hearing? Very effective. Who knows what I would've done. Maybe even painted those cranes pink, with Smuckers's face—"

"We'll pay!" Brett says.

"I don't want you to go," I say. "Brett is going."

"A bank transfer." She fishes out a checkbook and tears off a deposit slip. "Five hundred thousand and you'll never hear from me again."

"I wasn't pretending—you know I wasn't. Feel the truth of that. Of us."

Her eyes are cold. "If you follow me or try to contact me, I'll tell the *New York Tribune* the story of Vonda O'Neil and a dog and their hold over Locke Worldwide."

I get between her and the elevator door, but I don't touch her. I'm not Denny. Except it's too late. "I know what this looks like to you."

"Do you?" she asks. "Please understand when I ask you to leave me be. Respect me on that. Have the money in my bank account by bank open tomorrow. With that you'll get my silence and your company back." She stabs the elevator button. "If the money isn't there, you can kiss the stability of the Locke name goodbye. You'll learn firsthand about the power of the Vonda name."

"Screw the company. I want you," I say.

Brett grabs my shoulder. "Dude."

I shake him off. "We got this, Vicky."

Her eyes shine as she backs into the elevator. She stands in there alone, finger stab-stabbing the button like she always does.

"It doesn't actually go faster when you do that," I whisper, but the doors are already closed.

CHAPTER 30

VICKY

"The day after tomorrow?" Carly is inconsolable when I tell her we have to leave. Her eyes shine wild. "It's my junior year," she says. "We can't just *leave!*"

"We have to."

"But we can't! Please…"

"I'm so sorry."

She collapses in a heap on our ratty green couch. "And our show just went up. And Bess…oh my god, I'll never see Bess again!"

"You'll see her again." *I hope. I think.* I wrap my arms around myself.

"All my friends. Our whole life. If I leave school they'll never let me back in."

"I know, baby."

"Isn't there some other way? There has to be! You always think of something. You always do."

The hope in her eyes kills me. "I thought about it long and

hard. This is the best I can do for us."

She flops back, staring listlessly at the ceiling.

I'm letting her down. I tried to take too much. I tried to fly too close to the sun and I got torched. I wipe the thought of Henry from my mind's eye. He might be calling, but I've long since blocked him.

"All our stuff," Carly says.

I want more than anything to wrap her up in a hug, to give her the hug that I actually really want for myself, but she's not in the mood. "I'm sorry."

"What if I finished out the semester living at Bess's place? And then maybe it all dies down..."

"Connect the dots, Carly. Denny will spill. He lives to make my life miserable. Or somehow it gets out—too many people know. And Mom hears. She's going to want you back. Especially if she sniffs the money—she'll want you back and she'll figure out an angle."

"She's a drug addict! She didn't even file a missing persons report. Won't they see?"

"She's your mother and I'm Vonda—that's what they'll see. They'll put you back with her. You're leaving New York with me or her. You know I'm much more fun."

She picks up a bright green scarf and a soft sob escapes her lips. Deep down, she knows I'm right. She was young, but she remembers the scary guys, and they're still there. We know this because we secretly follow Mom on Facebook. We see her pictures, most of them from the inside of a bar or somebody's trashy living room.

I sink down next to her. "We can go a lot of places with that money. Where do you want to go?"

"Nowhere. I want to go exactly nowhere."

"Me, too," I say. I look around, despairing. Aside from the couch, the furniture isn't ours, but we collected a lot of little treasures over the years. We fought hard and we made a life.

"We'll never see the sad mimes or fierce protector guy again."

"I know." I set a hand on her forearm. "Let's think of a cool place to go where you can continue your theater training."

We go out to get stupid-amount-of-candy ice cream, passing the sad mimes on the way. We hug them and get white paint on our cheeks.

We talk plans at the ice cream place. I nix Los Angeles—it has to be overseas. I already spoke with my ultra-expensive fake ID guy—he feels like he can swing overseas work visas under different names.

We settle on London. It's the theater scene that sells it to Carly. And it's a big city like New York. A place to get lost.

We look for VRBOs on our phones, and when we find one, we pay a random neighbor to arrange it; that way we won't leave a trail.

We'll head to an airport hotel ASAP and arrange the rest of the move from there. It's important not to leave a trail, because if the story about me and Smuckers and the company pops, the media spotlight will be relentless.

Brett seems to think he has Denny contained, but he doesn't know that piece of shit like I do.

I leave Carly at our place, packing boxes to ship. A classmate of hers and her mother are taking over our parrot-sitting gig, because long-term pet sitting gigs on the Upper West Side are easy to fill. She's going to introduce them to Buddy and show them how it all goes.

I head out to meet Latrisha at the studio. It's dark outside when I get there. I thought I'd feel sad when I walked into the place, but I feel strangely proud. The space and the community made my life better. It was a family when I had none. I wander around, just connecting with people one last time, not doing the big dramatic goodbye.

Bron over at the smithy gives me a beer and tells me how my

order will be ready in a week. I tell him that I know it will be amazing.

Of course I tell Latrisha I'm leaving. She senses it's trouble. She thinks it's Henry. I promise her it's not. She wants to rescue us, put us up in her high-security building, circle the wagons. She's a total Joan of Arc that way.

"You've been such a good friend," I say. "Trust me. It's better this way. A storm could be coming."

I make her come over to my space and look at my toolboxes to see if there are any tools she wants. I've got some great ones she can use for inlays and fine work.

"I hate this," she says. "It's morbid. You've been collecting these for years. You have to take them."

"I'm going on a plane with a dog and a teenager. I can't take my tools, too."

"How are you going to make jewelry?"

I swallow. "I'll figure it out."

"I'm taking them all," she declares with tears in her eyes. "And I'm keeping them for you for when you return. You belong here."

It's a sweet thing to say, but in the back of my mind, I think, *You don't know about Vonda.*

On the way back, I have the Lyft drive along Central Park past Henry's building. I make him stop across the street and I look up there, wanting to catch a glimpse of him. The kitchen light is on.

Is Henry there? Is he celebrating?

I wasn't pretending.

I'd be a fool to believe that. He lives for that company. He protects what's his.

I wasn't pretending. We got this, Vicky.

I sit there and let myself sink into the feeling of his words being true, like trying on a plush and beautiful coat that you can never afford but you want to feel it around you, and for a second, maybe you even believe.

And it feels so good.

CHAPTER 31

ONE MONTH LATER

Henry

It's three twenty-two in the morning and I'm lying in bed, thinking about her. Missing her.

I build a lot of residential projects, create a lot of homes for people, but the home I found with Vicky was beyond anything even I could've dreamed up.

Now it's rubble.

And not the cool kind you can turn into furniture. It's toxic and twisted up with unbearable loss, not to mention anger with myself.

And every time I see a griffin, or that ice cream she likes, or a mime, or a hundred other stupid things, that rubble pile gets deeper. And every time I get the urge to tell her some interesting news or a funny realization, I remember I can't.

And the pile gets deeper.

Why did I listen to her when she told me not to go after her that day?

Well, I know why. I wanted to give her a little space. I wanted to respect her in a way that the world hadn't.

Fool move.

I underestimated the trauma that sixteen-year-old Vonda endured, underestimated how deeply it burned.

A day later it was too late. She and Carly were gone. Vanished. When Vicky vanishes, she doesn't mess around.

I got the company, just like she said I would. I got it back—full control. Cold comfort.

I pour myself a scotch and wander out onto my veranda where she fed me cookies and joked about tea cozies. I know what they are now. I looked it up.

The night is mild for late October. I stare up at the moon, wondering if she might be looking at it this very moment. A cliché.

It's unlikely she's moongazing. It's probably daytime where she is; that's what our PI thinks. He had a lead for Hong Kong. A few continental European cities. Nothing panned out.

In the dark of the veranda, I open up my laptop. Before I even check my email, I click to a section of bookmarks that's all jewelry. It's a morbid ritual, perusing the latest debut designer collections of high-end boutiques around the world. I also look at solo designers.

She wouldn't be so stupid to start up her sequined dog bowtie business again. And she probably wouldn't create that Smuck U line I so loved and hated, either, but she has to do something.

She's a maker—it's in her bones—and women's jewelry was her passion.

She told me so many things. I could've told her about the hearing and the good cop thing, explain that I'd abandoned it. Was some little part of me holding all that back to protect my advantage? Covering my ass? Needing to arrange things to come off perfect to her? Not wanting to rock the boat of our time together? Not trusting her to understand?

I click through collections. It's not the names I'm looking at; it's the pieces. I feel sure I'll see a necklace or a pin or something, and I'll recognize her vision in it, her sense of humor, her spirit— something essentially *her* bubbling up out of the pages of baubles, unmistakable as a fingerprint.

I stay out there until dawn, clicking through the images. Then I switch to coffee and get ready to deal with the world.

Over the next few weeks, Latrisha completes the cool-as-hell furnishings for the Moreno, and we collaborate on the installation and interior finishes. I make sure the website is updated with plenty of pictures, just so Vicky can see.

Or should I call her Vonda? I don't know, but what I do know is that she'll check. She won't be able to help herself.

I throw myself into the Ten redesign. It feels good to do the place right. The neighbors are excited—we're experimenting with bringing them into limited sections of the process. Maybe it's arrogant, but I have this idea that one of these days, Vicky will pull up the website for that, too.

I want her to see it. I want her to see that beautiful things can be real. Or maybe that real things can be beautiful.

Not everything I do that autumn is noble. I have enough anger to go around, and my sights also happen to be set on Vicky's mother and the Woodruffs.

The *New York Nightly Reports* I-team is excited about the idea that I brought them for a news-hour segment about what really happened with Vonda O'Neil. Getting the salacious truth of the story. The mindfuck that everyone was wrong about her, and the opportunity to shame the true villains on camera.

That's how I find myself flying up to Deerville the week before Thanksgiving with a stack of cash—a hundred thousand, to be exact.

I got the idea for this whole thing after Brett told me that he thinks the mother still has evidence. He figured it out from something Denny said to him about the Woodruffs having to keep her quiet.

This little nugget doesn't put him back in my good graces, but it's a start.

Maybe.

The news crew is made up of Marv Jenkins, the on-camera personality, two camera operators, and a tech guy. The address they got for Vicky's mother, Esme O'Neil, is wrong, but we track her down to a trailer park and then follow the bread crumbs from there to a poorly lit local bar.

I recognize her right away, down at the end.

She's the skinny woman drinking alone, hair dyed red, skin wrinkled beyond her fifty-something years. She looks bewildered and angry when the lights and cameras fire up—it's an ambush and a half.

Newscaster Marv buys her a drink and coaxes her into repeating the lies on camera. My blood boils as she tells the world how surprised she was that her own daughter lied. She'd believed the girl—how would she know her own daughter turned out to be a liar? It's a well-worn speech, calibrated for maximum sympathy.

Her voice wavers when she meets my eyes. Does she feel my rage? Does she sense it's the end of the road for her story?

The cameras go off when she's done. I step up and slap the cash onto the scratched wooden bar. Bundles of fifties. The Woodruffs were paying her, but probably in the low five figures. My money adds up to more.

"Now you'll tell the truth," I say. "And after that, you'll deliver the evidence you're holding back. We know you have it."

She protests, but her gaze doesn't leave that money. When she looks up at me, there's defeat in her eyes, I know she'll bite. She'll take that money. She'll sell herself out.

Maybe I should have some compassion.

She lost the love of her life and couldn't cope.

I get it. I've been there.

I live there.

The footage they gather is insane. Esme O'Neil takes us to a safety deposit box where she has the shirt and a nanny cam—still inside a bear. There's a cop along to keep the chain of evidence right. The footage inside the bear is Papa Woodruff and Denny bargaining with her for the shirt.

We fire it up on a tablet. It's captured perfectly. The money exchange is clear as day. "Helloooooo," Marv says, sounding like a mustachioed, bathrobe-wearing porn star greeting his bedmate. "And with this, the story goes national."

They get Esme being sorry. They get actual lab shots of the shirt testing. It's like one of those hidden treasure shows or something.

The Woodruffs got a mayo-spattered shirt, as it turns out. You can never trust a drug addict.

The news feature crew does a Denny ambush at a black-tie gala—they actually hold everything under wraps just to surprise him at the gala. They make him repeat the lie about how Vonda must have fixated on him, and how he doesn't blame her for the lies.

They run the footage on a phone for him. They get it on camera, him watching himself standing behind his dad in the sad O'Neil living room all those years ago, paying Vicky's mother for the shirt.

He calls it fake news and storms out of there, lawyering up soon after.

There's a simultaneous confrontation with the Woodruffs on their doorstep that night—the same doorstep they stood in when they announced they forgave Vonda and that they'd drop the charges.

There's nothing the public loves better than liars getting caught on camera.

Marv and the I-team make it onto a sixty-minute news show, with the new material spliced up with old Vonda footage.

The statute of limitations has run out on Denny's crime as well as the cover-up, but there's no statute of limitations in the hearts of the public.

The story rips like wildfire through social media. Denny's friends and client base dry up overnight. The Woodruffs are ostracized by all but the hugest assholes.

Who knows, maybe they'll try to sue Esme O'Neil. But she's in rehab. It's more than she deserves.

She turned on her own child. A beautiful, honest girl who deserved love. Still does.

She has it—from me. My love for her bounces uselessly off the moon.

CHAPTER 32

ELEVEN MONTHS LATER ~ NEW YORK CITY

HENRY

I'M HAVING drinks with Smitty, an old college friend, and Theo Drummond, a chemist who might do some work with the Locke Charitable Foundation.

We're at one of the posh bars that cater to the Wall Street large-assets crowd.

The place is filling up. People come up to us now and then to say a quick hello. Locke is stronger than ever. Everybody wants in.

Small consolation.

Smitty has his eye on three women across the way. "Should we ask those three to sit with us?"

"Not me," I say. My heart's not in it. Hasn't been for a while.

"Theo?" Smitty tries.

Theo shakes his head. "You're on your own."

"I can't fuck all three," Smitty says. "Well, actually I could…"

Theo groans.

I point my finger into my empty glass, lit from the bottom

from the glowing bar. The bartender comes over and pours the scotch.

Smitty turns back to me. "Come on, Henry, when was the last time you had any?"

"A minute ago, and it tasted utterly amazing," I say.

"You know what I mean," Smitty says.

How long? The answer is a year and twenty-one days. It's been a year and twenty-one days since I had sex. A year and twenty-one days since Vicky disappeared. Literally disappeared along with her sister.

I try not to think what she'd say about my sex hiatus, how she'd tease me about losing my *most eligible bastard* status.

I don't care. It's only her. Her or nobody.

My PI hasn't turned up jack. It's a lot easier to hack through somebody's fake identity than to scour the planet for a person who knows how to disappear.

Last I heard, Denny was up to his eyeballs in debt, drinking heavily and trying to borrow money from the people he once snubbed for being beneath him.

A spate of *Where is Vonda?* articles came out, but nobody ever found her.

One year and twenty-one days.

"You sure?" Smitty tries.

"I'm not over my last thing," I explain. "Final answer."

He turns to Theo. "What's your excuse? You're not dating anybody. Look at them—smokin' hot!"

"I'm not *dating* anybody," Theo says. "But there is somebody."

"What?" I ask. This is the first I've heard of Theo with anybody. "Who is she?"

"I don't know who she is," he says. "That's the problem."

"I don't understand," Smitty says.

"This is going to sound a little crazy, but I've been having...*conversations*...with my wake-up call girl."

He's got our attention now. "*Conversations?*" I ask.

He gets this faraway expression. He sucks in a breath.

"Are we talking phone sex here?" Smitty demands.

"No. I mean, yeah, but it's more than that," Theo says. "We talk about everything," he says.

"But to be clear, phone sex *is* involved," Smitty presses.

Theo says nothing. I take it as a yes. "Jesus," I say.

Smitty just laughs.

"You've never seen her," I clarify. "You literally have no idea what she looks like…"

Theo shakes his head. "No information about her whatsoever. I'll find her, though. I'm scouring this fucking city."

"You know she could be a total troglodyte," Smitty points out with his usual sensitivity.

"I don't give a shit." Theo gazes out the window at the people going by. "I have to find her."

He looks exhausted. Is he even sleeping?

I nod. "Dude. Hard to find a woman who doesn't want to be found." I should know.

He tells us the scant details he has on her. We brainstorm ways to find her.

I tell him about my attempts to find Vicky. How I sometimes scour the jewelry collections, but nothing I see ever comes close to what she'd make.

Nothing feels like her.

Or maybe I'm just getting further away.

"Speaking of makers and their studios, you put a bid in for that London thing?" Smitty asks me.

"What London thing?"

"The huge warehouse share studio—Redmond or something?"

"I haven't ever heard of it," I say.

"That's weird. You have a UK presence. I would think Locke would be the first firm they'd invite to bid. It's the kind of shit you guys have been getting off on lately. It's some big cooperative makers space. Freaking huge. Reclaimed urban ruin, neighborhood integration..."

I sit up, interest piqued.

He goes on to outline more features...*familiar features.* "We bid it, and it's not even our thing."

"Are there places to eat, sleep?" I describe the ideas I had for the Southfield Place Studio.

He nods his head. "So you do know about it."

"The owner's not named?"

He gives me a funny look. "No."

"You have access to the RFP?" Request for proposal. I nod at his phone.

"What? And let you bid against us if you weren't even invited?"

I nudge his phone toward him. "Forward me the RFP."

CHAPTER 33

LONDON

VICKY

IT'S a rare sunny day in London. I step out from the funky share space where I have an office onto the street with Smuckers trailing behind.

We skirt around puddles like pale mirrors on the pavement, reflecting gray skies and the gray buildings all around, and the colorful lights of signs. There's a scent of diesel in the air, mixed with the sweetness of hops from a nearby microbrewery.

We head up the street toward a bright-red phone box. A woman named Hanna converted it into a coffee booth—I was relieved there isn't just tea here.

"Hi, Veronica!" Hanna says.

I tell her hi. I buy a muffin and coffee and hang around and talk to her, like I do every day. She always has a nice treat for Smuckers.

I love the colorful, international bustle of London. I love my fun, fashionable neighbors at the office shared space, but I miss New York.

The Vonda story broke after Christmas. My mom, of all things, found it in herself to confess and produce evidence that shows what the Woodruffs did to me. There's speculation she was paid.

It was a big TV news-hour-style story that got picked up all over—it even made the front page of the *Washington Post*.

I cried when I watched it. And then I watched it again and again and again. And I just felt so clear. Like something painful inside me got washed clean in tears and rain.

But, strangely, I didn't want to go back.

That thing that got washed and cleared is perfectly preserved, fragile in a nice ribbon. Going in front of the cameras as vindicated Vonda doesn't appeal to me much more than going as hated Vonda.

Maybe I'm tired.

Carly is attending a great school, and she's got a part in a musical on the West End that will be amazing on her résumé when she goes back to New York. I don't want her to go, but she'll be eighteen and done with school soon. I want her to be free to chase her dreams.

I'm using the money I got from Locke as seed money to build my dream co-op studio in the ruins of an old warehouse. I've got a few investors lined up, and I'm in the process of quietly soliciting bids, blending elements of the Southfield studio with Henry's vision and some ideas of my own.

I try not to think of him too hard these days or about the way things ended with us. And how I loved to be with him.

How he helped me remember who I was. I sometimes wonder if he had a hand in my mother's one-eighty.

I still don't think he meant it when he said he wasn't pretending. Or, at least, most of me doesn't think he meant it. A tiny sliver of me thinks he did.

But I still won't reach out to him. Does that sound screwed up?

It's just that the memory of him saying he wasn't faking his feelings for me is like a lottery ticket where you never go and check if you won. So you can never be disappointed that you lost. And when you look at it, you can think maybe it's something good.

The balsawood griffin sits up on my dresser like that, faithful and loyal and full of possibilities, as if there is still some magic in the world. Like a lottery ticket I never followed up on.

I look at it when I wash dishes. When I make food. When I feel happy. When I feel unhappy.

The studio keeps me busy. There will be subsidized spaces for artisans from all over the world. It's exciting.

I say goodbye to Hanna and head back to the share office with its hip interior of brick walls and green corrugated metal partitions between desk after desk. I make my way down to my area, saying hi here and there.

I'm surprised to find a large box has been set in the middle of my desk where I have my inspiration photos scattered. It's addressed to me. No indication of the sender.

I ask the woman who sits next to me if she saw who brought it.

"Courier," she says, shrugging.

Large as it is, it's light as a feather. I grab a knife and slit the tape, opening the top.

My eyes don't know what I'm seeing at first. My mind interprets everything as packing materials, like a company that doesn't have its shit together decided to go into the packing peanuts business.

But my heart sees. It starts racing, dangerously racing. Fear. Happiness. Wonder.

The box is filled with hundreds of tiny balsawood griffins, intricately carved—I recognize Henry's hand in every claw, every tiny wing.

I dig my fingers through them and I draw up a handful.

"Four hundred twenty-five."

I spin around. My eyes meet his. My breath hitches. Shivers skim over me.

He's leaning on a partition behind me in a deep brown suit, dark hair tousled and just a little bit too long.

Smuckers jumps at his legs, tail wagging.

"Henry."

"I carved one every day you were gone," he says.

My voice shakes. "You can't be here."

He pushes off the partition and comes to me, defiance sparkling in his eyes.

I grip the table edge behind me like that might stop the room from spinning.

He stops in front of me. He stands there, watching my eyes.

He's all posh polish in a thousand-dollar suit, but his pulse drums in his throat. When he speaks, there's the faintest crack in his voice. "I want us back. What do I have to do?"

My heart aches—it actually aches. "I don't know if there was an us." Even as I say it, some little voice in me screams that it's a lie.

"There was an us for me," he says. "There always will be an us for me."

Henry's here. In front of me. "You carved more than four hundred of those?"

His gaze sears my heart. How many he carved isn't the question, and he knows it.

I can barely think. This is everything I didn't dare want.

"It feels like too much to believe," I say finally.

"I know. I get it. You've been burned." He takes my hand like my hand belongs to him. He knits his fingers between mine, warm and soft. "I burned you when I didn't tell you everything," he says. "I should've, and I didn't. I could stand here and give you excuses, but I won't. I just need you. Give us a chance."

"I can't."

His hand tightens, just a bit, like if he doesn't hold me tightly, I might get away. "Let me love you enough for both of us."

"What?"

"I love you." His words are calm and sure. "That's real. Everything was wrong, but that part's real. It always will be."

Instinctively I'm looking for the trick, the lie. But all I see is love, the vulnerability of Henry's love. Of his coming here. Of his griffins.

Henry's gaze is deep-blue honesty and miles-wide loyalty. He's been burned, too, but he's showing up.

Like some things can come true.

"And of course..." He lifts our joined hands, brushes a kiss on my middle knuckle. "You have to let me design and build your studio share project. I mean, please. You think anybody else can do it halfway as well as I could?"

I smile. "There's the Locke Kool-Aid that I know and love."

He pauses and everything seems to still. Like, do I mean I love him?

"It's just about the Kool-Aid?" he asks.

I smile so wide, I think I can never stop. "If I tell you I love you, if I tell you how much I love you and how scared I am for it not to be real that you love me, will it stop you from carving more tiny griffins like a psycho?"

"No," he says. "I'll keep carving them for you. As long as I can carve."

CHAPTER 34

ONE YEAR LATER ~ NEW YORK CITY

VICKY

THICK RED CURTAINS crash to the stage, and Henry and I leap to our feet, clapping. Latrisha springs up on my other side. She sticks her fingers in her mouth and gives an earsplitting whistle.

It was an amazing show, a super funky musical adaptation of *Shakespeare in Love*. Carly got the part of Lady de Lesseps—a huge feather in her cap for her age. She even got a duet, which was heart-stoppingly beautiful, though I might be biased.

After several long minutes of applause, the leads come out, two big Broadway stars. They take their bows, and then the supporting cast all run out, including Carly, who catches my eye and grins wide before taking her bow, holding hands with her scene mates.

The curtain goes down one final time, the lights go on, and we make our way to the aisle—slowly.

It's Locke night at the show, meaning Locke Worldwide bought out half the tickets for employees and vendors as a way to support the show early on. Brett's idea.

Things are better with Brett. I came around to forgiving him —it was right around when we got back to the States, once Carly finished her school term in London. I know he was fighting for the company, not unlike Henry. And Brett's going to be family now—Henry and I got engaged over Christmas.

Henry was slower to forgive, but they're on good terms again. Back to their golf and scotch and strategy walks around Battery Park.

Henry shakes hands, kisses cheeks, and remembers names left and right. And I love him like crazy for it.

"Vonda!" Mandy comes and squeezes my hands. She's in a dazzling green dress. "Your sister! So good."

I thank her, grinning like a proud parent.

Other Locke employees are there, as well as some of Henry and Brett's society set, complimenting my sister. Renaldo asks about Smuckers and I confide that he's home resting up in preparation for a long day at the Sassy Snout groomer.

A woman comes up to me wearing a Smuck U necklace—I put them up on Etsy and they're a huge hit. It's fun to be back to jewelry designing.

We also bought the Southfield makers space and we're making it bigger and better. I got my area back. Right next to Latrisha.

Coming back to New York publicly as Vonda was a revelation. Naturally, I didn't want to. I dreaded the attention. Even after the Woodruff scandal broke, even after having long talks with Henry—he felt certain the attention wouldn't hurt this time —I just didn't want it.

But I wanted to be with Henry, wanted to return to New York. The London share studio was on its way by the time Carly finished high school. I had a great person to run it. So we packed up our flat and I steeled myself and we flew back on Henry's jet.

He set up a press conference for the day after we returned.

I wasn't so sure about that plan, but I trusted his experience with the paparazzi. "Feed them a nice meal and they won't go following you for crumbs," he said.

So I steeled myself. I might have even put on a dark sweater set and slim skirt. "No!" Carly cried, tugging at my sweater. "Noooooo!"

I grinned and hugged Carly to me. But I needed body armor. Something to cover my heart.

I stepped out in front of the cameras with Henry, holding his hand in a sweaty death grip, waiting for the insults, the onslaught of hurtful questions. Braced, steeled, pulse racing like I was entering a war zone.

The battle never came.

It was just waves of goodwill, stunning and warming me. People empathizing with me. Apologizing. It was beyond cathartic.

I can't count the number of people who have come up to me since I got back, telling me their own stories of not being believed, of being scapegoated, pilloried on social media.

None got to the level of national shaming I did, but I also know that when it's happening to you, it feels like the whole world is doing it. Sometimes I know I'm the only one listening.

We finally reach the chandelier-draped lobby. There are vintage posters all around. People are happy—buoyant, even, from the show.

I'm pulling forward but Henry tugs me back and spins me into a corner, hands curled around my waist. He kisses me hard. "That dress. God, need you so bad," he says. "You're beautiful. You're like a firebird."

I grin and nip his lip. I've let my hair go back to red, and my dress is bright orange. Fire doesn't burn me anymore.

"Need to strip you out of it," he grates in a voice that has me wishing that lobby-to-limo teleportation was a thing.

"Need to get you out of that wristwatch," I say.

He pulls me in more tightly against the powerbrokery hard body that I love.

We do eventually get out of there, but not to the limo. We sneak around the dark side of the building to the cast exit and wait for Carly, which involves making out like teenagers. And then he pushes back into the bricks and fixes me with a serious stare.

"I love you," he says, his voice full of wonder. "So much."

I gaze up at his beautiful face and lopsided dimples that I like to kiss. "I love you, Henry." And the stars in the night sky seem to brighten behind him.

I'm going to be honest—the stars up there still make zero intelligible pictures as far as I can see. But the picture Henry and I make together means everything to me, lines scribbling between our hearts to create an amazing new world.

~The End~

ALSO BY ANNIKA MARTIN

STANDALONE ROMANTIC COMEDY

~READ IN ANY ORDER~

Most Eligible Billionaire

The Billionaire's Wake-up-call Girl

Breaking The Billionaire's Rules

The Billionaire's Fake Fiancée

Return Billionaire to Sender

Just Not That Into Billionaires

Butt-dialing the Billionaire

Find a complete list of books and audiobooks at www.annikamartinbooks.com

ACKNOWLEDGMENTS

I'm so grateful to have so many smart, creative, generous friends in my life—you guys are always up for reading my stuff at different stages and lending me your expertise and it means the world. It definitely meant the world to this book. Joanna Chambers came through with the most brilliant insights and tough love ever—omg thank you! M. O'Keefe blazed in with beautiful emotional ideas and key fixes; Katie Reus had great catches and character insights. Thanks also to Courtenay Bennett for a fabulous eagle-eye read and ideas on *certain terms*. Hugest thanks to my local writing group—Elizabeth Jarrett Andrew, Marcia Peck, Mark Powell, and Terri Whitman—your thoughtful read and insights were absolutely inspiring and just golden to me! Deb Nemeth did a great developmental edit, Sadye Scott-Hainchek did an early proofread, Judy Sturrup proofed and Judy Zweifel of Judy's proofreading delivered on a wonderfully helpful final proofread. Thanks also to Michele of Catalano Creative for the cover beauty, and kisses to Nina Grinstead and the gang at Social Butterfly for amazing energy and invaluable support. All of you! Hugs!